A COWBOY'S TOUCH

Other Novels by Denise Hunter Include:

Driftwood Lane
Seaside Letters
Sweetwater Gap
The Convenient Groom
Surrender Bay

A Cowboy's Touch

Denise Hunter

**Doubleday Large Print
Home Library Edition**

THOMAS NELSON
Since 1798

NASHVILLE   DALLAS   MEXICO CITY   RIO DE JANEIRO

This Large Print Edition, prepared especially for Doubleday Large Print Home Library, contains the complete, unabridged text of the original Publisher's Edition.

Published in Nashville, Tennessee, by Thomas Nelson. Thomas Nelson is a trademark of Thomas Nelson, Inc.

Publisher's Note: This novel is a work of fiction.
Names, characters, places, and incidents are either
products of the author's imagination or used
fictitiously. All characters are fictional, and any
similarity to people living or dead is purely
coincidental.

ISBN 978-1-61129-505-4

Printed in the United States of America

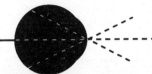

**This Large Print Book carries the
Seal of Approval of N.A.V.H.**

Jesus answered, "I am the way and the truth and the life."

JOHN 14:6

A Cowboy's Touch

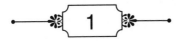

1

Abigail Jones knew the truth. She frowned at the blinking curser on her monitor and tapped her fingers on the keyboard—what next?

Beyond the screen's glow, darkness washed the cubicles. Her computer hummed, and outside the office windows a screech of tires broke the relative stillness of the Chicago night.

She shuffled her note cards. The story had been long in coming, but it was finished now, all except the telling. She knew where she wanted to take it next.

Her fingers stirred into motion, dancing

across the keys. This was her favorite part, exposing truth to the world. Well, okay, not the world exactly, not with *Viewpoint*'s paltry circulation. But now, during the writing, it felt like the world.

Four paragraphs later, the office had shrunk away, and all that existed were the words on the monitor and her memory playing in full color on the screen of her mind.

Something dropped onto her desk with a sudden thud.

Abigail's hand flew to her heart, and her chair darted from her desk. She looked up at her boss's frowning face, then shared a frown of her own. "You scared me."

"And you're scaring me. It's after midnight, Abigail—what are you doing here?" Marilyn Jones's hand settled on her hip.

The blast of adrenaline settled into Abigail's bloodstream, though her heart was still in overdrive. "Being an ambitious staffer?"

"You mean an obsessive workaholic."

"Something wrong with that?"

"What's wrong is my twenty-eight-year-old daughter is working all hours on a Saturday night instead of dating an eligible bachelor like all the other single women her age." Her mom tossed her head, but her short brown hair hardly budged. "You could've at least gone out with your sister and me. We had a good time."

"I'm down to the wire."

"You've been here every night for two weeks." Her mother rolled up a chair and sank into it. "Your father always thought you'd be a schoolteacher, did I ever tell you that?"

"About a million times." Abigail settled into the chair, rubbed the ache in her temple. Her heart was still recovering, but she wanted to return to her column. She was just getting to the good part.

"You had a doctor's appointment yesterday," Mom said.

Abigail sighed hard. "Whatever happened to doctor-patient confidentiality?"

"Goes out the window when the doctor is your sister. Come on, Abigail, this is your health. Reagan prescribed rest—R-E-S-T—and yet here you are."

"A couple more days and the story will be put to bed."

"And then there'll be another story."

"That's what I do, Mother."

"You've had a headache for weeks, and

the fact that you made an appointment with your sister is proof you're not feeling well."

Abigail pulled her hand from her temple. "I'm fine."

"That's what your father said the week before he collapsed."

Compassion and frustration warred inside Abigail. "He was sixty-two." And his pork habit hadn't helped matters. Thin didn't necessarily mean healthy. She skimmed her own long legs, encased in her favorite jeans . . . exhibit A.

"I've been thinking you should go visit your great-aunt."

Abigail already had a story in the works, but maybe her mom had a lead on something else. "New York sounds interesting. What's the assignment?"

"Rest and relaxation. And I'm not talking about your Aunt Eloise —as if you'd get any rest there—I'm talking about your Aunt Lucy."

Abigail's spirits dropped to the basement. "Aunt Lucy lives in Montana." Where cattle outnumbered people. She felt for the familiar ring on her right hand and began twisting.

"She seems a bit . . . confused lately."

Abigail recalled the birthday gifts her great-aunt had sent over the years, and her lips twitched. "Aunt Lucy has always been confused."

"Someone needs to check on her. Her latest letter was full of comments about some girls who live with her, when I know perfectly well she lives alone. I think it may be time for assisted living or a retirement community."

Abigail's eyes flashed to the screen. A series of nonsensical letters showed where she'd stopped in alarm at her mother's appearance. She hit the delete button. "Let's invite her to Chicago for a few weeks."

"She needs to be observed in her own surroundings. Besides, that woman hasn't set foot on a plane since Uncle Murray passed, and I sure wouldn't trust her to travel across the country alone. You know what happened when she came out for your father's funeral."

"Dad always said she had a bad sense of direction."

"Nevertheless, I don't have time to hunt her down in Canada again. Now, come on,

Abigail, it makes perfect sense for you to go. You need a break, and Aunt Lucy was your father's favorite relative. It's our job to look after her now, and if she's incapable of making coherent decisions, we need to help her."

Abigail's conscience tweaked her. She had a soft spot for Aunt Lucy, and her mom knew it. Still, that identity theft story called her name, and she had a reliable source who might or might not be willing to talk in a couple weeks.

"Reagan should do it. I'll need the full month for my column, and we can't afford to scrap it. Distribution is down enough as it is. Just last month you were concerned—"

Her mother stood abruptly, the chair reeling backward into the aisle. She walked as far as the next cubicle, then turned. "Hypertension is nothing to mess with, Abigail. You're so . . . restless. You need a break—a chance to find some peace in your life." She cleared her throat, then her face took on that I've-made-up-my-mind look. "Whether you go to your aunt's or not, I'm insisting you take a leave of absence."

There was no point arguing once her

mother took that tone. She could always do research online—and she wouldn't mind visiting a part of the country she'd never seen. "Fine. I'll finish this story, then go out to Montana for a week or so."

"Finish the story, yes. But your leave of absence will last three months."

"Three months!"

"It may take that long to make a decision about Aunt Lucy."

"What about my apartment?"

"Reagan will look after it. You're hardly there anyway. You need a break, and Moose Creek is the perfect place."

Moose Creek. "I'll say. Sounds like nothing more than a traffic signal with a gas pump on the corner."

"Don't be silly. Moose Creek has no traffic signal. Abigail, you have become wholly obsessed with—"

"So I'm a hard worker . . ." She lifted her shoulders.

Her mom's lips compressed into a hard line. "*Wholly obsessed* with your job. Look, you know I admire hard work, but it feels like you're always chasing something and never quite catching it. I want you to find some contentment, for your health if nothing else. There's more to life than investigative reporting."

"I'm the Truthseeker, Mom. That's who I am." Her fist found home over her heart.

Her mother shouldered her purse, then zipped her light sweater, her movements irritatingly slow. She tugged down the ribbed hem and smoothed the material of her pants. "Three months, Abigail. Not a day less."

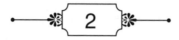

2

Moose Creek—Gateway to Yellowstone—
Population 1,923. The wooden sign, propped
on two spindly log legs, stood just outside
town on the corner of a tiny park. The picture
Abigail had conjured in her mind matched
reality.

The cabbie drove her through town—
Main Street the sign read. She noted the
old brick shops with sun-faded canopies
jutting out over boarded sidewalks. Vehicles, mostly trucks, occupied the diagonal
parking spaces that lined the two-lane
street.

Just past town, they turned down a country road in need of a good paving. What was she going to do here for three months? Her mother's words flittered through her mind. *"You need a break—a chance to find some peace in your life."* She wasn't sure there was anything to be found in Moose Creek, Montana, *except* peace.

Thank God she'd brought her laptop. She could only hope Aunt Lucy had Internet. *Please let there be Wi-Fi.*

Several minutes later the cabbie turned down a long drive. A weathered log archway straddled the lane, bearing a sign that read *Stillwater Ranch.* Gravel crunched under the tires as the driver accelerated down the road. Hills and evergreens marked a land so vast, Abigail felt small and lost. The lane dipped and rose and curled between spring-green hills.

About a mile down the drive, she told the cabbie to turn onto a side lane, as her directions instructed. Ahead, a tiny cabin was tucked at the base of a hill, centered in a grove of evergreens and surrounded by a plethora of colorful flowers.

The driver applied his foot to the squeaky brakes. Abigail exited the cab and stepped onto the grass, surveying the tenant house. Her mom had told her that Uncle Murray worked this ranch for years as a cowhand. After he'd passed on, the owner allowed Aunt Lucy to stay in the home for a small fee.

Abigail hoped the fee was as small as the cabin. Have mercy, would they both fit?

She paid the cabbie, then toted her bag toward the cabin. The flowers were so— Abigail squinted and frowned as she approached the colorful blooms—*fake*. Hundreds of vibrant plastic blossoms protruded from the soil. Only Aunt Lucy.

The screen door squawked open and out popped her aunt, a smock hugging her generous waist. She seemed to have shrunk since Abigail last saw her, and her short hair was whiter than Abigail remembered. Her thick glasses perched on her nose, magnifying her brown eyes.

"Abigail!" She waddled across the porch, the marionette lines beside her mouth deepening as she smiled.

"Aunt Lucy!" A smile spread across Abigail's face.

The woman crushed her in a hug, never mind that her aunt's face was somewhere in the vicinity of Abigail's bosom. Abigail patted her back.

"You're so tall and slim, like your father! Ten years is too long." Aunt Lucy pulled back. "Let me look at you. You're so lovely and grown up, and look at that beautiful complexion! But those pretty green eyes look tired. Marilyn said you work too hard." She patted Abigail's cheek, then brushed Abigail's hair over her shoulder.

"Mom's overreacting."

"Well, you must be exhausted from your travel. Come in, come in. You know I hate to travel. Ever since Murray went away, I stick close to home."

He'd died years ago. All Abigail remembered was that he'd worn a cowboy hat and smelled like leather.

The door opened to a small room full— and she did mean full—of stuff. Lamps and knickknacks and books and boxes and *dolls*. The little cloth creatures perched on the armchair in the corner, lounged on the back of the sofa like sleeping cats, and lined up across the shelf over the TV, staring blankly at her with their button eyes. It was just this side of creepy.

"Everyone welcome Abigail!"

Nothing in the house stirred except Aunt Lucy, who moved toward another room. She stopped on the way and repositioned a doll on the love seat. "Don't be rude, Dorothy, make room for our guest. You want a nice tall iced tea, dear?"

It took a moment to realize Aunt Lucy was speaking to her. "Uh, yes, please."

Abigail sat opposite Dorothy. The doll's stitched-on smile seemed to mock her.

"Still making dolls, I see," she said when her aunt returned with the tea.

"Oh yes, I still have my little shop in town. You passed it on the way in. The girls keep me busy."

Ah . . . the "girls" from her letter.

Aunt Lucy adjusted the Western skirt on the nearest doll. "I'm so excited you can stay all summer. It's been ages since I've had family around, and I can't wait to show you off to my friends at church."

She'd be going to church then. It had been awhile.

"I'm just so happy to see you." Her aunt's eyes turned glassy, and she dabbed at them with the corner of her smock, knocking her glasses askew. "You favor your father so much." She sniffled. "Oh, I'm being a wet rag!"

"I'm glad to see you, too, Aunt Lucy. You were always Dad's favorite."

"Well, enough of this." She straightened her glasses. "It's tight quarters, as you can see, but you'll get to know all of us, and you can keep me company at the shop if you like."

Abigail pictured a dusty shop full of Aunt Lucy's friends. "Well, I was hoping to research my next story while I'm here. I don't suppose there's any Wi-Fi around here."

"Why what?"

"Wi—Internet. You know, for the computer."

"Oh, the Internet. The main house has it, but I don't have a computer. You could check the library. They might have some Internet."

Well, what had she expected to find out here in the boonies? "Maybe I'll do my research there."

Aunt Lucy fingered her white curls. "Oh, whatever you want, dear, whatever you want. I'm just tickled to have you." She gave her cloth companion a sip of tea.

Aunt Lucy might not be so tickled, Abigail thought, when she found out why she'd been sent.

※

Abigail ran a duster over the glass counter at the Doll House. Only a few days in Moose Creek, and she was already bored out of her mind. Aunt Lucy had run to grab a bite at the Tin Roof, leaving her in charge.

Abigail scanned the dozens of dolls staring blankly into space and pointed her duster at them. "Behave yourselves, girls."

Holy cow. Five days in Moose Creek and she was losing it.

But her perpetual headache was tapering off, and she hadn't had palpitations in a few days. She checked her pulse to make sure she was still alive, then set the duster down and stretched her back, twisting to one side and then the other. Sleeping on the couch was putting the hurts on her, literally. The old tweed sofa was lumpy, hard, and about eight inches too short.

For a couple days she'd done research at Mocha Moose, which offered free Wi-Fi and tasty espresso. Abigail hadn't found a single issue of *Viewpoint* in town, but her mom had forwarded a few e-mails from readers. It was gratifying to see her work in print and get feedback, though that was secondary to the thrill of exposing the truth.

But the coffee shop's Internet had been down for two days, and she'd somehow become her aunt's assistant in the stagnant shop. Her mom called twice for her initial assessment on Aunt Lucy. Abigail's diagnosis so far: eccentric but not fatally so. No reason to rush her off to assisted living just yet, but she realized after some Internet research on dementia that she needed to watch her aunt for signs of forgetfulness.

The bell over the door tinkled, and a woman and a little girl walked in.

"Good afternoon," Abigail said. "Can I help you find something?" Probably not, since she knew nothing about the dolls other than a few of their names.

"We bought a doll here for my daughter's birthday last summer, and she'd like another. We're passing through on our way to Yellowstone."

"I want a blond-haired one." The little girl tucked her own swingy hair behind her ear.

Abigail smiled. "Well, we have lots of those. Look around and see who catches your eye. Any one of them would love to have a mommy like you."

The child frowned at her. "I'm just a little girl."

The mother laughed as the bell tinkled again, announcing Aunt Lucy's entrance. Saved by the bell. Her aunt led the customers to the back of the store, and Abigail resumed dusting. She'd just cleaned out the window display by the front door and returned the dolls when the door opened again.

A girl of ten or eleven entered. She walked as if the floorboards might snap under her slight weight. Abigail didn't see her tears until the light from the window hit her face.

"Hi, honey," Abigail said. "Are you okay?"

The girl looked toward the back of the store where Aunt Lucy was pulling a doll from the shelf, then back toward the entrance.

Abigail squatted in front of her. Now that she was closer, Abigail noticed her wide-set green eyes and a light smattering of freckles on her nose. "Is that your mom?"

The girl shook her head. "I need to talk to Miss Lucy."

"Miss Lucy's with a customer right now. Could I help? I'm Miss Lucy's niece, Abigail. What's your name?"

The girl turned her eyes on Abigail for the first time, and a fat tear slid down her face. "Maddy Ryan." Her lip trembled. "Somebody took my bike." Another tear tumbled down her cheek.

Abigail frowned and took her hand. It was cold and wet from her tears. "Tell me what happened."

"I . . . I rode to town 'cause Dad said I need a haircut, and I wanted to buy some candy 'cause I saved some money. I parked outside the market." She reached into her hoodie pocket and pulled out a handful of Twizzlers. "When I came out, my bike was gone." Maddy drew a shuddery breath that threatened to turn into a full-out bawl.

Abigail glanced at Aunt Lucy, who was introducing the customers to another blond doll, then turned back to Maddy. "Well, here, put your candy back in your pocket. Let's go back to the store and see what we can find out." She placed a hand on the child's shoulder and led her out the door. "Did you call your parents or tell anyone at the store about your bike?"

"No, I came straight to Miss Lucy." She wiped her face with her sleeve.

"Well, let's see if anyone at the store saw something."

When they reached Pappy's Market, Maddy gestured to the walk along the building. "I parked right here."

Abigail glanced along the building, down the street, and all around, as far as she could see. Pedestrians and cars bustled by on what was probably a busy Saturday for Moose Creek. No sign of a bike.

"Are you certain?"

"Positive. I always park here." She pointed to the empty spot. "My dad got it for my birthday." Her lip quivered and her eyes filled again.

"Do you want to call him? I have a cell phone."

Maddy looked down at her cowboy boots and shook her head. "He's working, and his cell phone doesn't work too good out there."

Abigail squatted in front of her and took both her hands. "I know you don't know me, Maddy, but it just so happens I'm very good at getting to the bottom of things. I promise I won't give up until we figure this out, okay?"

Maddy nodded.

But an hour later, after reporting the missing bike to the sheriff and questioning the clerk at Pappy's Market, they were no closer to finding the missing bike.

"I still haven't gone to the Hair Barn," Maddy said. "Miss Greta—she's our housekeeper—is going to be mad if I'm not home soon."

"Well, let's see. How about if you get your hair trimmed, then I'll take you home in my aunt's car." A thought hit her. "But your dad wouldn't want you riding in a stranger's car."

"Miss Lucy's not a stranger. She lives in one of our houses."

"Oh—your dad owns Stillwater Ranch then. I'm staying at my aunt's for the summer. Do you want to call your mom and make sure it's okay to get a ride with me?"

"My mom died. But my dad trusts Miss Lucy. I go to her house sometimes."

She was young to have lost her mother.

"Well, let's do this then. Go get your hair cut, then come to the doll store when you're finished and I'll give you a ride home."

"But what about my bike?" Hopeful green eyes looked up at Abigail.

"Don't give up; every mystery has a solution. We'll figure out what happened to your bike, even if we don't do it today."

Ten minutes later Maddy was safely ensconced in a chair at the Hair Barn, and Abigail returned to the Doll House.

"Can I borrow your car in a few minutes, Aunt Lucy?"

"Certainly, dear, the keys are by my purse." The mother and daughter were gone, and Aunt Lucy sat in her rocker sewing a half-finished doll.

"I met a friend of yours: Maddy. Her bike was stolen down at the market, and I told her I'd give her a lift home. You think her dad would mind?"

"Oh no, the poor dear. She loved that bike."

"I told her I'd help her track it down."

"Well, if anyone can find it, you can."

"She seems young to be wandering through town alone."

"She's eleven, and this is a very safe town. Why, the stolen bike will probably make the front page of the *Moose Creek Chronicle*." Aunt Lucy eyed the bald doll in her lap. "Now, what color hair do you want, Victoria? . . . Oh yes, black will suit you very well." She pulled a skein of fuzzy black yarn from her bag, then nudged her thick glasses up on her nose.

"She seems kind of lonely. Maddy, I mean," Abigail added, in case her aunt thought she referred to the doll. "She said her mom died."

"She is lonely, I think. Comes to the house sometimes to visit, her and destiny."

Destiny? Her aunt said the strangest things. "So you don't think Maddy's dad would mind my driving her home?"

"Oh no, I've known Wade since he moved here. He's famous, you know. Voted Sexiest Man Alive by one of those movie star magazines."

Sure he was. And Abigail won the Pulitzer last year.

Aunt Lucy smoothed the black yarn for Vanessa. Or was it Victoria? All the names were running together in Abigail's head.

"Did the little girl find a blond doll?"

"Oh yes, she adopted Lillian. They're a perfect match."

"They were on their way to Yellowstone, they said? How far away is it? I noticed the Moose Creek sign called the town the Gateway to Yellowstone."

Aunt Lucy nodded. "Used to be, dear,

but then they built other highways into the park. Most folks don't come this way anymore. Mayor Wadell is trying to change that, but he's not having much luck."

"It's a quaint town."

"There's been many a fuss over a national advertising budget, but those tightwads on the council won't spend a dime. Meanwhile, shops like mine are struggling. But God has it under control. He's taken care of me this long."

Abigail frowned. "If only people knew about it." It was a shame for the town to go unnoticed. And for the shops to struggle. She looked around the quiet store and was sure it had seen better days.

Well, she couldn't solve the world's problems, or even Moose Creek's, but she could give one little girl a ride home.

She snatched up the keys. "I'll run Maddy home."

"All right, dear."

Abigail headed out to her aunt's old yellow VW bug. Who would steal a lonely little girl's bike? She didn't know, but one thing was sure. She was going to find out.

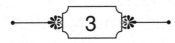

3

Wade Ryan felt the same way every year when calving season was over: proud and disappointed. There was still plenty of work left before summer. He and the neighboring ranchers would pitch in with branding, vaccinating, and earmarking, and then another summer would begin.

Wade closed the pen, letting his hands linger on the splintered rail. The cows and their calves made soft lowing sounds. Twilight swallowed the valley, and a bright moon rose over the Gallatin Range.

He should get inside to Maddy and relieve Greta. His stomach let out a rowdy grumble, reminding him he'd worked past suppertime again. Turning, he tried to tell himself he was glad that calving season was over and summer perched on his doorstep.

But summer meant Maddy was home, meant another nanny was coming, meant worrying about his daughter and how she spent her time. She was growing up, getting to the age where a girl needed a mom. Even he could see that.

Wade steered his thoughts a different direction. Today had enough worries of its own. He'd hired a young preschool teacher, who was off for the summer, to look after Maddy this year, and he was sure the girl would be good for his daughter. Well, as sure as you could be about anything, he reckoned.

Maddy burst through the front door, trotted down the porch steps, and met him in the yard. She curled her arms against the chill in the air.

"Get your hair cut, squirt?" Even in the dim light he saw it was pulled back as always.

"Can't you tell?"

Should an eleven-year-old girl wear the

same hairstyle every day? He wouldn't know what else to do with it. He pushed back the guilt. "It's not hanging in your eyes, at least." He ruffled her bangs. She had Lizzie's fine, soft hair, but the rich mahogany brown came from his mother's gene pool.

They traipsed toward the house side by side.

"My bike got stolen in town," Maddy blurted.

Wade frowned. "Stolen? You sure?" Not that bad things didn't happen in Moose Creek, but these were neighbors. They worked together, worshiped together, celebrated together. Practically extended family, whether you wanted them or not.

"I parked it at the market, and when I came out it wasn't there."

He hated she'd lost her bike and figured chances of finding it were slim. Maybe he should buy her a new one—wasn't like he didn't have the money. But Greta said he spoiled his daughter, and maybe she was right.

"Need to file a report," he said.

"Abigail already did. And she asked

people questions and stuff too. She's going to help me find it."

"Who's Abigail?"

"Miss Lucy's niece. She's visiting for the summer, and she said she's good at solving mysteries."

Probably would've seen her around if it hadn't been for spring works season. He'd been gone dawn to dark for days. "A mystery, huh?"

"The Case of the Stolen Bike. She thinks we can figure it out pretty quick. Hope so. I don't want to go all summer without it. We're going to start looking on Wednesday."

"What about school?"

"Dad. Tuesday's my last day, remember?"

Had he told the new nanny that? It had been weeks ago. He couldn't remember. Wade made a mental note to call her tomorrow after church.

He opened the door for Maddy, and she ducked under his arm. She was getting tall. He noted the frayed hems of her jeans as she passed through to the kitchen. Blame it all if they weren't hanging three inches above the toes of her boots. The sleeves of her Western shirt were turned up at the cuff despite the chilly May weather, and the shirttail wasn't long enough to stay tucked in.

Why was he always two days late when it came to Maddy? Why hadn't he noticed she'd outgrown her clothes?

"Supper's in the oven, Wade," Greta said as he entered the kitchen. She tugged her thick sweater over her ample frame and flipped her gray hair over the collar.

"Smells great," he said. Greta hadn't noticed that Maddy had outgrown her clothes either. That made him feel a little better.

Greta and her husband, Pee Wee, lived in one of the camp houses. Pee Wee wasn't much taller than Greta, but he was Wade's cowhand, and a fine one too. Greta did the household chores a few hours a day, but she'd made it clear from the beginning she wasn't a nanny. The couple had never had kids of their own, but neither one had said why, and he sure wasn't asking.

"See you at church," she said.

"Thanks, Greta."

The back door clicked quietly behind her.

Wade hung his hat on the peg, then turned to help Maddy get the food on the table. She waited for him every night, no matter how late he was.

Once supper was on the table, he said grace and they dug into Greta's roast beef. The woman could cook. Once the worst of his hunger was satiated, he slowed down.

"Homework done?" he asked.

"When I got home from school yesterday."

"Grades okay?"

She shrugged. "I'll make honor roll."

Wade didn't know what he'd done to deserve a daughter like Maddy.

"Can I help with branding when school's over?" she asked.

He pictured the anxious calves kicking up a ruckus as they were heeled, held, and worked. He'd received more than his share of knots and bruises when they dragged calves. "Not this year, Maddy."

Her sigh filled the quiet house. "You say that every year. I have friends at school who've been holding down calves since they were seven."

Wade knew it was true. His neighbor's kids, younger than Maddy, helped every year. Still, it only took once. One kick to the head, one blow to the face. "You can watch."

Maddy pursed her lips, her gaze sliding down to her food.

Was he overprotective? Maybe so, but he wasn't taking any chances with his daughter. She was all he had.

"Can we go somewhere this summer, Dad? Just you and me? Everyone at school is going somewhere."

He shook his head.

"Just for a long weekend? Wouldn't have to be far . . . just someplace else, like Seattle or Salt Lake City—"

"You know we can't, Maddy. We might be recognized." It broke his heart to say it, to see the light in her eyes go dim. But what could he do? They were trapped here, like it or not.

She looked down at her food, moved the roast beef around with her fork. A minute later she pushed her plate back. "I'm going to bed."

He should insist she finish. A growing girl needed nutrition, and her height was stretching her out, making her skinny. But she was already putting her plate in the sink.

"Get a shower first," he said.

She turned at the doorway, one hand on the wide woodwork. "Dad. I'm almost a teenager. You don't have to tell me that anymore." She said it with more patience than he probably deserved.

"Sorry." He watched her turn the corner, heard her bare feet padding up the wood stairs, heard the shower kick on, and wondered if he knew anything at all about raising a teenage girl.

❀

Wade found the number on a scrap of paper in his desk drawer and dialed the old phone. The mammoth computer hummed on his desk, and outside the open window Maddy encouraged her horse.

Charlotte answered on the second ring.

"Hi, Charlotte. Wade Ryan from Stillwater Ranch, just checking in to make sure you're arriving on Tuesday or Wednesday."

"Oh. Hi, Mr. Ryan."

Something in her tone of voice troubled him. Maybe he'd caught her at a bad time.

"Listen," she continued. "I'm afraid I have some bad news. Well, I mean, good news for me, but not so much for you."

He didn't find her chuckle amusing.

"Thing is, my boyfriend, he's like from Billings, and he asked me to move in with him. I mean he only asked me Friday night, and I should've called you right away, but I spent all day yesterday moving and—" She muffled the phone and spoke to someone else. "Sorry about that. And sorry I didn't call yesterday. This probably leaves you in a lurch with Marley."

"Maddy," he said absently.

"I'm really sorry about quitting last minute, but he—my boyfriend—lined up a job for me at a day care in Billings, and well . . ."

Wade wanted to tell her she was inconsiderate, rude, and irresponsible. Instead he sent up a silent petition for patience, then cleared his throat. "I understand. Don't suppose you know of another teacher needing a summer job?"

"Sorry . . ."

He could hear the cringe in her tone. Well, so what, he was cringing too. Cringing because he had two days to find someone to keep tabs on his daughter.

He wished Charlotte good luck and hung up the phone. Two days. He glanced out the window and watched Maddy set her boot in the stirrup and swing her leg over her horse's back.

Maybe she could manage without a nanny. He tried to think back to eleven. He'd made plenty of extra trouble for his parents, he was ashamed to admit.

No, eleven wasn't old enough. In another summer or two, maybe, but not yet. And he knew better than to ask Greta. He planted his elbows on the desk and scraped his fingers through his hair. Two days to find someone responsible, trustworthy, and available.

Where am I going to find a woman like that in two days, God?

4

Abigail was on her third set of squats when she heard the noise outside Aunt Lucy's cottage. She walked to the door and peeked out the half-moon window to see Maddy dismounting a brown horse as easily as Abigail could dismount a bike. The horse neighed, tossing its white-streaked nose. Its hooves danced in the grass, dangerously close to Aunt Lucy's fake spring blooms. Oh well. Not like she couldn't just stick them back in the ground.

Abigail opened the door. "Hi, Maddy."

The girl looped the reins around the

porch post. Her sloppy ponytail looked like it had been slept in, and dirt smudged her too-short jeans.

"Want a soda? Aunt Lucy's taking her Sunday afternoon nap, so we'll have to keep it down."

"Sure."

Abigail let her in, wondering if it was normal around here to let an eleven-year-old girl ride all over creation on a big horse. What if she fell and hit her head or broke her leg?

"Have a seat. You might have to move a couple dolls. Pepsi okay?"

"Sure."

Abigail went to the kitchen for the soda and a glass of water. She'd been thinking about Maddy's bike in church. Okay, so she should've been listening, but at least she'd gone. That's more than she'd done in a long time.

"That your horse out there?" Abigail handed Maddy the can.

"His name's Destiny."

Ah . . . Destiny. "I like that."

"Dad got him for me when we moved here."

"His hair's the same color as yours. Do you take care of him? I've heard horses are a lot of work."

The pop of her soda tab sounded loud in the little cabin. Maddy sipped from the can. "I like taking care of him. When school's out I can ride him all the time."

"Doesn't your dad worry?"

She made a face. "I have a nanny in the summer."

"But he knows you're riding today?"

"He's helping the O'Neils today—they're our neighbors. But Miss Greta knows I'm here."

"Your housekeeper, right?"

"Yeah." She pointed to the thin mat on the floor. "What's that?"

"My exercise mat. I was working out when you got here."

"Why don't you just take a walk?" The confused crease between her brows made Abigail laugh.

"Good point. Guess I'm just used to doing it the city way. Plus I'd probably get lost."

"You could go with me and Destiny if you want. I don't have to be home for forty-five minutes."

"It would give us a chance to talk about your bike." And maybe it wasn't a bad idea to stay with the girl awhile. At least Abigail would know she was safe.

"I was hoping you'd say that."

After changing into a pair of jeans and a clean T-shirt, Abigail joined Maddy outside where she was stroking Destiny's nose.

Abigail reached out to touch the mane, wondering at the texture, but drew back at the last moment, suddenly aware of the horse's size. "Will he mind?"

Maddy shook her head. "Most horses like people. You just have to be careful not to sneak up on them. That might earn you a good, hard kick."

"Duly noted." Abigail touched the mahogany mane tenuously at first, then ran her fingers through the coarse hair. The horse tossed his head, and Abigail jumped back.

Maddy laughed. "You really are a city girl."

"I've never even seen a horse up close."

Maddy untied the horse and they started off, Maddy leading Destiny. "I can teach you to ride sometime if you want."

"I'll think about it." The cool air felt good on Abigail's heated skin, and her leg muscles were shaky from the intense workout. "Was your dad upset about your bike?"

"Naw, he doesn't get upset much. I told him you'd help me find it . . ."

Abigail noted the uncertainty in her tone. "You bet I will. In fact, I was thinking about it this morning. Why would someone in a town this size steal that bike? Only a girl would want a pink bike with a white basket. If the thief intended to use it, you'd be bound to see it at some point, unless they painted it and removed the basket."

"Or sold it somewhere."

"Possibly. But if that were the case, there'd probably be other stolen bikes, and the sheriff said there hadn't been any."

Abigail questioned Maddy about her friends at school. She wasn't so far removed from childhood that she didn't remember how petty girls could be.

The green hills rolled out before them, and Maddy turned off the gravel road, heading up one of them. The spongy ground gave beneath Abigail's tennis shoes. Their feet swished through the grass, and

Destiny's saddle creaked and clicked with his movements.

". . . So I guess there are two girls at school who really don't like me," Maddy was saying. "I don't like them much either, but Miss Greta says I have to love everyone because God tells us to—even if they're stinkers."

Abigail tugged her ponytail. "They're probably just jealous."

Maddy gave a rueful laugh. "Of what?"

"Your beautiful hair and twinkling green eyes."

Maddy turned a smile on Abigail that warmed her heart, reminding her that the girl didn't have a mother to tell her such things. She wondered about Maddy's relationship with her dad. Even as the thought crossed her mind, her foot caught on something and she stumbled. "Whoops."

Maddy reached out, but Abigail had already recovered.

"The ground's pretty uneven," Maddy said.

"I should probably stick to sidewalks."

"Good luck with that."

They walked in silence for a few minutes, Abigail taking care with her steps.

"So, do you think Haley or Olivia might've taken my bike just to be mean?"

"Did they know what it looked like?"

Maddy rolled her eyes. "Everybody 'round here knows everything about everybody."

"Well, I wouldn't count it out." Abigail checked her watch. Going on five. "You know where they live? Maybe we could drive by their houses. We could do it now."

"I have a bunch of chores, and Greta said to be home by supper."

"Oh, that's right. Well, tomorrow then?"

"Okay. What should I say at school tomorrow?"

"Don't even mention your bike." Last thing they needed was a bunch of drama. "If someone from school took it, we don't want them aware we're looking for it."

Maddy shrugged. "Okay."

They reached the hill's crest and stopped. Abigail scanned the miles of green hills that stretched into distant mountains. "It's so vast. So beautiful."

"I thought you'd like the view. It's my favorite. That's the Absaroka Range, and the river down there is the Yellowstone."

Abigail stared in silence for a moment,

taking in the colors and textures of the land. It looked so much like a painting she wanted to reach out and touch it. Behind her, Destiny whinnied. Abigail checked her watch. "It's getting close to suppertime."

"Yeah, I should get back. You want me to take you back to Miss Lucy's?"

"I think I can find my way." They turned and headed toward the gravel drive.

When they were halfway down the hill, Maddy darted a shy look at Abigail. "Thanks for helping with my bike."

She was only doing what was second nature. First nature really. "You bet," she said.

※

Wade was doing the bills when Maddy entered the office. In her pink pj's with her hair hanging in wet strings, she looked like the little girl he rarely got a glimpse of these days.

"Aren't you supposed to be in bed, squirt?"

"Do I *have* to go to school tomorrow?"

He planted his elbows on top of the bills. "Maddy."

"We'll only clean out our desks. We never do anything the last couple days."

"Enjoy your friends—you won't see much of them till fall. Besides, there's been a glitch with the nanny. Wouldn't be anyone here to watch you and won't be all summer if I don't do some quick thinking."

"I don't need a nanny."

Wade rubbed his wrist where a rope had burned through the skin when he heeled an ornery calf the day before. "Answer's no, Maddy. To both." He still had two days. He'd asked his neighbors and folks from church, but their teenaged daughters had already lined up summer jobs.

He might have to resort to an agency. Man, was he that desperate? Could he trust Maddy to a stranger? There was little time to check references. At least an agency would've done that already. "I'll put a call in to an agency in the morning. In the meantime—"

"No, Dad. I'll wind up with some starchy old lady who makes me stay inside all day. Let me try the summer on my own. *Please?* I'll be good." She clasped her hands, begging.

If he'd learned anything about fatherhood, it was that doing the right thing sometimes made you unpopular. "Sorry, Maddy. Mind's made up."

His daughter dropped her hands, and her shoulders gave in to gravity.

"If I'd known a few weeks ago, maybe I could've found someone around here. But everyone either has a job or doesn't want—"

Maddy straightened. "Abigail can be my nanny!"

"Abigail . . ."

"Miss Lucy's niece. Remember, I told you about her, how she's helping me find my bike, and she's here for the whole summer and doesn't have a job!"

"Maybe she doesn't want a job." If she was Miss Lucy's niece, she was probably old enough to be retired, which explained the extended visit.

"It's worth a try, Dad. I could ask her tomorrow after school 'cause she's helping me with my bike again. Besides, she really likes me."

He couldn't help but smile at her confidence. He saw little enough of that. Maybe he should talk to the niece first, or at least ask Lucy about her. If Lucy thought she'd be interested in a summer job, he'd talk to her then. "You can mention it to her. *Mention*. I don't want her to feel obliged."

Maddy's smile was stunning, and the sparkle in her eyes reminded him of Lizzie in the early years. "I'll be very subtle."

He'd seen his daughter in action when she wanted something. Miss Lucy's niece wouldn't know what hit her.

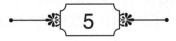

5

That's where she lives." Maddy pointed down a long dirt lane.

They'd already tried Haley's house in town; now they were investigating Olivia's.

The one-story house looked miniscule in front of the mountains. Abigail was sure it was as small as Aunt Lucy's cabin.

She slowed the VW bug and turned down the lane. Clumps of grass dotted the dirt drive, and when they neared the house, she saw no one had gotten around to mowing in a while. Or painting. The flower bed spawned nothing but hearty weeds, and there were no cars in the drive. No bicycles either.

Abigail eased the car along the side of the property, and a small shed came into view. Nothing there either.

"Doesn't look like they're home," Maddy said.

"Hardly looks like anyone lives here. You sure this is her house?"

"I'm sure. We were kinda friends in the third grade, and I came over a couple times. She lives here with her mom."

Abigail wondered what had become of Olivia's father. She was starting to feel sorry for the family. "Well, that's about all we can do for now. My aunt's closing up shop, and I need to give her a ride home—seeing as how this is her car and all."

She smiled at Maddy, but the girl was looking out the window, forlorn.

Abigail put the car in drive and headed back up the road. "Don't worry, Maddy, I won't give up. I'll call the sheriff again tomorrow and see if he's learned anything. And I called a used bike shop in Bozeman today. They haven't seen your bike, but they said they'll keep an eye out. Someone always knows something. It's just a matter of finding the right person. So cheer up, okay?"

Maddy worked her lip. "I actually wasn't thinking about my bike. I mean, I'm worried about it and everything, but there's something else."

"What is it?"

"I have to ask something, and I don't know how to say it."

"Just ask."

"Dad said I should be subtle."

Now Abigail was curious. "I'm more a fan of blunt, actually."

Maddy tossed her a relieved smile. "Oh, good. Blunt is my specialty."

Abigail laughed as she turned onto Main Street. "Out with it then."

"Would you be my nanny for the summer?" The words spilled out like a tipped carton of milk. "My dad says I have to have one, and the one he hired quit before she even started, and now he's going to call some agency, and I just know I'll get stuck with a dud for the whole summer!"

Her nanny? Abigail tossed the idea around a little, trying it on for size. It wasn't like she had other things to do. In fact, she'd been bored silly with her aunt working all day—and it wasn't like Aunt Lucy needed her at the shop. Abigail would still be close enough to check on her.

"You totally don't have to say yes. I mean, you've already been so nice to me."

Maddy had kind of grown on Abigail in a short time. She felt a kinship with the girl, having lost a parent herself. Plus, didn't Aunt Lucy say something about the main house having Internet? She'd be able to do research in her spare time without having to find a way into town.

"Are you mad?" Maddy asked.

Abigail pulled up to the curb in front of the Doll House and put the car in park. "No, honey, not at all. I was thinking it through. Does your nanny stay at the house with you?"

"Yeah. Dad works late a lot, and sometimes things happen and he has to be in the barn all night."

"Your dad is okay with you asking me?"

Maddy nodded. "He said I could. He'll want to meet you and ask you questions and stuff. You could come over tonight after he's done working. If you want to, that is."

Did she? Abigail envisioned a summer with Maddy, with research opportunity at her fingertips, maybe even a soft bed instead of her aunt's lumpy, too-short sofa.

She turned to Maddy, smiling. "Actually, I think I do."

Maddy punched a fist in the air. "Yes!"

❧

Abigail crossed her legs, adjusting the white crepe skirt over her knees while she waited for Maddy to return with a photo album. She was supposed to be meeting with the girl's dad, but his work was keeping him late. Abigail knew all about that.

Her mom would have a conniption if she took this job. And Reagan wouldn't be too thrilled either. Abigail was pretty sure this wasn't what her sister had in mind when she prescribed rest and relaxation. Still, being at the ranch with Maddy would be restful compared to her job in Chicago.

She'd already met Greta, and the smells drifting from the kitchen were reason enough to take the job as Maddy's nanny. Aunt Lucy's culinary skills were limited to canned food, and Abigail never went far beyond macaroni and cheese and hot dogs.

Maddy entered the room with a thick leather-bound album and plunked it on her lap. She opened the cover and ran her small hand over the glossy page. "These were taken at the Fourth of July festival. It's so much fun. There's a parade and games and fireworks and lots and lots of food."

"Looks like a good time."

"You'll still be here in July."

"Sure will. Till the end of August, actually."

"Maybe we can go together. I can show you around."

"Sounds like fun."

As Maddy flipped the page, a male voice sounded in the kitchen.

"Dad's home. He'll need to clean up, then he'll be right in. That's him right there." Maddy pointed at the photo of a man somewhere in his thirties.

He was very attractive. In the photo he'd turned to look at the camera with a guarded grin. He wore a brown cowboy hat low over his eyes. Abigail recalled Aunt Lucy's declaration about Wade being named Sexiest Man Alive. The crazy notion didn't seem so crazy suddenly.

"This is my dad with one of his trophy buckles—he was the World All-Around Champion more times than anyone else."

"No kidding." The photo showed a younger man, smiling wide, holding up his trophy buckle on a stage. In his Western shirt and fitted jeans, Wade Ryan was any woman's definition of a total hunk.

❧

Wade hung his hat on the peg and pulled off his boots, caked with dirt from an afternoon spent cleaning the corrals.

"I know, I'm late," he said before Greta could get on him.

"Supper's keeping warm in the oven, and your daughter's entertaining your applicant in the living room."

"She upset?"

"Not as I can tell." Greta grabbed her purse from the low bench by the door, then slipped into her sweater and tied the belt around her thick middle.

The smells wafting from the oven set a low grumble in his belly. "Thanks, Greta."

"See you tomorrow."

"'Night."

The screen clacked quietly into place. In the sudden silence of Greta's departure, Wade heard his daughter's voice.

He went to the sink, rolled up his sleeves, and washed the dirt and grime off his hands and forearms. Snagging a towel probably not meant for hands, he followed the sound of Maddy's voice to the living room doorway, stopping shy of the threshold.

Around the corner, on the couch, he could see the bottom half of them, his daughter's denims and the woman's white skirt and sandals.

Maddy was jawing about some rodeo and his finish. A lifetime ago.

"Here he is in the newspaper after he won that All-Around," Maddy was saying.

"You must be very proud." The woman had a soft, soothing lilt to her voice.

"Greta says he's the most eligible bachelor in all Montana. But he doesn't date."

Enough of that. Wade cleared his throat and stepped into the room, and Maddy looked up from the photo album.

"You're late, Dad."

His eyes drifted to the woman beside his daughter. *Miss Lucy's niece, my foot.* The woman couldn't be a day past twenty-five. She had flawless skin and large eyes of questionable color.

When she stood, her honey-colored hair swung over her shoulders. The top of her head reached his lips, which made her tall by anyone's standards.

"Hi. I'm Abigail."

"Wade. Sorry to keep you waiting." And he was especially sorry he smelled like cow flesh and wore the grime of a day spent in the corral branding a hundred feisty calves.

He ditched the towel and extended his hand. At least that was clean.

"I've been enjoying talking to your daughter." Her grip was firm, her skin soft.

He pulled away quickly. "Maddy, why don't you run along and let us talk."

Maddy gave Abigail a small smile before heading up the stairs.

He ran his hand through his hair, aware he no doubt had a bad case of hat head. When he heard Maddy's bedroom door close, he gestured toward the album. "Sorry. Looks like she got a little overzealous with the family history."

"Not at all. I met Maddy the other day in my aunt's store, and we've become fast friends. I guess she told you I'm Lucy Bowers's great-niece."

He took a seat in the recliner across

from her. "She did." With the exception of the "great" part.

"I like Maddy a lot."

"She's at ease around you already. I'm surprised."

"She was shy at first, seemed a little lost. But then she opened up. I think she's a loyal and curious girl. Strong, too, though she may not know it yet."

He kept his expression blank only from years of practice. The woman knew his kid better after a couple days than her past nanny had after three summers.

"Sorry if I offended you," she said, absently playing with the silver ring on her right hand.

He cleared his throat. "Appreciate your honesty."

"I have good intuition, or so I'm told."

The announcement and proof of its accuracy made Wade want to don a lead mask. But some things couldn't be intuited, no matter how discerning the woman, and those things he would carry to his grave.

"I have a great deal of respect for your aunt," he said. "She's a fine Christian woman, and she's been good to Maddy. You're visiting for the summer?"

"My mom wanted me to check on Aunt Lucy, as she's getting up in years. I have a three-month leave of absence from my job in Chicago."

Long leave of absence.

"Health reasons," she added as if sensing his question.

He wondered if it would be rude to inquire. Would her health limit her?

"Nothing serious." She waved her hand. "Just needed a break and a change of scenery—which this certainly is."

"No doubt." He eyed her getup and wondered if she had ranch duds.

"I have jeans," she said. "And I should probably buy a pair of boots."

It was a little disconcerting, the way she read his mind. "Probably should."

"I like the ranch name—Stillwater. Did you name it?"

"Got it from Scripture. You know, 'He leads me by quiet waters.'"

"Ah, Psalm 23. A popular one."

"Seemed fitting." Before she could question his comment, he changed the subject. "Our nanny usually stays here in the main house—my hours aren't exactly nine to five." He looked her over, feeling a twinge of something he hadn't felt in a while. "But if you want to stay at your aunt's—"

"Actually, I wouldn't mind staying here. I'd be more available to Maddy, and honestly, the couch at Aunt Lucy's? Not so comfy." Her wide smile kicked him in the gut.

He was so in trouble. "Fine."

"I hope you wouldn't mind us checking on her now and then. I don't have a car, but we could walk over."

"You're welcome to use my truck. Maddy likes visiting your aunt, so that'd be fine. Sundays off?" He named a wage that seemed fair, considering the free room and board.

"Perfect. When does school end?"

"Tomorrow's the last day. You can come the next morning and settle in if that suits."

Abigail smiled again. "Suits me fine. Thanks for your time." She stood and swung her bag onto her shoulder.

He moved to tip his hat, then remembered it wasn't there. "'Night then."

After she walked through the door, he turned on the porch light and watched her walk to the yellow bug, skirt swishing around her long legs, and wondered if he hadn't just bought himself a whole heap of trouble.

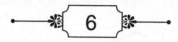

6

Dust plumed behind the wheels of the VW as Abigail drove down the winding gravel driveway toward the main house. She'd been worried Aunt Lucy might feel slighted by her new job, but instead the woman had seemed relieved.

"You'll be good for Maddy. I worry about that child," she'd said when Abigail had broken the news two nights ago. "And now you won't have to sleep on my lumpy old sofa, but you'll still be nearby."

Abigail had promised they'd visit often. But now, with her bags packed and stowed in the backseat, she recalled Wade's dark good looks and slow Southern drawl and wondered if the summer wasn't going to be more challenging than she'd planned.

When she pulled the bug up to the porch to unload her belongings, Maddy ran out to meet her.

"No more school!" The girl's smile spoke for itself.

"Yay, summer!" Abigail exited the car and pulled her bags from the backseat.

"I can help."

Abigail handed her a case. "Careful with that. It's my laptop."

"You're so lucky! My dad won't even let me on his computer."

"Well, maybe he won't mind if you play games on mine."

"Sweet! I'll show you to your room."

Abigail followed Maddy into the house and up the staircase. The steps creaked as they ascended, and when they reached the top, Abigail followed the girl down the short hall to the second room on the left.

She opened the door and flipped the switch, lighting a bedside lamp. The clean scents of pine and lemon permeated the room. A fluffy patchwork quilt covered the high double bed, and a braided rug hugged the wood plank flooring.

Abigail set her bags by the foot of the bed, then trailed her fingers down the nubby stitching on the quilt. "It's lovely."

"The drawers are ready for your things, but there's a bunch of junk in the closet." Maddy set the laptop case on the white-painted desk. "Wanna see my room?"

"Of course."

Maddy gestured to the room across from Abigail's. "That's the bathroom we'll share." A towel lay bunched on the floor against the sink, and various toiletries lined the countertop.

"Here's my room." It was next to the bathroom and across from the other bedroom door—Wade's, she presumed.

Maddy plopped on the bed, making it squeak.

The room was a bit larger than Abigail's, with basic white walls and honey-stained furniture. The sculptured brown carpet was a few days past its expiration date. Two photos sat framed and propped on the dresser, one of Destiny and the other of a young Wade with his arm around a pretty young woman—Maddy's mother?

"Very cozy," Abigail said.

The only splash of color in the plain-Jane room was a green pillow on the bed. Maybe they could redecorate. After they tracked down Maddy's bike. Speaking of which . . .

"I called the used bike shop yesterday, and they didn't have any news for us. I have some other ideas, but I wanted your input."

"Can we do it later? I want to show you the corral and stuff. They're branding right now, and it's pretty fun to watch."

"Sure."

"You need a snack?" Maddy pulled Twizzlers from her desk drawer.

"Don't mind if I do." She took the red sticks from Maddy and followed her into the hall.

"That's Dad's room." Maddy pushed open the door and flipped the switch. A masculine scent wafted into the hall. The lamplight revealed a room with dark walls and simple mahogany furniture. Tidy. Plain. A cowboy hat and shirt hung on a tree in the corner and a pair of black boots sat on the floor below them.

She found herself curious about the

man who occupied the room. Why was he all alone out here with his daughter? Why didn't he date? Was he still mourning his late wife?

"Come on, I'll show you where the action is."

Abigail stuck the licorice in her mouth and bit off the tip, her mind still on Wade as she followed Maddy down the stairs and out the door. He'd seemed nice enough, not strange or rude or arrogant. How did a man who looked like that stay single all these years? And exactly how long had it been since his wife passed away?

She remembered her aunt saying something about Wade and Maddy moving here and recalled the photos Maddy had shown her. She hadn't realized it at the time, but the terrain was different in some of them. Flat and arid looking. Plus, there was Wade's Southern drawl.

"Maddy, where did you move from when you came to Montana?"

"Texas. Don't really remember it though. Dad bought the ranch when I was seven. It was called the Flying B, but he changed it to Stillwater Ranch."

Her mother must've died before they

moved. Abigail didn't know many men who could go five years without a woman. But then, Maddy couldn't know everything about her dad.

Abigail could hear the ruckus from the corral when they were still a distance away. Cows mooing, hooves pounding, men's voices.

They walked along the barn to the fence that enclosed a herd of calves and cowboys. It was a noisy affair. Her eyes scanned the men until she found Wade on horseback. One of the cowboys wore a big silver belt buckle that looked like the ones in Maddy's album.

Abigail gestured toward him. "Did he win a rodeo contest too?"

"Uncle Dylan? Yeah, he used to rodeo with Dad. Moved up here a couple years after we did. Trophy buckles are a big deal, so cowboys like to show them off."

She looked at Wade. "Not your dad though?"

Maddy shrugged. "He doesn't talk much about his rodeo days."

"You have any other family here, other than your uncle Dylan?"

"No, and he's not really my uncle. He's dad's best friend, so I just call him that."

Wade twirled his rope, then tossed it. It sailed in a misshapen loop toward a calf.

"Got it." Maddy set her knee on a low fence rail.

Two young muscular cowboys closed in on the calf as it came to the ground.

"Nobody's better at heeling a calf than Dad. That's why he does the roping."

Abigail couldn't help but feel for the animal as it was dragged across the ground.

"That's the branding pot, where they heat the irons." Maddy pointed to the low machine at the feet of another cowboy. The calf was dragged to the heater, and a gloved man grabbed a long metal tool protruding from the heater. Two men held down the calf and blocked her view, but she turned her head anyway.

When the calf squealed, she wanted to cover her ears. She glanced distastefully at her half-eaten Twizzler.

"They vaccinate and notch her ears as another way of marking—you're not watching."

"Tell me when it's over."

Maddy laughed. "Be thankful it's not a bull calf."

Abigail didn't ask why.

"You can look now," Maddy said a moment later, wrinkling her nose at the smell—an awful stench that smelled like burning hair.

Abigail scanned the pen until she found the branded calf trotting wild-eyed to her mother's side. Poor thing. Abigail scanned the scores of calves. "They have to do that to all those calves?"

Maddy shrugged. "Part of ranch work. Cowboys love this stuff."

"Where did all these men come from?"

"Most of 'em are neighbors. Dad'll help them with their branding too."

Abigail watched Wade trot the horse across the pen. He looked tall in the saddle. Masculine. He had fawn-colored chaps over his jeans and gloves on his hands. He and the black horse moved as one.

It seemed like it would take forever to get all those calves done. "They do this all day?"

"Till supper."

Abigail imagined Wade and the others would be beat after a day of wrestling frightened calves.

Just then he turned in the saddle as if sensing their presence.

"Hi, Dad!" Maddy waved.

Wade lifted a gloved hand to his daughter, his eyes lingering. He touched the brim of his hat, and Abigail felt his gaze clear down to her dirty tennis shoes.

"You ready to go in and unpack?" Maddy asked.

"Sounds like a plan."

❀

Abigail took a bite of roasted chicken, her gaze darting between Wade and Maddy. Was it always this quiet at dinner? The silence felt awkward, though the other two seemed at ease.

Abigail couldn't stand it anymore. "The branding was interesting."

"Abigail couldn't watch," Maddy said.

She shrugged a little, embarrassed at her weak stomach. "I felt sorry for the poor little things."

"Keeps 'em safe in the long run," Wade said. "No different than kids. Sometimes what's good for them is less than pleasant. They get over it soon enough."

"The calves or the kids?" Abigail asked.

"Both."

"Hey, I'm right here, you know."

Wade winked at Maddy.

He hadn't come in until eight thirty, and Maddy said that was normal. That didn't give her much time with her dad during the summer, much less during the school year when she presumably had an earlier bedtime. But then, he was a single dad, and if ranch work was that time consuming, what choice did he have?

"All settled in?" Wade asked Abigail.

When she looked at him, his gaze flickered away. He never held eye contact long.

"I am. And I have to say, I'm looking forward to a real mattress."

"Hope your aunt doesn't think we stole you away."

"We'll visit plenty, won't we, Maddy? Plus, I promised I'd attend church with her on Sundays. Anyway, I'm still trying to assess her mental faculties. It's kind of . . . challenging."

"She's always been eccentric," Wade said. "Least, since I've known her."

"I think she's fun," Maddy said. "She has a great imagination."

Abigail smiled. "I'll say. She talks to her

dolls like they're her children, and she told me you were voted Sexiest Man Alive for some magazine."

"Ewwww!" Maddy said.

Abigail realized immediately that she'd made it sound like an impossibility. "I didn't mean . . ." She stopped at the look in Wade's eyes.

A deer in headlights. Then, just as quickly, his lids shuttered his eyes and the feelings behind them. What had she seen in those blue eyes? Not embarrassment or even offense. She watched him covertly as he gulped down his milk and Maddy chattered. He'd looked . . . caught. Which was awfully strange, given Abigail's benign comment. Unless . . .

But how could it be true? Some obscure rancher given the notorious award? Even if it had been back in his rodeo days, the celebrity world didn't pay attention to ordinary cowboys, did it? She'd never followed celebrities or read those ridiculous tabloids, though, so what did she know?

Well, it was easy enough to check. One Internet search, and she could put the silly notion from her mind.

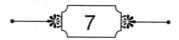

7

Abigail didn't remember her resolve to do an Internet search on Wade until the next morning. By the time Maddy had turned in the night before, Abigail was tired and ready for a real mattress, which turned out to be as comfy as it looked.

After Maddy had eaten and gone to get dressed, Abigail turned on her laptop. When she tried to get online, she found the wireless secured. She'd have to get the password from Wade, but he was busy with branding now. It would have to wait until evening.

Once Maddy was ready, they watched

the branding again. Maddy was itching to help, especially when one of the cowboys' sons worked a small calf. The boy straddled the wiggling calf, and with the help of his dad, held him down while the others did their thing.

Maddy scowled. "That kid is way littler than me." She hopped down from the fence. "Can we eat now?"

After lunch they went to Abigail's room so she could get the number for the bike store in Bozeman. Maddy flopped across the bed while Abigail checked her cell phone for the number. "Maybe there'll be news today."

A message waited on her phone. Marla at Pappy's Market had seen a pink bike in front of Movie Magic Video on her way to work. She'd just left the message four minutes earlier.

"Maddy, we've got a break on the case."

Maddy's eyes went to the laptop case. "I didn't do it. I was real careful when I brought it in."

Abigail laughed. "The *bicycle* case. That was Marla from the market." She repeated the message. "The bike might still be there. You know where the truck keys are?"

"Sure do!"

They retrieved the keys from a hook in the kitchen and trotted to the old red truck. It started with a cough and a sputter, then Abigail maneuvered it out of its space. They stopped by the corral to let Wade know, then headed down the drive.

"You think it's my bike?" Maddy asked once they were on the main road.

"Are there any other pink bikes in town?"

"Not that I know of."

They were so close. If they could only get there before the bike disappeared, they'd catch their thief red-handed.

"Can't you go faster?"

"I'm going the speed limit." Her foot itched to press down, but she had to be mindful of setting a good example.

When they reached town, Abigail turned toward the video store. They both leaned forward in their seats, peering around the parked cars in front of the stores.

"There it is!" Maddy said.

"Is it yours?" Abigail parked on the opposite side of the street.

"Sure looks like it. It's got a white basket. Mine had a scratch on the frame from when I took a spill on the driveway, so I'll know for sure when we get close."

They exited the truck, waited for a pickup to pass, and darted across the street.

Maddy squatted in front of the bike. "There it is! Look!"

Abigail leaned over and eyed the long silver scuff on the frame. "Wait here," she told Maddy, heading toward the store's entrance. But before she could grasp the handle, the door opened.

A girl slipped past Abigail, turned toward the bike, and stopped short. From behind, Abigail could see the child's shoulders lift and draw inward. Her fingers tightened convulsively on the plastic bag in her hand.

Maddy rose to her feet, her eyebrows drawn together. "You stole my bike."

The girl turned to run and smacked into Abigail's stomach. Abigail took the girl's shoulders. "Wait just a minute, young lady."

Tears welled up in brown eyes that were wide and frightened. "I'm sorry!"

"You knew it was my bike, Olivia."

So it was the girl from school, the one without a father. "Stealing is a crime, Olivia. Why did you take Maddy's bike?"

"I'm sorry! I figured she didn't need it! I knew her dad would buy her a new one."

"That doesn't mean it's yours to take!" Maddy said.

Abigail looked at Olivia. The girl's stringy brown hair hadn't been washed in days, and she fairly swam in her white T-shirt and jeans.

"She can have it back." Olivia dragged her hand across her wet cheeks. "I won't do it again. I'm sorry, Maddy!"

The girl seemed earnest, and Maddy had her bike back, but they weren't finished. Abigail hated to burden Olivia's mom, but the woman needed to know her daughter had stolen.

"Can I go now?" Olivia cradled the video bag.

"I'm afraid we need to talk with your mom, Olivia."

"Please! I wanted a bike so bad, and we can't afford one. I said I won't do it again."

Abigail glanced at Maddy. Her face had softened, and she stared back at Abigail, uncertain.

"I'm sorry, Olivia, but your mother needs to know the truth."

Abigail stowed the bike in the truck as

Maddy and Olivia climbed into the cab. She pulled the truck onto the street, then turned toward Olivia's property. The girls sat silently beside her. The road stretched before them and seemed to lengthen with every sniffle.

When they finally turned into Olivia's drive, Abigail breathed a sigh. In the distance, the girl's house loomed bleak and gray under a cast of clouds. Her mother's vehicle, an old white truck, sat in the drive.

The girl's lips were trembling by the time they started up the overgrown walk to the house. Maddy had fallen in behind them.

It was up to Abigail to be strong. "Olivia, go get your mom. If you like, you can tell her yourself, and we'll wait for her here."

Olivia's head dropped as she entered the house slowly.

"Maybe we don't have to talk to her mom," Maddy said. "I have my bike back."

"It's very sweet that you're concerned for Olivia, honey. I feel for her too, but stealing your bike was a choice she made, a bad one, and she might do it again, or even do something worse. It's hard for Olivia now, but it might save her a lot of trouble later."

"I know, I just wish . . ." Maddy scanned

the house and yard. "I don't think she has much. And she's right. Dad probably would've bought me another bike."

A woman appeared at the door. Through the screen, Olivia's mom didn't look much older than Abigail. She had flawless olive skin and wore a low ponytail.

"I'm Shay, Olivia's mom. Olivia told me what she did."

"I'm Abigail, Maddy's nanny."

Shay's eyes shifted to Maddy. "I'm truly sorry, hon. She won't do it again." She turned to the side. "Livy, come here and apologize."

"She already did," Maddy said, but Olivia appeared and whispered an apology anyway.

"I'll be grounding her for a suitable length of time, and maybe she can come out to your place and work to pay you back for your trouble. But I'd be obliged if you didn't press charges."

"No, we won't," Abigail said. "I'll call the sheriff to let him know it's been resolved, but I thought you should know."

"Thank you," Shay said, nudging Olivia.

"Yeah, thank you," Olivia whispered.

Abigail nodded and smiled, then she

and Maddy turned away from the house and got into the truck. They were to the end of the lane before either spoke.

"I'm glad I have my bike back," Maddy said in a somber tone, "but that was hard."

"I know. Sometimes telling the truth is the hardest thing to do." And sometimes, not telling the truth would haunt you for the rest of your life.

❀

Abigail peeked out the front door where Maddy and Wade sat on the porch swing. Darkness had long since enveloped the yard, swallowing all but a glowing cone of porch light. It cast a golden light across their faces, lighting Wade's dark hair like a shimmering fire.

"I'm headed to my room," Abigail said.

"'Night," they said.

"Wade, could I get the wireless password? You have a secure network."

He lowered his copy of *Livestock Weekly*. "Didn't set that stuff up, but I might've used our phone number. Or the word *password*."

"All right, I'll try them both. Thanks."

Abigail retreated to her room and pushed the door closed. After getting into her pajamas, she settled against the feather pillows with her laptop.

"Let's see if we can get this to work." She opened Network Connections and tried the word *password*. Denied access, she fumbled through her purse for her cell phone to find the ranch phone number and entered it.

Bingo.

Wi-Fi was a beautiful thing. She'd be able to conduct research for her identity theft story now, not to mention stay in touch with family via e-mail.

She checked her messages and found one from her mom and one from her sister. Reagan mentioned that their mom was concerned about *Viewpoint*, but she didn't go into detail. Mom hadn't said anything in her e-mail, but she was probably trying to shelter Abigail, especially where *Viewpoint* was concerned. She knew Abigail would be back at work in a blink if she thought she could help. Abigail replied to them both, assuring her mother she was getting plenty of rest, despite her new job, and that her headaches and palpitations were better, and asking Reagan just what she meant.

Once that was done, she Googled

"Wade Ryan sexiest man alive," rolling her eyes at her own stupidity as she hit Enter.

Please, don't ever let him snoop through my Internet history.

The links page came up. *No results found*. Well, duh. What did she think she'd find?

On impulse, she did another search, this one more general, and clicked on a link for a list of Sexiest Man Alive winners. She was nothing if not thorough.

Abigail scanned the list for Wade's name, starting with the most current year and going backward. When she reached 1998, she stopped and scanned back toward the most recent entry.

This was ridiculous. She couldn't believe she was following up on a wacky statement from Aunt Lucy, backed only by an odd look from Wade. So much for intuition.

She started to close the page, but her eye caught on a name. *J. W. Ryan*.

Right last name, but she'd never heard of J. W. Ryan. Even Abigail had heard of the other winners. Whoever J. W. Ryan was, he was the winner of the contest six years ago. She clicked on the name, and a new page began opening.

A photo appeared, and Abigail's breath caught in her lungs and held there. It was a younger Wade. He wore a black cowboy hat and a cocky, almost ornery, grin. His hat was pulled low over his eyes, which looked startlingly blue against his tanned skin.

Talk about palpitations. They were back with a vengeance.

Someone knocked on the door, and Abigail jumped. She snapped the laptop closed. "Who is it?" Her voice came out sharp.

"It's me, Maddy."

She tried for casual. "Come in."

Maddy slipped inside. "Just wanted to say thanks for finding my bike. Sorry if I didn't seem grateful before."

"You were just concerned for Olivia."

"I wish I'd been nicer to her at school."

"It's never too late. Maybe we can have her over sometime."

Maddy perked up. "I'll bet she'd like to go riding."

Abigail smiled. "I'll bet she would. We could take a picnic and make an afternoon of it."

"There's a spot by the river that has a great swimming hole . . . when it's a little warmer."

"That sounds like fun."

Maddy shifted toward the door. "Great. Well, I'm going to take a shower. 'Night."

"'Night, honey."

When the door clicked closed, Abigail laid her head against the headboard and drew a breath. For heaven's sake, it was like she'd been caught with her hand in the cookie jar.

She opened the laptop again and watched as the photo of Wade appeared on the screen. She read the paragraph beside the picture.

J. W. Ryan may be the world's most deco-rated cowboy, with five World All-Around titles, but he's also a treat for the eyes. Standing at 6'2" and weighing in at 194 pounds, he's without a doubt made of tough stock. But according to those who know him, he's a focused competitor, an attentive husband, and a tender father to daughter Madison, 5. And with a grin like that, it's no wonder he's become the world's most famous cowboy.

Abigail stared at the screen. Amazing. The man was apparently famous, or had been a handful of years ago, and yet here he was on a cattle ranch in Middle-of-Nowhere, Montana.

Why had he come here? Did the townspeople and neighbors know who he was? Aunt Lucy knew about the award; did everyone else? Maddy hadn't seemed to know. Of course, she'd only been five at the time, but hadn't anyone told her? Why did he go by Wade and not J. W.? Was he trying to hide? And if he was, why?

Curious, she did another search, this time typing *J. W. Ryan*. Pages and pages of links followed. There were articles about him in *Cowboy Sports News, Rodeo Magazine, People, American Cowboy, ESPN*, and the *Denver Post*, not to mention all the trashy tabloids.

How had she never heard of the man? Of course, she'd been immersed in college at the time, and her sister had always said she was clueless when it came to celebrities.

Abigail clicked on a link for the *Houston Chronicle*, wanting something more substantial than a fluff piece and figuring the Texas paper might have the scoop on their local cowboy celebrity. The headline read *J. W. Ryan Questioned in Wife's Death*.

Abigail frowned at the photo of Wade walking into a building with two uniformed officers. She read the article.

World Rodeo champion J. W. Ryan was brought in for questioning yesterday following his wife's unexpected death. Sources say Elizabeth Montgomery-Ryan died unexpectedly in the couple's home late Friday night. J. W. Ryan reportedly found his wife and called 911. The police say they have no suspects at this time and that their questioning of Ryan is standard procedure.

Abigail didn't know what to feel first. The thought of Wade losing his young wife and then being questioned about her death was horrific. Was he with his wife when she died? Was Maddy? Abigail could only hope not.

Had the police's questioning really been standard procedure? Surely he hadn't been involved in the murder of his wife—his daughter's mother. But why else would he have moved so far away, and under a different name? What had happened after the questioning?

She could find out easily enough.

She did another search, confining it to the investigation of his wife's death, and clicked on an article in the *Houston Chronicle* dated several weeks later.

Nearly a month after the death of rodeo celebrity J. W. Ryan's wife, police have declared the death an accident. Speculations about the cause of Elizabeth Ryan's death have been fueled by a heated argument the couple reportedly had the night of her death.

So he was cleared. Abigail felt a blanket of relief cover her, for Maddy's sake, not to mention her own safety. The rest of the article turned up no new information.

Why did Wade move? Was it only to escape the speculation and gossip? Surely that died down when the police cleared him. Why move so far away, go by Wade instead of J. W.? Why give up the rodeo circuit, which had apparently earned him a fortune?

Abigail clicked on another link, but it restated the same information. She skimmed articles for more details and found only redundant pieces from the Associated Press.

It was too painstaking to search through links. Where could she get more information? Who would know the details?

Reagan. Her sister had read celebrity tabloids since she was twelve. She'd know about this story. Abigail checked her watch, surprised to see over an hour had passed since she'd begun. It was an hour later in Chicago, but Reagan would still be up.

She unplugged her phone and dialed her sister's number. It rang four times, then voice mail kicked in. Abigail considered leaving a message, but changed her mind. She'd call Reagan back when she was sure there was no one around to hear.

She closed the phone, plugged it into the charger, and reluctantly shut down her computer. It was late, and Maddy rose early. Abigail needed to turn in, but she knew from past experience that questions would hover like pesky mosquitoes until she found answers.

8

Abigail woke before dawn the next morning. Moonlight still filtered through her eyelet curtains, illuminating the silver case of her laptop on the nightstand. All she'd read about Wade the night before came rushing back.

She sat up and glanced at her cell phone. It was too early, even in Chicago, for a phone call. It would have to wait until tonight. Besides, she admitted to herself as she rubbed the sleep from her eyes, the speculations she'd read last night seemed less substantial now.

The police had ruled the death an accident. Regardless of how the accident occurred, Wade had suffered a tremendous loss. According to the articles, he'd found the woman he loved lying dead in their home.

Abigail rubbed her temple, realizing as she did so that she'd woken with a headache. She fumbled through her purse for Tylenol, then padded into the bathroom, hoping for a glass. No such luck.

Resigning herself to an early morning, she felt her way down the stairs, cringing at the creaks, hoping not to wake Maddy or Wade. Especially not Wade, as she was still in her pajamas, her hair a tousled mess.

In the kitchen, she filled a glass, took the pills, then headed back to her room. The floor was cold against her bare feet, and outside the living room window she could see the purple fingers of dawn stretching across the sky.

She found the stair railing and followed it up the flight, congratulating herself for missing the squeaks this time. Now if she could just go back to sleep for a couple hours. Maddy wouldn't be up for another—

Her body collided with something hard. She braced herself against it.

There was warmth to the hardness. Motion. Not it.

Him. She was such a klutz.

"What the—"

"Sorry . . ." she whispered. "I didn't expect anyone to be up." She couldn't see his face, but she felt his hands on her arms, warm against her bare skin. Then they were gone.

"Always up this early." His voice was a sleepy drawl.

Now that she'd recovered, she realized her own fingers were on his shirt, realized she was absently stroking the soft—flannel?—fabric.

She jerked her hands away, feeling like a fool. Thank God he couldn't see the heat flooding her face. "I was just—I needed some water. I'm going back to bed."

She ducked her head and dodged past him. When she reached her room, she slipped inside, closed the door, and told herself the fluttering of her heart was only from the fright of Wade's sudden appearance.

❧

Wade nudged Ace toward his friend Dylan as he watched Pee Wee and his neighbor

O'Neil work a big calf that was putting up a fight.

Dylan laughed. "My grandma could do better'n that, O'Neil."

O'Neil tightened his hold on the calf's hindquarters, swearing when one hoof got loose and kicked off his hat.

Wade sat back in the saddle, grinning. The calf was definitely winning. He was glad Maddy was watching. It gave credence to his caution.

Wade removed his hat, ran his sleeve across his face. Ever since Maddy and Abigail had appeared at the fence ten minutes ago, he'd been distracted by their presence.

Not their presence, he corrected. *Her* presence. He didn't know what it was about Abigail that had him all hot and bothered. Sure she was attractive, but it was more than that. He felt like she could look right through him, and it was disconcerting.

Yeah, that's all it was. He was disconcerted. Especially this morning when her soft body had smacked up against him.

"Who's the pretty young thing?" Dylan jerked his head toward the fence.

"My daughter."

Dylan tossed Wade a look.

Wade didn't like the way his friend eyed Abigail. "Maddy's new nanny from Chicago."

He grinned. "That's some nanny. She got a boyfriend?"

"What happened to Brittney? Or Bridgett or whatever?"

"Got bored. What's the story on the nanny?"

Wade shoved his hat on his head. "Name's Abigail. Miss Lucy's great-niece. Here short-term, for the summer."

"Wouldn't mind me a summer romance."

Wade frowned at Dylan, but it was lost on his friend, who was still checking out Abigail. Dylan would consider the short-term part a bonus. Wade loved the guy like a brother, but his friend didn't know the meaning of the word *commitment* when it came to women.

"Unless you're interested," Dylan said.

While Wade's mind had wandered, Dylan had shifted his attention to Wade's face, which no doubt reflected his thoughts.

"'Cause if you're interested," Dylan continued, "I'd consider it a good thing. A man needs a little feminine companionship, know what I'm saying?"

Wade's gaze darted to Abigail, and just as swiftly his mind sifted through all the reasons Abigail didn't deserve him. All the reasons no woman deserved him.

"Not interested," he said finally. Amazing that the lie came out steady and firm. You'd think he meant it.

"Been a long time, buddy."

Dylan meant well, but he didn't understand. Wade wasn't sure he understood it himself. "Got a daughter to raise and a ranch to run. All I'm thinking about now." He nudged Ace forward.

"Then you don't mind if I have a go?" Dylan said.

Wade scrambled for reasons and came up empty. "Suit yourself," he called over his shoulder.

He could've kicked his own behind as he watched his friend saunter toward Abigail. Dylan was missing nothing in the looks department. He had a dimpled smile that beckoned every filly in a fifty-mile radius and a certain charm that gathered a female crowd wherever he went.

Why was he so bothered? Because there was something going on with Abigail's health, that's what it was. She didn't need some philandering cowboy messing with her heart.

Maddy came off the fence, and Wade heard her squeal from clear across the pen.

"Hey, Uncle Dylan!"

Traitor. He scowled as Dylan set his hat on Maddy's head. A minute later, Maddy went skipping toward the barn. Dylan must've sent her on an errand. Smooth.

Ace shuffled under him. Wade dismounted and pretended to adjust the bridle, discreetly watching the scene between Dylan and Abigail. He'd give his best pair of boots to hear them.

Abigail perched on the fence, her long legs dangling over the side. Didn't look much older than Maddy with her hair back in a ponytail. His gaze traveled down the length of her jeaned legs. Yeah, he'd bet that wasn't the way Dylan saw it.

His friend leaned on the post next to Abigail. Close. Wade watched her face for clues, but she was too far away. Then Dylan shifted, putting his body between Abigail and Wade.

Daggonit. Wade checked out the calf being worked. They were vaccinating, finally.

He set his boot in the stirrup and mounted, hoping for a better view of the action at the fence. Maddy ran from the barn with a pair of gloves. Good girl. She handed them to Dylan, but he stood there still chatting up Abigail.

Activity in the corner caught his eye when the worked calf scrambled to her feet and ran for mama. The cowboys at the heater ribbed one another, no doubt casting blame and calling each other's manhood into question.

"All right, boys," Wade called. "Back to work."

A moment later Dylan took his hat from Maddy's head, set it on his own, then sauntered back toward him. Wade worked his rope, readying it for the next calf, telling himself he didn't care if Abigail had fallen for Dylan's charm, didn't care if they were going out tomorrow night, didn't care if they got hitched and had a passel of kids.

Dylan was slipping on the gloves Maddy had fetched as he passed Wade. "Must be losing my touch," he mumbled.

Wade smothered the grin that fought for release.

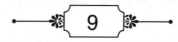

9

I'm going for a walk, Maddy," Abigail said. "Want to come?"

Maddy didn't look up from the computer game. "No thanks."

"All right. I won't be long."

Wade had given Maddy permission to use Abigail's laptop as long as she stayed in the living room and used it for games only. The girl was already a Ball Maze fanatic.

Abigail stepped onto the porch, letting the screen fall behind her. The night was getting cooler, and the moon rose in the sky, big and round, blanketing the treetops with a pale, silvery light. She trotted down the porch steps and started up the lane at a brisk pace. She'd neglected her exercise.

Wade had come home for dinner, then he was off again—to the barn, if the light up ahead was any indication. He was as passionate about his work as she was, apparently. It was hard being away from her job, the action, the satisfaction she got from writing her column.

She glanced at her watch, turning it so the moon illuminated the face. She'd give her sister another hour. It was a Friday night after all, and Reagan might have a date. It could happen.

Abigail breathed deeply, drawing in the fragrance of fresh grass and the loamy smell of dirt. Even the moonlight seemed to have a fragrance out here. It was a different world, a different planet. The pace was slower, and everything worked on nature's schedule.

As Abigail neared the barn she heard a rustling, a low voice, and she turned into the doorway. The smell of fresh hay and cow flesh packed a wallop. She followed the sounds to the end of the barn where Wade squatted by a sleeping calf.

She heard the low murmur of his voice and stopped, wondering if he'd be embarrassed to be caught crooning to a cow.

As if sensing her presence, Wade turned. It was the pose from the Sexiest Man photo, minus the ornery smile.

"Maddy okay?" he asked in that low, Texas drawl of his.

"Fine. I was taking a walk and heard you. Everything all right?"

He faced the calf as Abigail approached. "He's sick."

She squatted beside Wade. The calf didn't open his eyes as she ran her hand down his hide. The fur was smooth, not as soft as she expected. "What's wrong with him?"

"Stress or allergic to the vaccine. They're vulnerable after they're worked—little ones like this guy especially."

"He'll be okay?"

"Probably not."

Abigail stroked him again. Poor little guy. Mama stood nearby, and Abigail wondered if the cow knew, if she would grieve her baby.

Wade went to a stall where another calf

lay. The animal eyed Wade with huge brown eyes.

"That one sick too?"

"Just weak and stiff. He'll be fine." Wade darted a glance at her. "You and Maddy getting on okay?"

Abigail wondered if he'd ever hold eye contact long enough for her to get a read on him. "Sure. She's a great kid." Maybe this was a good time to address a couple issues, since he'd asked . . . "She's at that age where she's growing like a weed. Would you mind if I took her shopping for a few things?"

She didn't think she imagined the relief that chased across his features.

"Be fine." He reached for his wallet.

"We can settle up afterward."

He nodded once and turned his attention to the calf.

One issue down. One more to go. "We're thinking of having a picnic lunch soon as it warms up, going for a swim. I know you're busy, but maybe you could join us."

Wade tugged his hat. "Got my hands full right now."

"You have to eat." She laughed lightly. "How about a picnic dinner? We could have a moonlight swim." She kept her tone light, but the look in his eyes heated her skin through. Gave her images of a swim that didn't include Maddy at all.

What's gotten into you, Abigail? He's your boss.

Just as quickly, Wade looked away, pulled off his gloves. "Too cold at night."

"A Sunday afternoon then." She didn't mind using her day off. If it brought father and daughter closer, it was worth it.

"We'll see."

She knew a blow-off when she heard one. "Maddy could use some attention. Girls need their daddies, you know."

His posture stiffened. "Thought you said she was fine."

"She is fine, but that's not to say—"

"I love my daughter. Reckon I know what's best for her."

"I didn't mean—"

"Don't come in here and presume to know what's what. You've known Maddy a week. I've had her since the day she was born. I've raised her alone since—" He looked away, then back in Abigail's general direction. "We've been on our own for a while, and we're doing just fine. I'll thank you to remember that."

Warmth flooded Abigail's face. She hadn't been scolded in years, certainly not by a boss. "I'm sorry." She felt the sudden sting of tears and a desperate need to escape before she humiliated herself. "I think I'll turn in now. Good night."

She brushed past him, made her way out of the barn and toward the house. She was only trying to help. So much for her walk. Wade had shattered her peace. How could he be so tender with a sick cow yet disregard his daughter's needs? He was the only parent the girl had. Couldn't he see she needed him?

Abigail blinked away the tears, quickening her steps. Why'd he have to be so snippy anyway? He'd asked how Maddy was, and Maddy's business was Abigail's business. It wasn't like she'd butted into his private affairs.

When she entered the house, she saw her laptop on the coffee table. The shower was running upstairs. With Maddy readying for bed and Wade in the barn, it was a good time to call Reagan . . . and put the confrontation with Wade from her mind.

In her room, she retrieved her cell phone and placed the call.

"Sis!" Reagan said. "How's life in the boonies?"

At the sound of Reagan's voice, some of Abigail's stress drained away. "Much as you'd imagine. I would've called you earlier, but I figured you'd have a hot date."

"I did—with an appendix."

"He make it?"

"*She* made it just fine." Reagan filled in the details until Abigail was sorry she asked.

"I have a question for you," Abigail said when Reagan wrapped up her surgery summary. She lowered her voice, just in case. "You remember anything about a rodeo star named J. W. Ryan in the news several years ago?"

"Well, duh, who doesn't."

"Me?"

"If only you read the tabloids . . ."

"Spare me."

Reagan chuckled. "He was a cowboy, a total hunk, in every celeb magazine you could find. His wife died—or got murdered, depending on whom you ask. There was a lot of speculation, then he just disappeared. Which, of course, made everyone suspicious."

"What do you mean, *disappeared*?"

"I mean fell off the face of the planet. No more interviews, reporters gossiping about what happened to him and his daughter. Why the sudden interest?"

Abigail was supposed to be resting, and having a potential murderer for a boss wasn't exactly restful. "I ran across some articles online and was curious."

"You were doing research! Stay off the Internet, Abigail, or I'm telling Mom. How are your symptoms?"

"Better."

"That's nice and vague."

"Stop being a worrywart. How much trouble can I get into in a town the size of Moose Creek?"

"You? Plenty."

"Ha-ha. Stop worrying and get some sleep before you get another emergency."

Abigail said good night, then checked on Maddy, who was crawling into bed. She tucked the girl in, retrieved the laptop from the living room, then returned to her room and booted up.

※

Abigail closed her laptop, her mind reeling. Reagan had been right. There'd been plenty of gossip about Wade's part in his wife's death. Some of the articles were over the top—clearly he hadn't killed his daughter and himself, but he had disappeared.

Had he just grown tired of being the subject of gossip, or was there something more? Something more sinister? He seemed like a nice guy—tonight's dispute aside—but Abigail knew better than most that appearances could be deceiving. People, seemingly normal people, were capable of awful things.

Several articles mentioned a heated argument. Was there another man or woman involved? Did Wade have a temper, had he lost control? The police's conclusion of accidental death didn't hold much weight with her. They could be fooled or even bought off.

Was there a connection between Wade's emotional distance from Maddy and guilt? Was he capable of murder? If he was,

Maddy could be in danger. Abigail had seen too much to believe all parents had their children's best interests at heart, despite what they said.

Her thoughts crept back to the one piece of evidence she couldn't escape: his running. If Wade had nothing to hide, why not face the questions and state the truth until the gossip died down?

Abigail smothered a yawn and realized she'd gone way past her bedtime. She set the laptop on her nightstand and slipped under the covers, making a decision as she tucked the quilt under her chin.

She wasn't going to stop until she had answers. One thing she knew from the stories she'd covered: someone always knew something. She just had to find that someone and extract the facts. The truth was out there somewhere, and she was going to uncover it.

10

On Sunday Abigail went to church with Aunt Lucy and made a point of listening to the sermon. The preacher taught on the fruit of the Spirit and managed to hold her attention, and Aunt Lucy's friends were as welcoming as they'd been the week before.

She and her aunt ate a simple lunch in the cabin. Abigail stayed alert for signs of dementia. Aunt Lucy had asked her twice if she wanted ice cream and had once been unable to come up with the word *futile*. But that could happen to anyone, right?

Through the afternoon, Abigail also tried to draw information from her aunt about

Wade. Abigail went into it determined to take every comment seriously, no matter how absurd it sounded—after all, the Sexiest Man Alive had panned out. But Aunt Lucy had nothing new to share, ridiculous or not.

So Abigail left that evening, feeling troubled about Aunt Lucy's health and disheartened that she'd turned up nothing on Wade. She had to keep trying.

There were a few ways of collecting information. The Internet, questioning others, and Abigail's least favorite, snooping. She'd continue her online research and question people in Wade's life. Wade was the one who knew for sure, but he also had the most to lose and would therefore be the hardest one to crack.

Her next step was to see how much Maddy remembered. Also, Wade may have confided in Dylan. They seemed to have a long history together. Greta and Pee Wee were potential sources. Wade may have shared information with his cowhand, and if Pee Wee knew something, it was likely he'd shared it with his wife.

The summer was looking more interesting. She would continue to observe Aunt

Lucy, take care of Maddy, and investigate Wade's past on the side. If he was guilty of murder, she was going to find out and make sure justice was done.

Her mother wouldn't be happy if she found out what Abigail was doing. But she could hardly stand by and let a potential murderer get off scot-free, could hardly risk a young girl's safety.

❧

Abigail eyed the blond horse skeptically. Her huge buggy eyes stared back, and Abigail was sure the horse was just as dubious about her.

"Are you sure she's gentle?"

"Yep. Her name's Trinket, and Dad said she's the best in his string for a beginner."

The word *beginner* didn't set well with Abigail even if she was officially, and okay, unofficially, exactly that. "Hi, Trinket." She stroked the horse's side. "She's kind of big."

"You can reach the stirrup. Put your foot in there."

Abigail slipped her sneakered foot into the hole. Sure, she'd seen it on done on TV, but seeing and doing? Not the same thing, as she discovered when Trinket lumbered forward, knocking her off balance.

Abigail dragged her foot along the ground. "Stop!"

"Whoa, girl." Maddy took the reins. "Swing your leg over."

"Here goes nothing." Abigail put her weight in the stirrup and swung her leg over. Next thing she knew, she was in the saddle. "Hey, I did it."

"Told you it was easy. We should've gotten you some boots Saturday."

"I know, I know."

Maddy adjusted Abigail's stirrups, mounted Destiny like she'd been born in the saddle, then led them past the corrals toward open pasture.

Abigail grabbed the saddle horn as Trinket plodded along. There was more movement up here than she'd expected.

"Let your body kind of roll with it," Maddy said.

Abigail made an effort to relax, letting her body sway. Slowly she began to trust that she wouldn't fall. She even released the horn and gripped the leather reins with both hands.

"Hey, I'm doing it."

"You're a real pro."

"No need for sarcasm."

Maddy shot her a smile.

"Did your dad like your new clothes?"

Maddy shrugged. "Guess so. You know men. They don't notice clothes so much."

"Guess you're right. That purple sure does look good on you."

"Thanks. I wore the blue plaid shirt yesterday, the one with the dark stitching."

"I like that one." Abigail had taken Maddy shopping on Saturday. Despite the limited clothing stores in Moose Creek, they'd turned up some pretty cute clothes. They'd even visited the undergarment section. Abigail thought Maddy might be embarrassed, but the girl had been eager to have her first bra and probably relieved her dad wasn't present.

The rolling hills, covered in soft green grass, seemed to go on forever before rising into mountains that glowed pink in the morning light. A clean blue sky stretched from one side of the world to the other, and the air smelled like dew and fresh grass. A black and white bird flittered past and settled on a nearby tree.

Maddy went through a myriad of horse commands and noises like clucking and kissing sounds, but it took all of Abigail's concentration to stay upright, especially when they hit an incline. Besides, Trinket seemed to be on autopilot.

After her instructions, Maddy questioned Abigail about life in Chicago. Abigail told her about everything from the Magnificent Mile to Navy Pier to the famous deep-dish pizza.

After thirty minutes in the saddle, Abigail shifted, loosening her lower back. At least Trinket was nice and slow. She took in the scenery as they plodded along. "It's easy to see why they call this Big Sky Country."

"It's pretty. And it looks different every season, like a whole new place. Summer's my favorite, even though it gets really hot."

"I guess it's a big change from Texas."

Maddy shrugged. "Don't remember much about Texas. I was young."

Still, Abigail wondered . . . "It must've been hard losing your mom and moving away from your friends."

"Don't remember much about my mom. Wish I did."

Abigail heard the sadness in her tone. "You were so young." She hesitated to

ask, but it had to be done. "What happened to her?"

Maddy shrugged. "It was an accident.
Dad doesn't like to talk about it. Makes
him sad."

"That's understandable." Probably guilt.
Abigail shifted gears. "What's your favorite
memory of her?"

Frown creases formed on Maddy's forehead, and she was silent so long Abigail
wondered if she'd answer. "I guess I don't
have one," she said finally.

"I'm sorry for your loss, Maddy. She'd
be very proud of you."

"You think?"

"Any parent would be. You're a smart,
strong girl. I lost my dad too, but I was
older than you. Fifteen."

"How'd he die?"

"Heart attack. It was sudden and scary.
No time for good-byes or anything. I used
to write my dad notes to say things I
wished I'd told him."

Maddy's ponytail swung as she looked
at Abigail. "Never thought of that."

"It helped. He used to leave me notes
all the time, on my pillow or in my gym
bag." Abigail smiled, remembering. "Some-

times he wrote something serious like *I'm proud of you, baby girl*, and other times he'd stick a silly note on my pillow like *Don't forget to brush your teeth*, even though I was fourteen and didn't need reminding. I still have the last note he left me. I wish I'd kept them all."

"What's it say?"

Abigail envisioned the white square paper, a smiling red apple caricature in the corner, probably Christmas stationery from a student.

"Oops, sorry," Maddy said. "I shouldn't have asked."

"I don't mind. It says *Win one for the Gipper. Love, Dad*. That's a saying from an old movie we used to watch together. I had a championship volleyball game that afternoon. He never got to see it."

"That's sad."

Abigail leaned forward as they started up a grassy hill. "I have good memories. He taught at my school, so I got to see him a lot."

"What grade?"

"Fifth."

"That's what I just finished!"

"He would've loved your curiosity."

"Miss Greta says I'm nosy."

Abigail laughed. "It's a fine line, I guess."

"Huh?"

"Never mind. I like it, and you can ask me anything you want. The worst I can say is 'None of your business.'"

"You wouldn't say that." Maddy's eyes teased.

"You're right, I wouldn't." Trinket rocked her from side to side as they climbed the hill. The leather saddle creaked under her, and Abigail tightened her hands on the reins. "We going somewhere in particular?"

"Toward the Yellowstone River. It's pretty there, and we might even see Dad. I heard him tell Mr. Pee Wee he'd be in the red barn meadow—that's just over that ridge."

Abigail had a feeling the whole ride had been about catching a few minutes with Dad. She hoped for Maddy's sake they caught up with him.

"What did you do yesterday after church?" Abigail asked.

"Went to town for supplies, then over to Uncle Dylan's. He owns the Circle D over that way." She pointed back toward town, then turned to Abigail, her eyes twinkling. "He's sweet on you."

"He doesn't even know me."

"I heard him tell Dad your legs go clean up to your neck." Her giggle sounded every bit the eleven-year-old. "That's silly."

Abigail felt warmth flood her face. "That is silly."

"Dad told him his eyeballs are going to get him into hot water. What's that mean, anyway?"

Abigail grinned. "I think it means he likes the ladies too much."

They rode awhile in silence, and Abigail was glad Maddy dropped the subject. She wondered how much Dylan knew about Wade's past. The fact that he was attracted to her could work in her favor. As quickly as the thought appeared, she cringed. Using someone's feelings was wrong on so many levels. But she needed to question him one way or another.

The hill never seemed to end, and it was only one among dozens. She wondered how cowboys kept track of their whereabouts on thirty thousand acres without a GPS.

Awhile later they crested another hill,

and Abigail arched her back. She was going to find a whole new set of muscles in the morning. The view from the top, however, was worth it. The river meandered through the pasture, rippling and turning, its banks shaded by tall leafy trees and towering evergreens. Wildflowers dotted the meadow with vibrant reds and yellows.

"We're here," Maddy said.

"Wow, it's beautiful." Abigail scanned the horizon as they began the descent. "Where's the red barn?"

"Oh, it's long gone. They just call it that 'cause there used to be a red barn here. Hey, there's Dad!" Maddy nudged Destiny, and the girl and her horse went sailing down the hill at a pace that made Abigail's heart skip a beat.

"Don't even think about it," she told Trinket. But the horse continued her plodding steps downhill, following Destiny without direction. It might be dinnertime by the time they reached the bottom, but at least she'd be in one piece.

She watched Maddy racing toward her dad, who hadn't spotted her yet. Abigail's body swayed to and fro with Trinket's steps. She was getting the hang of this. She held her reins to one side like she'd seen in the movies. Oh yeah. She was good.

The next moment Trinket hit a hole, flinging Abigail forward in the saddle. She gripped the reins against the horn, brought her legs in. Her feet thumped against Trinket's side, knocking twice as Trinket regained her footing. Abigail's left foot slipped from the stirrup.

Trinket took the nudge as some kind of signal. Her hooves dug in and she picked up speed. Abigail leaned forward, hung on to the reins, the mane, anything she could grasp. Her knees clamped onto the horse's side.

"Stop!" she called. No, not *stop*. "Halt! Stay!"

Her body jolted against the saddle. She was slipping. The noises Maddy demonstrated, what were they? She made a clucking sound. Trinket didn't respond. She made a kissing sound.

And Trinket's speed increased. They raced down the hill. "Noo-ooo-ooo-ooo!" The jarring broke her word, was breaking her breath, her rear end. *Gentle, my foot*.

Air rushed past Abigail, tore at her hair. She slipped sideways. She was going to fall. She was going to be trampled. She was going to die on her relaxing trip to Montana. Not from complications of hypertension, but from sheer stupidity.

She slipped further, tilting, bumping, her one foot still caught in the stirrup. She had visions of dangling from the stirrup while Trinket raced merrily along.

Jump or fall? Those were her options now. A braver soul might choose the first, but she clung to the shred of hope that neither would happen. That she could somehow hang on until the horse stopped.

One slip, tipping her crazily to the side, relieved her of that notion. She was going down. She shook her foot free of the stirrup as gravity had its way.

Abigail extended her arms, hoping to break her fall. She heard hooves thudding the ground. So close. *Please, God!*

The next jolt made love pats of the earlier ones. Her body thudded on the ground, her head slammed into the hard earth. How could something so soft-looking be so hard? That was her last thought before darkness closed in.

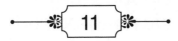

11

Wade nudged the stray Hereford from the riverbank, through the wooded copse, and toward the hill where the others gathered. The sun was getting higher in the sky, and the cows had stopped to graze. Soon they wouldn't budge, but the meadow was just over the ridge.

"Dad!" Maddy approached on Destiny, a smile stretching across her face. The sun gleamed on her mahogany hair in copper sparkles. Destiny neighed as they neared, then Maddy reined her in.

Wade frowned, looking around. "You didn't come out here alone."

"Abigail's with me." She pointed to the ridge where his dun mare was lumbering down the slope. Abigail leaned back in the saddle, tense.

"Can we help you awhile?" Maddy asked.

"Sure." Wade removed his hat and wiped his sleeve across his forehead. "You can help me get them up the hill."

He heard a muffled scream and followed the sound across the valley and up the hill.

Trinket was trotting down the slope, and Abigail flopped around in the saddle like a rag doll.

Son of a gun.

"What the heck's she doing?" He nudged Ace forward. "Stay here, Maddy," he called over his shoulder.

The mare was half a mile away, and Abigail clearly had no control of the horse. He hoped he could reach her in time. Even as he had the thought, Trinket spurted forward like she'd shifted gears. He watched Abigail keeling to the side and felt a dread he hadn't felt since he'd pitched head over heels two summers ago. That had ended with two broken ribs and a fractured shoulder.

"Pull back!" he called, but the wind snatched his words.

Abigail's foot was free of the stirrup, he could see that now, and she caught air, slipping, slipping. *Help her, Lord.*

He watched helplessly as she flew from the saddle. Her arms stretched out. She cleared Trinket's hooves, then hit the ground hard. Bounced and rolled to a stop. Trinket galloped past Wade, and he let her go.

He raced toward Abigail's still form and dismounted before Ace reached a stop. She was facedown in the long grass, her limbs sprawled. No odd angles, thank God.

"Abigail." He went to his knees, reluctant to touch her for more than one reason. The woman's stillness weighted his gut. "Abigail, you okay?" What if she'd hit her head on a rock? Broken her neck?

Another image flashed through his mind, a different time and place, another lifeless body. He pushed the image back where it came from, removed his glove, reached toward Abigail's neck. He forced himself to take her pulse, realizing last time he'd done this he'd found nothing but cold, stillness.

Abigail's skin was warm, smooth. *Please, God*. He gulped, his fingers finding the artery and stopping. A slow steady pulse beat against his fingers. His own heart seemed to skip a beat in response.

Abigail moaned. Her hand flinched at her side.

"Don't move."

Despite his instruction, her hand inched toward her side.

"Hold still." Her hair hung in her face, and he itched to brush it aside. He clenched his hand into a fist.

Her eyes fluttered open. "What—what happened?"

"Took a spill. Lie still. Tell me what hurts."

"Everything."

Still had a sense of humor. "Good. Means you're not dead."

Nearby, Maddy dismounted Destiny and approached. "Is she okay?" Her voice wobbled.

"I'm fine," Abigail mumbled into the grass.

Sure she was. "What hurts?" Wade asked again.

"My head." She closed her eyes, wincing.

"Anything else?"

"Nothing serious, I don't think. Can I move now? I have grass up my nose."

"Go ahead."

As she rolled, Wade noted a knot already rising on her forehead, scrapes on her cheek.

Her hand covered her eyes in slow motion. "Turn off the lights."

He set his hat on her head, careful to avoid the knot. "I think you lost consciousness."

"Mmm."

She probably had a concussion. He should check her pupils, which meant he'd have to touch her. Couldn't be helped. "Need to check your pupils."

"They're still there."

"Wise guy." Wade held open one eye and watched it react to the light. Her eyes were mossy green with flecks of amber. Not that he noticed. He checked the other, and pulled back as soon as the task was completed. "Think you'll live."

Dirt and grass clung to her cheeks. He wasn't going to be the one to brush it away.

Maddy went to her knees beside Abigail. "I'm sorry, Abigail. I shouldn't have ridden off without you." Tears and guilt glimmered in her eyes.

"My fault," Wade said. "Guess Trinket's not as steady as I thought."

"No," Abigail said. "I—I think I gave her a signal accidentally—and then I couldn't remember your instructions. I should've listened better."

"Feel like sitting up?" Wade asked.

"What if she broke something?" Maddy asked.

"Nothing broken." Abigail pushed herself up, wincing as she came upright. "See?" The angry knot on her forehead bulged.

Wade had to admire her tenacity. He knew from experience her head was ringing. "Dizzy?"

Her gaze bounced off Maddy. "No."

"Liar," he whispered. Inside, he shrank. There was no way he could let her ride back alone. She could pass out. Another fall wouldn't do, and she couldn't ride back with Maddy. The girl wasn't strong enough to keep her on the horse if she blacked out.

"Maddy, get Trinket."

His daughter scurried away, and Abigail felt the lump on her head, knocking his hat to the ground in the process.

Wade retrieved it and put it on. "How's that head?"

"Beating like a jungle drum."

"Need to get some ice on that bump. Sure nothing else hurts? Move your arms around, wiggle your fingers."

She followed his instructions, still wincing against the light.

"Can you stand?" Gritting his teeth, he took her hands and helped her to her feet. She was light as a reed and twice as pretty in her form-fitting jeans. Wade scolded himself for noticing. Just because Dylan went all gaga over a pair of long legs was no reason he had to go there.

Abigail took a tentative step forward. She was as unsteady as a foal. She wasn't riding alone.

Wade took her elbow and guided her toward Ace. "We'll take mine."

Abigail eyed Ace skeptically. "Yours is further from the ground than Trinket. Do I really have to go up there?"

"Unless you want to sleep out here."

"No thanks. The ground is harder than it looks."

"So's your head, apparently."

She sent him a mock glare.

"You'll be fine. Ace is steady as a rock." He stopped in front of Ace. *All right, Ryan, buck up.* He reached out and scooped Abigail into his arms.

She gasped. One arm flew around his shoulder, and her other hand clutched his shirtfront. "You could've warned me."

Her hair smelled like sunshine and flowers. Her curves fit into him like she belonged there.

You could've warned me.

The smell of her, the feel of her, made him miss all the things he could never have. Wade set his jaw and placed her gently in the saddle. The moment he released her, his empty arms—who was he kidding?—his empty *heart*, complained.

Thoughts like that'll get you nowhere fast, Ryan.

"I can't reach the stirrups," Abigail said.

"Don't need to. Scoot forward and make room." He put his foot in the stirrup.

"For what?"

Swinging his leg over, he settled behind Abigail.

"*Oh.*" She squirmed forward, but only got so far. She finally settled in the cradle of his thighs in a way he found most disturbing. *Can't be helped. Just this one time. Be over before you know it.*

He reached around Abigail for the reins, then nudged Ace forward and took Trinket's reins while Maddy mounted Destiny.

"Go slow," he told his daughter.

"I second that." Abigail white-knuckled the horn. She was stiff as a barn door.

Even though she leaned forward, the heat of her body seeped through his clothes. The sweet smell of her teased his senses. He leaned back, determined to think of something else. Something less soft and curvy. Something that didn't smell so good and feel so right.

Instead of swaying with Ace's movement, Abigail fought it. She was going to be in worse shape than she already was if she rode home that way.

"Relax." His breath stirred her hair. "I won't let you fall."

"Easy for you to say." Despite her words, her shoulders slowly dropped and she sank into the curve of his chest.

Wade gritted his teeth. *You asked for it, Ryan.* He was thankful he held Trinket's reins in one hand, because the urge to wrap his arms around her was as compelling as it was absurd. What was wrong with him?

Then again, what did he expect when he'd been without a woman so long? Hadn't so much as touched one since Lizzie.

But it was more than that. He wasn't that shallow, and Abigail wasn't just any woman. In the short week he'd known her, he'd come to appreciate her. She was considerate and patient, and he liked her self-deprecating humor. She somehow seemed strong and vulnerable at the same time. And she was completely unaware of her feminine charms.

He hoped the thudding of Ace's hooves covered the thumping of his heart. Last thing he needed was his nanny thinking he was interested. 'Cause he wasn't. Not a bit.

The ride home was long and arduous. The word *torture* came to mind, but he tossed it out, refusing to admit he was so bothered by Abigail's proximity. When the house came into sight, he breathed a sigh of relief. Almost there.

He pulled Ace's reins as they drew up to it, then dismounted. The instant he left the saddle, a weight he didn't care to define settled in his midsection.

"Maddy, take the horses." He handed off Trinket, and his daughter led the mare toward the barn.

"Your turn," he said to Abigail.

"I got it." She slipped down until she could reach the stirrup and swung her leg over.

Wade held her steady at the waist until she was on her feet, refusing to admit his touch might've been unnecessary.

"Thanks." She didn't quite meet his eyes.

The knot on her forehead had swelled and colored. "Get some ice on that."

"I will." She turned toward the house, steady enough.

"You get nauseated or have blurry vision, tell Greta."

Abigail started to nod, then checked the motion.

He hoped she wouldn't overdo it. He'd known one too many cowboys to take a fall, keep working, then keel over later.

"Lie down and take it easy," Wade called.

"Yes, Dad," Abigail said saucily.

Wade clamped his lips together. Last thing he wanted was Abigail thinking fatherly thoughts of him. Heaven knew, his own weren't going that direction.

❦

Sergeant Greta wouldn't let Abigail off the couch all day. The woman wanted her to see a doctor, but when Abigail refused, Greta relented. She pressed her lips together. "Suit yourself," she said before returning to her cleaning.

Two Tylenol tablets later, Abigail's head settled to a dull pounding. Maddy brought ice packs on the hour and retrieved the laptop to keep Abigail occupied.

When Maddy went outside to play and Greta went upstairs to vacuum, Abigail looked up articles on Wade. A pang of guilt hit her even as she typed in the search words.

She couldn't reconcile the man who was accused by some of murdering his wife with the man who'd tended her in the meadow.

Not to mention the man who'd swept her into his arms and deposited her so gently in the saddle. She sure hadn't been thinking about his past when she'd been cradled against his chest . . . when his arm had curled around her . . . when his breath had stirred the nerve endings in her ear and tingled all the way down her spine.

She'd been thinking about lots of things, but not his past.

Maybe her instincts were off. Maybe he really was a lonely widower who'd been left to care for his young daughter and pursued relentlessly by the nosy paparazzi.

Well, she wouldn't know for sure until she researched thoroughly. It was *fact* that mattered, not emotion. She couldn't let her decisions be clouded by feelings.

Not that there were *feelings*. She barely knew the man, for heaven's sake. And she sure didn't trust him. Even if he did seem gentle and caring.

She clicked on a link, then another and another. Twenty minutes later she was browsing photos of Wade at a National Finals Rodeo when she realized she'd gotten off track. Way off track. Sure the photos were interesting, and he was attractive from every angle, but it was getting her nowhere with her research. Shaking her head, she started another search, determined to stick to business.

She turned up an article written after Wade and Maddy disappeared that included details Abigail hadn't come across before. Supposedly there was a large lapse of time between Elizabeth's time of death and Wade's 9-1-1 call. Between eight and nine hours, the article said.

The original article had appeared in a small magazine, but when she searched the website, there was nothing more recent. The magazine was now defunct, she supposed.

Abigail was surprised the article was still online. There wasn't even a writer attributed. If she could find the person who'd written it, she could find out if there was any credence to the detail.

But if it was true, why had the police let him off the hook so quickly? She'd seen Wade's enormous earnings from his rodeo wins. Had he paid off someone?

Abigail didn't want to believe it. She wanted to think Maddy's father incapable of the heinous crime. What kind of man killed his daughter's mother? And yet, people committed atrocious crimes all the time. It was up to her to find the truth.

She was unaccustomed to this tug-of-war. She was a journalist, the Truthseeker, not the Bleeding Heart. She had to stick to the facts and not let her relationship with Maddy or Wade cloud her judgment. Which, she realized as she exited the website and shut down her computer, was easier said than done.

12

Something pulled Abigail from the oblivion of sleep. Her head pounded. Surely someone was hitting it with a sledgehammer. She lay motionless, trying to gather the will to hunt down the Tylenol.

Before she could move, she sensed a change in the room. Her eyes snapped open. It was dark, save for a sliver of light beneath the door. Even as her eyes skimmed past, a shadow fell at its base. She heard the quiet click of her doorknob turning.

Abigail's heart raced, the pounding in her head all but forgotten.

It's just Maddy.

She watched the gap between the door and frame widen. The article from the night before surged to her mind, adding fuel to her thudding heart.

A hulking silhouette formed against the background. Broad shoulders, trim waist. Why was Wade coming in here? Did he know about her research? Had she left the laptop in the living room? Had he looked at her history? She couldn't turn her head to check her nightstand, couldn't let him know she was awake.

Think, Abigail!

Wade took a step toward the bed and then another. What should she do? Better he think her asleep and helpless, she decided, tensing at his approach. The floor creaked quietly under his feet as his form swallowed the light from the hall.

He held something. The light flashed off it. Her breaths became shallow puffs.

Then he was there. Beside her bed. Leaning over.

Oh, God, what do I do? She pressed her lips together, forbidding the scream that gathered in her throat.

"Abigail," he whispered.

She clutched the sheet between them,

a pathetic barrier. Killers didn't wake their victims, did they? Except the cruel ones. If he'd wanted her dead—

"Abigail?" His voice was louder, more insistent.

He wasn't going away. "What?" The croak squeezed from her restricted throat.

"You okay?"

He woke her to ask if she was okay? "What?"

"Making sure you're all right—no concussion."

Her fingers relaxed on the sheet, and her pounding head reclaimed her attention. He hadn't come to murder her. He'd come to check on her. If there were a Ninny of the Year Award, she'd just earned it.

Abigail's heart rate slipped into a lower gear. "I'm fine." Fine as could be for someone who thought she was about to be slaughtered in her own bed.

"Brought you Tylenol."

Of course he did. She sighed.

"Head still banging?"

Was it ever. "Yeah." She sat up, took the glass, and downed the pills he offered. She set the glass on the nightstand and lay back. "Thanks."

Wade slipped quietly from the room, pulled the door until there was nothing but the sliver of light beneath it. The clock's hands read two. His gentle whisper still filled her ears, haunting her. She forced it from her mind, making herself remember the article, remember the new piece of evidence.

She hated inconsistency. Things were usually black-and-white for her. Sure, people had both good and bad in them, but in her experience one dominated. Wade's past looked black, but his present seemed white. It was confusing, and she couldn't think with the jackhammer going off in her head. She needed sleep. In the morning she'd be able to separate fact from feeling. That was the only way to get to the truth.

Abigail rolled over and closed her eyes against the banging. The adrenaline surge had left her weak and shaky. Instead of focusing on sleep, her thoughts rewound to earlier in the day when Wade had swept her into his arms. She was not a petite girl, had never been swept up into any man's arms. Had never desired a man to lift her from her two perfectly capable feet.

And yet there it was. She'd liked it. A lot.

Why was she thinking such things? About a man who may have killed his own wife? What was wrong with her? Maybe she did have a concussion after all. Brain damage, in fact, if she was harboring romantic thoughts about someone who might be a murderer.

But he didn't seem like the kind of man . . .

Are you going there again, Abigail Jones? Really?

No, she wasn't. It was easy for people to pretend to be something they weren't. She knew better than most. The memory fogged her mind, spreading, growing, until it was the only thing.

. . . She was ten years old, wearing her favorite periwinkle T-shirt and the matching braided friendship bracelet Julia had made her. She'd made Julia one too—a yellow one to match her pretty blond hair. After all, they had been best friends since Julia moved in four years earlier.

They were going to make more bracelets tonight and sell them during recess at school tomorrow for a quarter each. Abigail clutched her bag, traipsing through her yard and toward the sidewalk. Mrs. Burk's yard separated hers and Julia's, and Mrs. Burk didn't like her grass trampled one bit. Besides, Julia's yard had a thick privacy hedge that scratched your arms when you squeezed through.

Abigail stepped on crunchy leaves on the sidewalk as she went, calculating how much money they could make if they made bracelets every night for the next week. Maybe enough for an ant farm. Abigail had wanted one for a long time, but her mom said it was a waste of money, and her dad had only shrugged the way he always did when Mom put her foot down.

Abigail passed the hedge and turned up the drive that wound up an incline and turned sharply into the garage. Julia had the nicest house on the street and the best backyard, too, which was why they usually played at Julia's.

The garage door was up, and she heard voices coming from inside.

"Why do you always do that?" Mr. Kelley said in a tone Abigail had never heard.

She stopped near the garage opening. Maybe she should go home.

"I'm sorry." Julia's voice sounded small, afraid. "I'll clean it up."

"Those are *my* tools. How many times have I told you to stay out?"

"But Mom said—"

A sickening *thud* sounded. "Don't argue with me!"

Abigail winced, her breath trapped in her lungs.

A whimper. A scuffling sound. A sniffle. Abigail wanted to put her hands over her ears. Why was Mr. Kelley acting this way?

"Pick 'em up before your mom gets home! And stop that sniffling!"

She should go in. Say something. But what if Mr. Kelley hit her too? What if he told her she couldn't see Julia anymore?

Maybe she was imagining things. Mom said her imagination ran wild. Maybe she wasn't really here. Maybe she was at home, in bed, having a nightmare.

"Not like that!" Mr. Kelley screamed. "Worthless girl!" There was a loud ruckus, like metal cans falling.

Julia cried out.

Abigail slapped her hand over her mouth to keep the scream in. Her heart felt like a drum in her chest. Too big for her body. Why was he being so mean?

How could he hurt her? Mr. Kelley loved

Julia. Hadn't he bought her the Slip 'n Slide she wanted for her birthday? Hadn't he set up the swing set in the backyard?

She had to do something. But for the first time ever, she was afraid of Julia's father.

Tomorrow at recess Julia would tell her about this, and they'd come up with a plan. Together they'd tell her mom or go to the police. Abigail backed quietly away, hating the feeling that swelled inside her.

When she felt the hedge against her back, she ignored the sharp pokes and darted through it. She didn't feel the scratchy shrubs or think about Mrs. Burk's lawn as she put distance between herself and the man she didn't know anymore. As she put distance between herself and her best friend.

Now Abigail shivered in bed and pulled the quilt tight around her shoulders. Her heart raced as if she'd just witnessed the awful scene.

The next day at recess Julia hadn't said a word. There'd been no marks on her face or arms. Abigail had told herself she'd imagined it, had almost convinced herself of it because Julia acted so normally that day and every day after.

But Abigail could still hear the thud of Mr. Kelley's fist hitting Julia's body, feel the horror of somehow knowing it wasn't the first time and wouldn't be the last. Still feel the horror of knowing the truth and being too afraid to tell.

If only she could go back and change things. If only she'd been older and braver. If only she'd told. Then her best friend wouldn't have lived the nightmare of an abusive childhood.

When Abigail was thirteen, Julia's family moved out of state. The two girls wrote each other for a while, then they lost contact. Abigail was sure the abuse had continued, and the seed of guilt that started that day grew and spread until sometimes she thought it would strangle her.

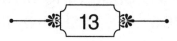

13

Outside the barn Wade heard Maddy and Abigail struggling with the manual tiller. Abigail had asked if they could start a small garden, and she'd chosen a plot of ground between the barn and the old well pump.

Maddy's loud laughter drew him, and he peeked out the barn door. Abigail was fighting the tiller and losing. She looked awkward against the ancient farm equipment, all arms and legs. But to her credit, she laughed along with Maddy.

He leaned against the door frame. Abigail was different from the other nannies.

It hadn't taken long to see that. She wasn't just present and accounted for; she clearly enjoyed the child. She made plans with Maddy, taught her, talked to her, and his daughter was blossoming under her care.

Wade hated the prickle of jealousy that stung him.

I'm obliged, God. Really I am. She's just what Maddy needed.

He wanted Maddy to blossom, and God knew she'd needed a female figure in her life for a long time.

Another burst of laughter caught his attention. He felt like the odd man out, peeking around the corner, then reminded himself he was doing what was best for his daughter. His own feelings didn't matter. As long as Maddy had what she needed, that was all that counted.

❦

Abigail turned off her phone. Her mom was keeping something from her. Something about *Viewpoint*. With so much news being read online, the magazine's circulation had been on a steady decline. But there was something more. She wondered if her sister would spill the beans.

Only one way to find out. Abigail punched

in Reagan's number. Saturday was a good day to reach her.

"Hey, sis." Reagan's tone was chipper.

"Aren't we in a good mood."

"I have a date."

"Well, ring the bells of heaven." Abigail dropped onto the bed.

"Shut up."

She heard the sound of clothing hangers screeching down the rod. "So, tell all. Who is it? Where'd you meet?"

"A doctor, and I met him at Mercy."

"You always said you wouldn't date another doctor."

"Well, he's in pediatrics."

"Good father material, possibly Mr. Right . . ."

"Exactly." Her sister growled into the phone. "I'm having a clothing crisis. I have business clothes and slop-wear, with nothing in between."

"Where's he taking you?"

"Dinner and the theater."

"You don't like the theater."

"Well, he's cute."

More hanger screeching.

"I so need to go shopping!"

"I'm thinking there's no time for that,"

Abigail said. "Wear your newish black slacks with your red Anne Klein blouse. Definitely the Kate Spade sandals. Dress it up with your layered silver necklace and dangly earrings."

"How do you *do* that?"

"It's a gift." Abigail flopped back against her pillow.

"That's great, thanks. Now I can have a bath, relax, and stop stressing about my clothes. Oh, please don't let me get an emergency tonight."

"At least he'd understand."

"What if he gets an emergency? Oh, why am I going out with another doctor?"

"Because he's cute?"

"Oh, yeah. Speaking of cute, how's your cowboy?"

"I never said he was cute."

"Didn't have to. I'm your sister, I heard the nuances in your voice."

"Wade's fine, and so is Maddy. I didn't call about them though. I'm calling to get the scoop on Mom. Or more precisely, on the magazine. I just got off the phone with her, and I could tell something's up."

The sudden whoosh of water sounded. "Sorry, didn't hear."

"Nice try. What's going on?" If their mom was in trouble and Abigail could help . . . "Reagan?"

"*Viewpoint*'s going through a rough spot, Abs. She's just worried."

"The new format isn't helping?"

Mom had worked with a designer to change the magazine's look. The overhaul was fabulous, and Abigail had been sure it was exactly what *Viewpoint* needed.

"There's been great feedback from your current readers, but I guess a new format isn't enough to persuade new readers to give it a try, and . . ." Her sister's words trailed off.

"There's something you're not telling me."

"Mom wants you to relax out there, Abs. And as your doctor, I second that—"

"*Viewpoint* is more than just my place of employment. It means everything to Mom, and if there's something going on, I need to know."

The sound of water grew fainter, and the click of the door sounded in Abigail's ear.

"Mom would kill me if she knew I told you."

"I won't say anything."

Reagan sighed into the phone. "BlueFly Publications is giving her three months to increase circulation by 30 percent. If she doesn't, they're shutting it down."

"Thirty percent in three months? That's impossible!" Abigail knew things were rocky, but it never occurred to her BlueFly would take such a hard line. "Mom's put thirty years into that magazine! Don't they know how many people that would put out of work?"

"I know. But supposedly they aren't turning enough of a profit to justify the magazine's existence."

Abigail popped upright. "I have to come home."

"No! You can't. Let Mom handle this. She's run the thing for all these years, she can figure it out."

"I can help. I can write a major exposé or something and—"

Wade's story flashed into her mind. If she found answers, if she could figure out what had really happened to Wade's wife, it would be a major story. With Wade's image splashed across the cover, thousands of readers would buy it. And once they sampled the new and improved magazine, she was sure circulation would increase dramatically. They only needed a story big enough to make people try it. And she had just the story to do it.

"Mom didn't want you to know about this. You can't come home."

"What if I can solve the problem from here?"

"What are you talking about?"

BlueFly had given them three months. "When did BlueFly notify Mom of their decision?"

"Yesterday. Where are you going with this?"

The July issue would release soon. If that was the first issue of the countdown, they had until the end of August, which would be the September issue. Abigail would have to dig around and find answers, turn in the column by mid-August at the very latest. She'd have to notify her mother earlier, so the cover and column space were properly planned.

"Hello?"

Abigail cracked open the door and listened. She could hear water running in the kitchen. Maddy was at Olivia's house, and

Wade was out feeding the cows or something.

Abigail clicked shut the door again. "I have a big story I'm working on," she said quietly.

"In Moose Creek?"

"Believe it or not." How much should she say? She supposed there was no point in holding back now. "It has to do with Maddy's father. You're not going to believe this . . . He's J. W. Ryan."

"What? J. W. the ex-rodeo—*that's* why you asked me about him last week?"

"He goes by Wade Ryan now. I can do research in my spare time, find out if he's responsible for his wife's death. I don't have answers yet, but I'll get them. Especially now."

"Just finding him is news, Abs. Are you sure it's him?"

"Positive."

"Holy cow. You said Wade was cute, but J. W. is a total hunk."

No kidding. An image of him flashed into her mind. The one of him from the Sexiest Man website, smiling, all cocky. It was a look she hadn't seen since she'd been here. Not even close.

"I don't know," Reagan was saying. "No doubt it's the story of a lifetime, probably enough to spur a ton of sales—"

"Probably?"

"Okay, definitely. There's not a woman who follows celebs who wouldn't buy that issue. But as your sister and as your doctor, I'm concerned about your hypertension."

"I'll monitor my symptoms."

"Mom's going to kill me. Are you taking your meds, watching your diet, exercising, limiting your sodium?"

"Yes, Dr. Jones."

"It's nothing to joke about. I want weekly reports of your symptoms, and I want you checking your blood pressure every week."

"Fine."

"I mean it, Abigail."

"All right, I will. I promise."

"It's not like there's anything I can say to change your mind anyway."

"You know me too well." She had a mission, and she was going to see it through. For her mom and all the people who worked at *Viewpoint*. Their livelihoods depended on her.

"If anyone can uncover the story, it's

you. And I agree it would be the sure thing to save the magazine. Just be careful not to overdo, sis, okay?"

"I'll be careful." Abigail heard the water shut off on the other end of the line. "You have fun with Dr. Right. I want a full report. Now, go soak away your worries."

"All right. Stay in touch."

"Will do." Abigail turned off the phone, her mind already on Wade's story. It would catapult *Viewpoint* to new heights. But she needed answers, and she wasn't finding them online. She was going to have to get them from people. Without their becoming suspicious.

She put the phone in her purse and left her room. A clank sounded in the kitchen, and she followed the sound. Greta was pulling something from a low cupboard.

"Need help with dinner?"

The housekeeper rose unsteadily, holding a large black pot. "No, thank you. Where's Maddy?"

"At Olivia's."

Greta frowned, her forehead puckering. "Isn't that Shay's girl? The one who stole her bike?"

"They made up. Olivia invited her over, and I encouraged her to go. I think they could both use a friend." Abigail saw what might have been begrudging approval. "Sure you don't want some help?"

Greta set a bag of potatoes on the counter. "Help yourself then."

Abigail opened the bag and took a paring knife from Greta. The woman set to work on a potato and had it peeled before Abigail was half done with her first.

"Have you worked for Wade long?"

"Pee Wee was his first hire, and I came with the deal."

Short and sweet. Greta wasn't going to be a fount of information. "Maddy must've been pretty young at the time."

Greta grunted.

Abigail tried again. "She told me her mom passed away. That must've been very hard on them both."

Greta's lips pressed together in a scowl before she spoke. "You leave that girl alone about her mama. She's been through enough without being quizzed about her loss."

Abigail was too taken aback to speak

for a moment. "I wasn't quizzing her. We were just talking. I lost my dad, and I thought it might be good for her to—"

"Maybe you should do less thinking and more peeling."

Abigail scraped the knife across the surface. Greta had plenty of bark, that was for sure. But Abigail wasn't dissuaded so easily. "I think it's great that Wade brought his daughter here to start a new life. Sometimes a fresh start is just what the doctor ordered."

Greta's knife made quick work of the peel.

"And the town seems to have accepted them. Aunt Lucy has nothing but kind things to say about Wade."

They worked in silence for a while. Greta was a dead end if Abigail ever saw one. When they finished peeling and washing the potatoes, she excused herself and wandered into the living room just in time to see Wade opening the door to his pickup.

Maybe this was a way to spend some time with him, ask a question or two. She hustled out the front door and down the porch steps. He was shutting the door when she reached the truck, and he rolled down the window when he saw her.

"Going into town?" she asked.

"Yep." He turned the truck over, and the engine groaned and sputtered before starting.

"Could I hitch a ride? I'm needing something from the market."

Wade tugged his hat, shifted in the seat. "I could get it."

Feeling mischievous, she hiked a brow and gave him a pointed look. "You sure?"

His eyes darted from hers to the steering wheel as a satisfying flush rose on his neck and flooded his cheeks. "Get in."

Abigail smiled. "Be right back." Feeling exultant at her success, Abigail trotted into the house for her purse, then back down the porch steps and to the truck. She jumped in the passenger side and buckled her belt.

"I have several errands, so I might be awhile."

She recognized his one last effort to ditch her.

"Great. I can visit with Aunt Lucy at her store while I wait."

He put the truck in reverse and backed out. "Suit yourself."

It was only a ten-minute ride to town and a ten-minute ride back. She had to be careful not to raise suspicions. Or to be distracted by the manly smell of leather or the nicely shaped fingers curling around the steering wheel.

Get a grip, Abigail.

She thought of the embarrassed flush she'd put on his face, which was only now fading away, and smothered a grin. The man had an eleven-year-old daughter, for heaven's sake. What was he going to do when he had to run to the store on her behalf?

"Where's Maddy?" Wade asked.

"She rode her bike to Olivia's. She said you wouldn't mind."

"They made up?"

"Maddy feels bad for Olivia, despite what she did. Your daughter is very compassionate. You should be proud of her."

"I am."

A few minutes later they pulled onto the road and turned toward town. She searched her mind for a question that wouldn't put him off. When they passed a neighboring ranch, she recognized the name.

"The Circle D. That's your friend Dylan's place, right?"

"Yep."

"Maddy said he moved out here after you and she did. You must be close."

He spared her a look. "Go way back."

"To childhood?"

"Something like that."

"What about your family? Did you leave them behind in Texas?"

"Dad passed on before I left, and I don't have any brothers or sisters."

"What about your mom?"

He darted her a look that said she talked too much.

Abigail shrugged. "Just making conversation."

He rolled his hands forward on the steering wheel, then relaxed his wrists. "She died a few years after my dad."

His words were matter-of-fact, but Abigail caught the vulnerability in his tone. She looked at his profile. A strong jawline, masculine cheekbones, and eyes shaded by the low brim of his hat.

"Must've been hard on her when your dad passed."

"It was."

"I'm sorry. I guess you and Maddy have something in common, losing your moms."

"Reckon so."

"Were you and your dad close?"

"What's with the twenty questions?"

"Knowing you helps me know Maddy."

He sighed hard. "Dad was a cowboy on a big cattle ranch. I worked beside him every chance I got. Yeah, we were close." He eased off the gas as a car passed them. "You?"

"There's just my mom and sister and me. Reagan's a doctor, she's the brains of the family. My dad was a teacher."

"And you?"

She'd known the question would come eventually. "I'm a writer. I write stories. My dad always thought I'd be a teacher like him. He taught fifth grade at my school, but he died of heart disease when I was a teenager."

"You were close?"

"Very. Aunt Lucy says I'm just like him."

"Hardheaded and too talkative?" His smile was a quick twitch of his lips.

Abigail stopped short of sticking out her tongue. "I think she meant tall and green-eyed. He had Scripture verses and other wise adages for every occasion. We called them Dadisms. And he took me to the theater and exhibitions. Reagan and Mom weren't into that stuff."

"Sounds like a good man. Can't imagine growing up in the city, though."

Abigail looked at the majestic line of mountains both to the east and west, at the valley in between with huge rolling hills, and at the blue sky yawning overhead. "It's beautiful here. I can't help but feel a little lost in the vastness."

"I'd feel lost surrounded by hordes of people and cars and houses crammed atop one another."

"Touché."

"Nothing like Big Sky Country. Clean air, open spaces, the wind in your face."

"We have wind in Chicago," she teased.

"Polluted, smelly wind."

"But we do have the theater. And Oprah."

"We have the Chuckwagon. And God."

She smiled. "God is everywhere, or hadn't you heard?"

"He's just harder to find in the city."

Abigail thought of her father when she thought of God. Of his faithfulness. He'd taken them to church, and Abigail had even asked Jesus into her heart as a child. But she'd been so busy the last, well, ten years.

"Maybe so," she admitted. "It's easy to let God fall by the wayside when there are so many distractions." *Like work*.

"Out here it's easier to avoid the hectic schedules and the trappings of religion. It's just you and God's creation."

"Never thought of it like that." Her mom had called her restless, but Abigail hadn't seen it at the time. Her busy life in the city had disguised it. But the slow pace of life here had made the truth apparent. She was restless.

If she were honest, she had to admit it had been a long time since she'd felt anything resembling peace. Not since . . . Her mind traveled in reverse searching for a moment of tranquility.

Not since childhood. She remembered swinging with Julia at recess and feeling completely all right with the world. Like she was safe and all was well. Before she knew people hurt each other. Before she knew she could keep awful secrets.

Abigail shook the unpleasant thought. Maybe her mom was right. Maybe she could find that kind of peace in Montana. Maybe if she got her spiritual life back on track, her soul would settle. God had been an important part of her dad's life, used to be an important part of hers.

Where did I lose my way, God? We used to be close.

She'd gone to church with Aunt Lucy but, Abigail admitted, she'd been present in body only. Maybe it was time to find her way back to God—if she could even figure out how.

14

Wade set the merchandise on the counter and pulled out his billfold.

"Hiya, Wade." Marla Jenkins flashed him a wide smile from behind the counter.

"Marla." Spotting the candy rack, Wade grabbed a pack of Twizzlers and set them on the counter.

"Getting ready for the week?" Marla asked as she rang up his purchases.

"Yep."

"Oh, these are really good." She held up the package of beef jerky. "My dad loves this brand."

Wade wondered what he'd do after

stowing his supplies. His errands hadn't taken as long as he'd made them sound, and Abigail had gone to visit her aunt.

"I'm so ready to get off work. My feet are killing me." Marla tucked her brown hair behind her ear.

Wade gave a polite smile.

"Big plans tonight?"

"Not really."

"My brother's band's playing at the Chuckwagon. Maybe I'll see you there."

The bell over the door jingled. "Hey, Wade." Dylan's familiar voice was a welcome distraction.

Wade nodded in Dylan's direction as Marla gave a total. He pulled the cash from his wallet and handed it over.

"The Silver Spurs go on around nine. Hope to see you there."

Dylan accompanied him from the store and nudged him in the ribs once they were out the door. "First you and the nanny, now Marla Jenkins. Dude, you da man."

"There is no 'me and the nanny.'"

"You were looking awful cozy riding through town twenty minutes ago."

"She needed a lift." They crossed the street, then Wade tossed his bags through the pickup's window and leaned against the door as another truck roared past. "What are you doing in town?"

"Changing the subject?"

"No subject to change."

"If you say so. It's Saturday, and I don't have a date yet."

"Marla was trolling for one."

"She was trolling for a date with *you*. Hey, I wonder if her sister's free. Or Shay. She's a looker. We could make it a double."

"First, Shay's a single mom—can't mess with a single mom. Second, I'm not interested in Marla."

"Well, your nanny then. Maybe Marla will be my date. Come on, a night out on the town—such as it is." He gestured up Main Street. "You like the Silver Spurs."

"I'm not going out with Abigail. She works for me."

"Fine. You ask Marla, I'll find someone else. Marla's cute, and she's a good Christian girl."

Wade glanced around the town, its old brick buildings and wooden boardwalks lining Main Street, as he searched for an excuse.

"Not interested in Marla."

"How about Shay?"

"Think I'll stay home and keep Maddy company tonight."

Wade scanned the sidewalks for Abigail but didn't see her. She must still be at her aunt's shop. He put on his best poker face.

Dylan had been his friend too long not to see through it. He folded his arms. "Come on, Wade, shoot straight with me. When are you going to move on with your life?"

"I moved a thousand miles."

"Not what I mean. Lizzie's been gone five years, man."

Wade clenched his teeth. He didn't want to talk about Lizzie, didn't even want to think about her. Hard enough to see her in Maddy every day. In her smile, in the way she pushed her hair off her face. To be reminded every day—

"It wasn't your fault."

"Never said it was."

"You don't have to. It's there in your eyes every time I say her name."

Wade turned and pulled the handle on the truck door. "You don't know what you're talking about."

Dylan held the door closed. "I've known you since we were eight. I know a thing or two about—"

"Don't know a thing about this."

"You've got some guilt thing going, and you're denying yourself anything that might actually make you happy."

Wade humphed, shook his head, tried the handle again. Dylan blocked his way. Wade rolled his eyes. Stuffed his anger down, laughed it off.

"It wasn't your fault," Dylan repeated.

"I don't date because I've got a ranch to run and a daughter to raise. I'm not a foot-loose single guy with nothing but my own needs to satisfy. Maddy needs me."

"Maddy needs a mom. But you're too busy punishing yourself to find her one."

Something in Wade shook loose. He shoved Dylan, knocking his friend away from the door. "That's too far."

Dylan's shoulders tensed. He could give Wade a run for his money, and they both knew it. But they hadn't gone at it since they were scrappy twelve-year-olds itching for a fight.

Dylan pulled himself straight. "You mean

I've stated the truth, and you don't like the sound of it."

Wade breathed a wry laugh. He'd had enough of Dylan for one day. He got in the truck without a glance at his friend.

When Dylan turned and crossed the street, Wade breathed a sigh of relief. He was stuck here until Abigail returned or until he fetched her, but he was in no mood to do that now.

Dylan's words rang in his ears. Even now, his muscles were taut, his nerves clanging. His friend rarely brought up Lizzie's name. It was a silent understanding between them. But he'd broken the agreement today and done it with style.

And he'd struck too close to the truth for Wade's comfort. Dylan couldn't understand what he'd been through with Lizzie. She'd been a spirited, happy soul when he'd met her, and he hadn't been able to stop her slow spiral downhill. Shouldn't a man be able to save his own wife?

How could he bring another woman into his life, knowing he'd failed one already? It was bad enough Maddy had him for a father. It might be true she could use a mother, but he didn't trust himself enough to put another woman at risk.

❀

"Abigail!" Aunt Lucy looked up from the Western doll in her hands. "I didn't expect you today."

"Hitched a ride into town with Wade." Abigail hugged her aunt.

Aunt Lucy settled back into her rocker and picked up her needle and thread. "Where's Maddy?"

"She's at Olivia's house."

"Ah, Shay's girl," Aunt Lucy said. "That child looks so much like her mom at that age. Shay lived with me awhile, you know, when she was eighteen."

"I didn't know."

"Felt bad for her, what with her upbringing. Then when that McCoy boy broke her heart . . ." She *tsk*ed. "Her parents turned her out for a few months."

"That was kind of you, to take her in."

"Poor thing. So brokenhearted. I don't think she ever did get over that boy, even after she married."

"She seems pretty strong now." Abigail noticed the layer of dust coating the display cases. She was sure they hadn't been

dusted since she'd done it two weeks earlier. She found the duster and went to
work.

"You don't have to do that, dear."

"Might as well make myself useful."

"How are you and Maddy getting on?"

"I love that girl. And I feel for her, having
lost her mom so young."

"She's precious."

"We're starting a vegetable garden, so
we'll see how that goes. I'm teaching her
to cook some simple dishes, and yesterday I helped her make something for her
dad for Father's Day tomorrow."

"That's very thoughtful. I'm so glad
Maddy has you for the summer."

"You don't feel neglected? I've been
feeling guilty leaving you all alone."

"I'm not alone!" She gestured to her
polyester-stuffed family. "I have all my girls
to keep me company."

"Uh . . . yeah, that's true." Abigail swept
the duster across the doll shelf, careful to
avoid hitting "the girls."

"I just hope you're getting enough rest.
Your mother won't be happy with me if
you're more worn to a frazzle when you go
home. What's that on your forehead?"

Abigail touched the spot, which was still a little tender. "I had a fall a few days ago—it's nothing."

"A fall from where? Is that a scuff on your cheek?"

"From a horse." Abigail gave a sardonic grin. "Leave it to me."

"You *are* doing too much!"

"No, no, I'm really not. Exercise is good for me—I just need to learn how to stay *on* the horse. I think I've got the hang of it now."

Aunt Lucy narrowed her eyes behind the thick glasses. "Well, I don't like it, and I don't think your mom would either."

"I appreciate your concern, but I'll be fine." A change of subject was in order. "I hope you'll pick me up for church tomorrow. I promised Maddy I'd help her fix a picnic for her dad after church, but I can come over later in the afternoon."

"That sounds wonderful, dear."

"Do you need help around the house? I could mow or clean or whatever you need done."

"That's sweet, dear, but I keep up the cleaning, and a high school boy mows for me. I've got it covered."

Maybe her aunt was as capable as

she'd always been. But there was the matter of her forgetfulness and, okay, her habits of talking to inanimate objects and planting plastic flowers.

"How's business?" Abigail asked.

"We're pretty slow here, aren't we, girls? But I'm sure it'll be just fine."

Aunt Lucy always looked so serene. Even in the face of what had to be a financial difficulty. "Maybe we can do something to help drive business."

"Everyone in town knows I'm here, and there's not much I can do to bring tourists someplace they don't know exists. Don't worry, child. God will provide. All I can do is remain in Him and keep making my dolls."

Remain in Him . . .

"John 15:5." Abigail pulled her ring from her finger. "That's the Scripture on the ring Dad gave me when I was baptized."

Aunt Lucy took the ring and traced her nubby fingertip over the engraved vines. "It's a nice reminder. Your daddy was a wise man."

"Yes, he was." Abigail slipped the ring back into place and resumed dusting. She hadn't thought about the words of that verse for years, but she still remembered them. *I am the vine; you are the branches. If a man remains in me and I in him, he will bear much fruit; apart from me you can do nothing.*

Had she remained in Him? If she was honest, she knew the answer, and it wasn't one that would've pleased her dad. Was Aunt Lucy's peace the result of remaining in Him?

Abigail finished dusting and gave the register a good cleaning while she and Aunt Lucy caught up on the happenings in town. By the time Abigail checked the clock, she realized almost an hour had passed. She was probably holding up Wade.

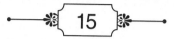

15

Abigail wrapped the chicken salad sand-
wiches and placed them in the tote bag
with the tub of warm beans, watermelon
slices, cans of soda, and place settings.

She handed Maddy the bag. "Okay, all
set. I put extras in there in case your dad
is especially hungry."

Wade glanced up from where he was
putting on his boots. "And I am. It smells
great."

"Maddy, don't forget the you-know-what."
She winked. "You two have a great time."

Maddy's face fell. "You're not coming?"

Abigail looked between Wade and Maddy.

"I thought you'd want to spend the after-noon with your dad."

"I do, but I want you to go too." Her sad eyes pulled at Abigail.

"Maddy," Wade said. "It's Abigail's only day off."

The last thing she wanted was Maddy thinking Abigail only saw her as a pay-check. Plus, it would give her a chance to talk to Wade. "I'm happy to go if you want me along. That is, if your dad doesn't mind."

His lips pressed together, and Abigail was sure he did mind. He shrugged any-way. "Suit yourself."

"Yay!" Maddy said. "I'll be right back." She ran to retrieve her dad's gift.

Abigail pulled an extra soda from the fridge, torn. She wanted to please Maddy, but Wade seemed unhappy about the change in plans.

"Sure you don't mind having me along?" she asked.

He stood and grabbed his hat from the peg near the door. "Not at all. I'll get the horses saddled." Wade slipped out the screen door, and it slapped quietly into place.

Well, obviously he minded, but if he

wasn't going to be forthcoming about it, served him right if she came along.

Maddy trotted into the kitchen, cradling the gift against her stomach, and they joined Wade by the barn. Soon the horses were saddled, and the three headed past the barn and toward Maddy's favorite swim hole, a spot she called Boulder Pass.

Maddy chattered as they rode. Abigail mostly focused on staying in the saddle and using the right commands with Trinket. Wade looked over his shoulder every few minutes, checking on her.

Abigail watched father and daughter riding side by side and thought how lucky Maddy was to have her daddy. The sight of them together made her miss her own father. Miss the things they used to do, miss his notes, his quick wink across the table when Abigail and her mom were arguing over some trivial thing.

He would've been proud of the way she'd listened in church this morning. The pastor had preached on fatherhood, and tears had stung Abigail's eyes twice. Then the pastor talked about God the Father and compared the two roles. She'd never considered how earthly fathers planted the seed of authority and uncon-ditional love in a child's life. How that relationship should mirror the heavenly Father's love.

She'd felt proud of her own father as the pastor spoke. She missed him so much it still felt like an empty ache in her middle even after all these years. She wondered if Maddy felt the same way about her mother. Maybe not, since she'd been so young and had so few memories. That in itself was sad.

It took thirty minutes to reach the spot where the river turned shallow around a wooded bend. Boulders, big and small, stood sentinel in the bubbling stream. The day was beautiful, sunny and midseven-ties, but the direct rays had heated her skin. She wondered how Wade bore the jeans and long sleeves during the hottest days of summer.

Abigail had developed a mild headache in church, but it worsened on the ride, and she wished she'd taken some Tylenol.

They dismounted and tied the horses. Abigail snapped out the quilt under a weeping willow, then she and Maddy set out the food and tableware. A fresh breeze blew, bringing the fragrance of pine and grass. Clean mountain air.

Wade sank onto the quilt, shrinking its size by half.

"Present first!" Maddy said after they were seated on the quilt. She handed her dad the gift, wrapped in silver foil they'd found in the attic and topped with a blue bow.

"What have we here?" Wade received the gift, smiling at his daughter.

"You have to open it to find out."

Wade loosened the dozens of pieces of tape sealing the package, then peeled back the paper to reveal a picture she'd drawn. It was good for an eleven-year-old. Wade wore a cowboy hat in the picture, and she'd drawn a five o'clock shadow on his jaw with the side of her pencil. Maddy was in the picture beside him, smiling, her hair in a ponytail, a few penciled-on freckles dotting her nose.

"Wow, Maddy, I didn't expect this. This is—this is just great."

Wade tugged his hat, a gesture of discomfort, Abigail was beginning to realize. He was touched by his daughter's effort. Abigail wondered what the girl had done for previous Father's Days. Maybe her other nannies hadn't encouraged her to make him something.

"Abigail helped me."

"Just with the proportions. It's your drawing. She's pretty good, eh, Dad?"

"Didn't get it from me. Even my stick figures don't look like stick figures."

Maddy leaned over Wade's shoulder, looking at the picture. "Was Mommy a good drawer?" The question was cautious.

Wade cleared his throat. "Maybe so." Wade held the picture up. "Think I'll put this on my desk. What do you think?"

Maddy nodded, obviously liking the idea. She was all smiles, soaking in her dad's attention, but Abigail had noticed how quickly he'd changed the subject. Didn't he see it was important for Maddy to remember her mother?

Abigail passed out the plates, and they helped themselves to the food. Wade bragged on how tasty it was, and Maddy glowed under his approval.

"Abigail's teaching me how to cook."

"Well, just some basics," Abigail said. "A girl needs to be able to feed herself."

Maybe she had misjudged Wade. He

clearly loved Maddy. Maybe he was just unsure of himself.

Abigail took in his manly form and strong jawline, hardly able to fathom that could be true. But men could be clueless when it came to relationships. Maybe he just didn't know how to be close to his daughter, how to communicate with her.

Or maybe he felt guilty about her mother's death.

The thought was so out of context with the quiet moment that Abigail discarded it. She didn't want to think about Wade's past or the ramifications of it. It was a beautiful sunny June day, and she was enjoying it with a sweet little girl and her dad. She would leave it at that.

They finished lunch, ate the watermelon, and had a seed-spitting contest, which Wade won soundly. Maddy stripped down to her bathing suit and tiptoed through the grass to the river's edge.

"You coming?" she called to them.

"In a minute," Wade said.

"I don't have a suit," Abby said.

"You can roll up your pants. It's shallow at the edge."

"All right. Let me pack up first."

Wade stretched out under the tree and crossed his feet at the ankles. With her own head throbbing, a nap sounded great, but she didn't want to desert Maddy.

Wade tipped his hat over his face.

"Naptime?" Abigail began packing up the leftovers.

"Just resting my eyes."

Abigail smiled, taking the opportunity to let her eyes roam down his long, muscular form. "My dad used to say that during Sunday afternoon football, right before he let out a big snore."

"I don't snore."

"That's what he said." Abigail put the last of the food into the tote bag and set it to the side. She pulled her knees into her chest and wrapped her arms around them.

Wade folded his arms under his head, the movement tugging his Western shirt from the narrow waistline of his jeans. Only his lower face was visible under the hat. His square jawline was freshly shaven. There was a shallow cleft in his chin she hadn't noticed before. His lips were relaxed, turning neither up nor down. His upper lip dipped in the middle, and she had a sudden image of herself leaning over and placing a soft kiss square on his mouth.

Disturbing.

She shook her head and pulled her eyes from him. Mercy. Just because he couldn't see her was no reason to let her imagination run wild.

She plucked a nearby dandelion puff and twirled it between her fingers. She should make a wish. She glanced at Maddy, who was splashing right into the water without so much as a pause. Her feet made quick work of the rocky bottom.

Wade still rested in the shade, his Father's Day picture at his elbow. Abigail closed her eyes and blew at the dandelion puff. When she opened her eyes, the spores were dancing away on the wind. She twirled the naked stem in her fingers.

"Make a wish?" Wade's eyes were open now.

"Maybe." She heard the flirtatious tone in her own voice. *Cool it, Abigail. Sheesh.*

She turned her attention to Maddy, who was waist-deep now. Maddy plunged forward and came up a moment later near a large boulder.

Abigail frowned. "How deep is the water?" she asked Wade.

"Waist-deep. She's a good swimmer, and the current is slow."

True enough. The water was almost still.

Near the edge, Maddy burst from the water, her entire torso above the waterline. Abigail might as well join her if Wade was going to nap.

"I didn't know she had artistic ability." Wade's tone revealed disappointment.

"Isn't that a good thing?" Abigail had a little bit of artist in her, enough to appreciate Maddy's talent.

"I should've noticed."

Abigail wanted to ease his guilt and didn't know why. "If it's the first time she's drawn you something, how could you know?"

Wade tipped his hat back on his head and propped his torso on his elbows, making his shoulders look broader than ever. He watched Maddy attempt a handstand, but the slight current worked against her.

"She doing okay, you think?" He darted a look at Abigail. "I mean, you being a woman and all." He shifted uncomfortably, like he had pieces of hay stuck in his shirt.

Abigail was charmed by his unease.

"Maddy's a good kid. Really. I like that she's curious and straightforward."

"You mean nosy and blunt?"

"She might come across that way every now and then, but those qualities will temper with age. At least you always know what's on her mind."

A frown puckered between Wade's brows, and Abigail realized that might not be true for him. Maddy might not feel free to tell her dad what she was thinking. Regardless of Wade's past, regardless of her investigation, maybe Abigail could help the father and daughter find firmer footing before she left.

"She might be a little lonely," Abigail said. "That was my first impression of her—'course it didn't help she was crying over her missing bike at the time."

"Watch this!" Maddy called.

"She's taken with you," Wade said as his daughter's feet shot skyward.

Abigail looked at him. "You say that like it's a bad thing."

"I worry about her. How she'll feel when you leave."

He didn't have to say what he was thinking. *She's already lost so much.*

"She's had a nanny every summer."

Maddy came up from her handstand and Abigail gave her a thumbs-up.

"That's different."

"How so?"

Wade sat up, rested his forearms on his raised knees. "I don't know. She wasn't close to them."

"I haven't been here two weeks." She realized as she said it that that was exactly what he found so disconcerting. If Maddy was this attached after a handful of days, how would she feel in three months?

"I'll miss her when I leave too." What did he want from her anyway? "Would you rather I just left her to her own devices?" She knew the frown made its way into her tone and didn't care.

Wade tugged his hat, then sighed. "Don't know what I want. Just don't want her hurt."

His concern for Maddy drained her irritation. "You can't protect her from everything."

The corner of his lip tucked in. He flicked a look at her, just enough self-deprecating humor in his eyes to show he knew he fought a losing battle. "I can try."

"Relationships teach us a lot about life

and ourselves, even the short-term ones. I'd like to have a positive impact on Maddy."

"You're right. God brings people into our lives for a reason. Sometimes I forget."

"Maddy's already aware that loss is a part of life. Besides, you're her dad, and she'll always have you."

His lips pressed slightly together, and Abigail wondered what that meant.

She rubbed her temple where it pounded. What she'd give for a couple Tylenol. It hadn't hurt this much since she'd been here. Well, except when she'd fallen from Trinket.

Wade reached toward her, then pulled his hand back. He'd done the same thing when he'd knelt at her side after her fall, something she hadn't remembered until now.

"How's your head?" he asked.

She swept her bangs aside and touched the knot, realizing he'd been about to do the same thing. It was better all around if he kept his hands to himself. His touch stirred things that didn't need stirring, certainly not by the man she was investigating.

"It's healing up." She tucked her hair

behind her ear. "It's a ghastly shade of yellow, though."

"You're still having headaches."

He must've noticed her rubbing her temples. "Not from the fall. It's the health condition I mentioned before— hypertension. High blood pressure can cause headaches."

Wade frowned at her. "None of my business, but maybe you're not getting enough rest. You don't have to entertain Maddy every moment."

"I'm fine, really. I like spending time with her."

A splash drew her attention to Maddy, who rose from the water like a wet mermaid. "Come on, you guys!"

"Maybe we should head back," Wade said.

Abigail wasn't cutting the Father's Day celebration short on account of a headache. "No way. I'm getting my feet wet." She removed her tennis shoes and socks, rolled her jeans until they reached the tops of her calves, and ran through the grass to the shoreline.

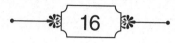

16

Abigail watched the school band approach the corner. The musicians looked spiffy in their starched red-and-white uniforms, marching forward in unison. The brass section blared "You're a Grand Old Flag," and the percussion beat out a snappy cadence. The Moose Creek annual Fourth of July celebration was under way.

The smell of grilling burgers and kettle corn continually wafted by, tempting her to break her low-sodium, low-fat diet. She'd seen a booth for Rocky Mountain oysters and hadn't been tempted in the slightest, though a long line snaked from the booth.

Abigail had lost Aunt Lucy to her friends from church, and Maddy was watching the parade with Olivia and her mom, Shay. Abigail spotted Dylan across the street, and he waved through the passing parade. As she waved back, her phone vibrated in her pocket.

Abigail darted into the nearest building, Mocha Moose. The smell of the rich brew was pure heaven, and she promised herself a cup after the call.

She pulled out her phone, checked the screen, then answered. "Happy Fourth, sis." It wasn't much quieter in the busy café. She meandered to the back, waving to new friends as she went.

"What's all the racket?"

"The Moose Creek marching band. And a thousand of my closest neighbors." Abigail rounded a bend and found a secluded nook. "That better?"

"Much. Aunt Lucy with you?"

"She was, but she ditched me for her friends. Actually, they wanted to put chairs out for the parade in the wee hours of the morning, and I decided my time would be better spent wandering the booths. Exercise, you know."

"Step away from the junk food."

"Yes, Dr. Jones." Abigail plopped into a stuffed leather armchair and wondered if she'd find the motivation to get up.

"How's Aunt Lucy? Are you seeing any signs of dementia?"

"Nothing too worrisome. She gets stuck on a word once in a while and repeats herself occasionally. I'm not sure what's normal and what's not."

"Either of those could be normal. Any signs of disorientation? Poor judgment? Misplacing things?"

"Not that I've noticed."

"Well, stay alert. Maybe you can talk her into a checkup."

"That's a good idea. How's my apartment?"

"Empty, much like it is when you're here. Now, tell me about your symptoms."

Abigail rolled her eyes. "Did you call just to nag?"

"No, I called to nag *and* snoop."

"Can we move on to the snooping?"

"Fine. What have you found out about J. W.?"

Abigail sighed. "Nada."

"It's been two weeks, Abs. We're into July already."

The band's patriotic tune permeated the walls as it turned the corner. "So that's why there's a parade . . ."

"Very funny. What's the holdup?"

"The holdup is I haven't found answers online—"

"Because nobody else knows the truth."

"Possibly. Maddy doesn't know anything, and the one person who does isn't exactly a fountain of information."

"Maybe he doesn't trust you."

"Well, hello, he's only known me a month. Why would he?"

"Is there someone else?"

Abigail had been down this road so many times she'd worn a rut in the pavement. "His best friend, Dylan, maybe. Beyond that, I don't think anyone knows."

"Think he'd talk?"

"He's pretty loyal. They go way back."

"Might be time to pull out the feminine charms."

Abigail laughed. "Right, because I have so much finesse."

"Just think Ginger from *Gilligan's Island.*"

"I'm more Gilligan, don't you think?"

"Ha. You can be charming when you want to be. You had Daddy wrapped around your little finger."

There was no animosity in her tone. Reagan had always been closer to their mom, Abigail to her dad. That's just the way it was.

"Maybe I can try." Abigail wouldn't lead Dylan on—that wasn't her style. But a little flirting never hurt anyone, she supposed.

"Good girl. You'll have J. W. eating from your hand in no time."

"J. W. . . . Thought we were talking about Dylan." Wade was a whole different matter.

"Why would you waste time charming his friend when you're not even sure he knows the truth? There's a deadline."

"Yeah, but—" Abigail bit her lip. But what? Wade was her employer? Wade was too much of a challenge? Wade was hazardous to her well-being?

"It's not like he's hard on the eyes. Come on, Abs, any single girl in her right mind wouldn't mind getting closer to the man."

"It's not like anything could come of it. He's the subject of my investigation." And he wouldn't be happy when he found out.

It's your job. She was the Truthseeker,

and it wasn't like she'd come here looking for this.

"Doesn't mean you can't enjoy the process."

"I'm not getting attached to a man I'm going to betray."

"You can't look at it like that. You do this all the time, Abigail. What's so different this time?"

"I don't usually get to know my subjects so well. I'm living here. He's Maddy's father."

"You'll have to find a way to separate all that. Maybe this is God's way of saving the magazine. Maybe you're there 'for such a time as this.'"

Abigail recognized the quote from the story of Esther. Was her sister right? Had God placed her here so she could save *Viewpoint*?

"You're right. It can't be a coincidence. All right, I'll see what I can do about getting closer to Wade." Abigail winced even as she said the words. She didn't even want to think about how she was going to manage that feat.

"Are there fireworks in Moose Creek? You might be able to do something with that."

"There's a small display." She imagined cozying up to Wade in one way or another and felt her face grow warm. "I don't know about this, Reagan."

"You don't have to throw yourself at him, Abs. You can be charming in a subtle and discerning way. I have confidence in you."

"Easy for you to say." She was so done talking about this. "So, how goes it with Dr. Right?"

"Three dates and counting. We're going downtown tonight for Taste of Chicago and the fireworks."

"Which kind of fireworks?"

"Hopefully both."

Abigail heard the smile in Reagan's voice. She shifted the phone to her other ear.

"He kissed me good night last time."

"And . . . ?"

"I think I'm a goner."

Abigail smiled. "You haven't said that since Robbie Lewis took you for a ride in his Camaro. Maybe he's the one."

"Oh, it's too early. We hardly know each other, right?"

"You have good instincts. But take it slow, all right?"

"You know me—I'll probably be weighing

the pros and cons for another year or two at least. If he hangs around that long."

"He'd be crazy not to."

"Spoken like a loyal sister."

A ring sounded on Reagan's end. "Oops, that's the answering service. Hope it's nothing major."

"Have fun tonight."

They said good-bye and Abigail pocketed her phone, her thoughts turning to their discussion about Wade.

As she waited in line for her coffee, the memory of sharing a saddle sprang to her mind. The heat of his legs against hers, the whisper of his breath in her ear, the rumble of his voice in his chest. The moisture in Abigail's mouth evaporated at the memory.

She could get closer without leading him on or behaving foolishly. As Reagan said, she could be charming when she wanted to be. The real question was, while she was busy tearing down Wade's defenses, would she be able to keep her own wall in place?

❊

After the parade, Abigail found Aunt Lucy and the gang in the craft barn and spent the afternoon perusing handmade afghans, quilts, and jewelry. Aunt Lucy had hired a teenage girl to man her doll booth, and she'd already sold more dolls than Aunt Lucy sold in a month.

They nibbled on goodies from junk food alley for dinner. Abigail gave in to her craving for kettle corn but skipped the fatty cheeseburgers, though the smell of them grilling was tempting. She decided to round out her meal with a barbecued chicken sandwich and hand-squeezed lemonade. Hey, it was made with fruit.

Abigail was getting in line at the barbecue booth, which was sponsored by Aunt Lucy's church, when Dylan and Wade stepped into line behind her.

"Hey, Abigail," Dylan said.

"Hi, you two."

Wade nodded hello.

"What do you think of our Fourth of July celebration?" Dylan asked. "Must be a far cry from Chicago's."

"Like two different worlds. This is great, though, and the food looks and smells so yummy. It's hard to choose."

"You picked the right booth," he said, all dimples.

She inched forward as the line moved.

"Have you seen Maddy?" she asked Wade. "I haven't seen her since I dropped her off with Shay and Olivia this morning."

"Reckon they're over by the games," Wade said. "She knows where to meet us for the fireworks. Where's your aunt?"

"We're meeting at the picnic pavilion once we have our food. Do you mind if I join you all for the fireworks? Aunt Lucy isn't sticking around." She widened her eyes the way she'd seen Reagan do, then wondered if her eyes looked like Aunt Lucy's behind those thick glasses.

"Sure," Dylan said. "We watch 'em up on Sugar Hill, just west of town." He pointed past the town square. "Great view from up there."

"Daddy!" Maddy appeared, followed by Shay and Olivia.

"Those look good," Abigail said, gesturing toward the caramel apples the girls were working on.

"They're over that way," Shay said. "Next to the funnel cakes, which is where I totally blew *my* diet."

"You hardly need to diet." Dylan's eyes flirted the way they did with anyone with a set of X chromosomes.

Shay's face blossomed a pretty shade of pink even as she rolled her eyes.

Abigail smothered a smile as she moved forward in line.

"Look what Olivia made me." Maddy pulled a knotted hemp necklace from the collar of her T-shirt. A horse charm hung from the bottom.

"That's beautiful, Olivia," Abigail said, fingering the fibrous cord. "Must've taken a long time."

"It looks just like Destiny." Maddy tucked the necklace into her collar.

"Hope you thanked her properly," Wade said.

"I did. Hey, Dad, can I watch the fireworks with Olivia? We're saving a spot on the fairground, right by where they're let off."

Wade's glance bounced off Abigail. "Don't know, Maddy. It'll be a madhouse getting out of here afterward. How will I find you?"

"We can drop her home," Shay said. "Olivia would love the company."

"Please, Mr. Ryan?" Olivia asked shyly.

Wade shifted, looked back toward the fairgrounds. Abigail wondered if he was uncomfortable without their buffer between them.

"Suppose so," Wade said.

"Yay!" Maddy said, and the group turned toward the town square.

"Don't get too close to the fireworks," he called.

Abigail moved forward, ordered her sandwich, and chatted with the teen she recognized from her aunt's church. Once her sandwich was in hand, she slipped past Dylan and Wade.

"See you in a bit."

She made her way to the pavilion where Aunt Lucy had saved them a spot at a picnic table, far enough away from the stage that the country music wasn't blaring in their ears. The sandwich was tasty, with only a hint of spice, and the lemonade was the perfect blend of sweet and tangy.

By the time they finished, Aunt Lucy and her friends declared themselves done in and called it a day.

"Do you need a ride, dear?" Aunt Lucy asked.

"No thanks. I'm staying for the fireworks."

They said good-bye and walked off in the dusk toward their cars. Abigail glanced around town. Fewer people cluttered the walks now, and the streetlamps had come on. Night was falling quickly, and everyone was finding a spot to settle for the display. It was time to find Wade and Dylan before it was too dark to navigate the hill.

She started the trek toward Sugar Hill, across the neatly clipped fairground grass. The evening was cooling off, and she wished she'd brought her jacket. Overhead, the stars were peeking through the dark shroud, and a large moon hung in the western sky.

Reagan was right. Tonight was the perfect opportunity to get closer to Wade. Maddy wouldn't be there, he was off work, and it was a romantic evening. She had to be more charming. She thought of Dylan's overt flirtation. Not a chance. She knew her limits.

Abigail glanced up at Sugar Hill, dodging spread-out quilts and children waving sparklers. The hill was lit with flares of fireworks and sparklers. She hoped she could find Wade. And if she did, what was she going to do with the opportunity?

17

Wade flipped out the quilt and lowered himself onto it. He pulled the pack of sparklers he'd bought for Maddy from his pocket and tossed them down. So much for that.

"Bring a lighter?" Dylan dropped onto the other side of the blanket.

Wade retrieved it and tossed it by the sparklers. There were at least a couple hundred people on the hill, but the sheer size of the butte allowed plenty of space for spreading out.

Dylan lit a sparkler and sat back, watching it flicker and flash. He'd been quiet since they'd run into his ex-girlfriend at the fairgrounds.

"So what's the deal with you and Bridgett?" Wade asked.

"No deal. We're friends."

"Didn't look like it to me. Couldn't take her eyes off you."

Dylan held the sparkler farther away, watching the light burn down the stick. "We're friends," he said firmly.

"Thought you liked her."

"I did." Dylan shrugged. "She wanted to take it to the next level, and I didn't."

"What's wrong with the next level?"

Dylan gave a wry grin. "It's the level preceding 'till death do us part.'"

Wade wondered if Dylan would ever tire of leaving a trail of heartbroken women and settle down. "Don't you want kids someday?"

"Don't know. I got Maddy."

"Maddy's *my* kid."

Dylan gave a crooked grin. "Exactly. I get to come around, tug her ponytail, then go home to my quiet house."

As Dylan's grin slipped away, Wade caught a flicker of something on Dylan's face and suspected that the quiet house was sometimes too quiet. Then again, the man was rarely home. He needed activity, socializing, fun. Maybe he needed all those things *because* his house was so quiet.

But Wade wouldn't verbalize the thought. Dylan would turn tables, and then Wade would be on the hot seat. It had taken almost a week for them to find their footing after their argument in town. The conversation was never revisited; they just bumped along until the conflict was forgotten. That's what men did.

Dylan's sparkler burned out, and he tossed the stick to the ground.

"Hey, guys." Abigail sauntered toward them on those long legs of hers.

Wade gave her a nod.

"Hey, gorgeous." Dylan stood, Wade just a second behind him.

She cocked her head and smiled as she approached, not at Dylan, but at him.

Wade gulped. There was something . . . different about her. About the way she looked at him, the way she carried herself. Something that stole the moisture from his mouth and made him wish he'd told Maddy no. No, you can't watch fireworks with Olivia. No, you can't leave me here with Abigail.

Abigail's foot caught on something and she stumbled, pitching forward. Dylan, who was closer, reached out and caught her. Abigail straightened, her eyes averted. "Sorry," she said, pulling away from him.

"You can fall into my arms anytime you like." Dylan winked. "Have a seat."

Wade took his spot on the edge of the blanket, Dylan sat on the other side, which left the middle for Abigail. She eased down between them. Wade wondered if that stumble was contrived, then recalled the genuine embarrassment on her face. Maybe not.

"Sparkler?" Dylan offered.

"Sure." Abigail took the stick and Dylan lit it. She extended it as it flared to life. "I haven't held one of these since I was a kid."

"Dylan!" Three women approached, one of them clutching a bulky blanket. "You have to come sit with us. Taryn's going to tell us about her disastrous trip to Yellowstone."

"Trust me, you don't want to miss it," another one of the women said.

Dylan cast Wade a glance. "You mind?"

Well, what was he supposed to say with Abigail sitting right here? He could hardly beg Dylan to stay.

"Nope."

Dylan hopped to his feet. "I heard you had an unfortunate encounter with a skunk."

The group walked off, skirting families and coolers, their chatter and laughter fading into the night.

"He's sure popular with the ladies," Abigail said, watching the group go.

"Disappointed?"

She shot him a look, and he read the surprise in her eyes. "I'm not interested in Dylan."

Wade looked away, denied that her words gave him any pleasure. He hoped she didn't think he was fishing for information. Last thing he wanted was Abigail thinking *he* was interested. She'd gone quiet, and he glanced her way.

She seemed mesmerized by the sparkler, apparently having shrugged off his comment. A pale yellow glow washed her face, and the reflection of light flickered in her green eyes. She narrowed those eyes, studying the sparkler as it burned down the stick, her brows bunching to-gether.

She turned the sparkler for a better view. "I wonder how these are made."

"Careful," Wade said, just as sparks spit onto her bare arm.

Abigail squealed, dropped the sparkler. Wade grabbed the cool end of the stick and tossed it onto the grass.

"Hope I didn't ruin your quilt." She brushed at the spot.

Wade tamped out the sparkler with his boot. The woman fell, tripped, and dropped things more often than a child. "Gonna start calling you Grace."

She lifted her chin. "You saying I'm clumsy?"

Wade shrugged. "Saying you've been here two minutes, and you've already dropped a sparkler and tripped over your own feet—unless that was on purpose."

Abigail frowned.

Wade cringed. Now why'd he have to go and say that?

"Why would I—" Her lips pursed. "I did not trip on purpose. I was mortified, if you must know."

"Makes no difference to me." Wade

wiped his boot on the grass and got resituated.

"If I were interested in Dylan, I'd go out with him—he's asked more than once, you know."

A twinge of jealousy flared. He didn't know Dylan had pursued that hard. "Like I said, no difference to me."

Abigail frowned and looked away.

He'd done it now. Managed to take things a couple levels past awkward. He really had a way with ladies. Stretching his legs in front of him, he looked skyward. The display could start anytime now. Anytime.

Was he really so incapable of making conversation with a woman? So out of practice? He shooed a mosquito from his face. Who was he kidding? It wasn't just any woman. It was Abigail, daggonit. She did something to him that didn't need doing. If she'd just keep her distance and stick to her job, everything would be just dandy. But no, every time he turned around, there she was. Falling off horses, inviting herself to picnics and fireworks.

Okay, so she hadn't invited herself to the picnic, and the fireworks was supposed to be a group outing. *Supposed to* being the key phrase. He looked in the direction Dylan had disappeared and scowled. *Thanks a lot, friend.*

His gaze passed over Abigail as he turned back. She sat with her legs crossed, twisting that ring on her finger. A breeze wafted by, and she shivered. He reached behind and pulled the quilt up, dropping it onto her shoulder, careful not to touch.

She looked at him as if suddenly remembering he was there. "Thanks." Her eyes were shadowed in moonlight, and Wade couldn't seem to tear his gaze from them. For the moment, she wasn't Abigail the nanny. She was just Abigail. Abigail with her easy nature, her quick wit, her nurturing ways. She bewitched him, was what she did. With those wide, questioning eyes. With those full lips that just begged to be tasted.

Her lips parted ever so slightly. His gaze darted back to her eyes.

Caught.

Wade turned away. Son of a gun. Why was he looking at her lips? Could he be more obvious? What had gotten into him?

Abigail. That's what. The fact that his

heart was galloping in his chest was just foolish. Crazy.

A boom sounded, and a second later a red starburst exploded overhead. The crowd *ooh*ed and *aah*ed. *Thank You, Jesus*. Now he could focus on something other than the woman cuddled up in his blanket.

Faint strains of "America the Beautiful" carried from the fairground speakers, and a blue starburst bloomed overhead, followed quickly by a loud boom.

Abigail was glad for the thunderous booms if only because they made the ones in her chest seem trivial. She stared into the sky, but all she saw was Wade's face, Wade's eyes when he'd looked at her. Another man might've kissed her—it was that kind of moment—and much as it pained her to admit it, she'd wanted him to. Might've even leaned a fraction of an inch toward him. She cringed at the thought.

But he'd turned away, leaving her feeling forsaken and confused. And embarrassed. Again. He had a way of bringing out the stupid in her.

What was her problem? Why couldn't she focus on her job? The subject of her investigation was right under her nose, living under the same roof, completely accessible. She'd never had it so easy. And yet.

When she was with him, she forgot her purpose. And it wouldn't be easier now that she'd upped the ante. She glanced covertly at him. He studied the night sky, a blue glow shining on his way-too-handsome face.

Of course she was having trouble focusing on her job. What woman wouldn't? Wade was a gorgeous cowboy. He was Marlboro man minus the tobacco. Could she help it if he made her go weak in the knees? If he made her forget herself and want things she couldn't have? She was only human.

You're the Truthseeker, Abigail. For heaven's sake, act like it. She had to think of *Viewpoint*, of what would happen if she *didn't* find the truth and write the story. The magazine her mother had started and nurtured for all these years would go the way of the dinosaurs. So many people would lose their jobs. People who needed their income and their health benefits. Starting with Mom.

It would be financially devastating for her mother, who couldn't retire for another ten years at least. Her father had been a good provider, but schoolteachers didn't exactly pull in the big bucks, and they'd had to take out a second mortgage when his health problems began.

A loud boom pulled her from her thoughts. Overhead, the sky exploded in shades of green, then red, then white. *Oohs* and *aahs* followed.

"Moose Creek does the Fourth proud," Abigail said, hoping to break the tension. The fireworks were more than she'd expected.

"Used to be bigger when the town was prospering, I heard."

"This your first fireworks without Maddy?" A breeze ruffled Abigail's hair, and she pulled the quilt tighter.

"Guess she's growing up, wanting to be with her friends and all that."

"It was bound to happen." Abigail smiled at him, then forced her gaze away before she got sucked in again. She watched the colors explode overhead. "I was a daddy's girl too. He never lost that spot in my heart, even after he died, so I think you're safe."

"You aren't close to your mom after all you went through with losing him?"

"We're close. My dad and I just had a special bond." This was as good a time as any. "Did it bring you and Maddy closer when her mother died?"

She waited through two loud booms for a reply.

"In a way. Definitely made me more protective."

Abigail took a breath and made the leap. "How did your wife pass away—if you don't mind my asking." She held her breath, wondered if she'd pushed too far.

"It was an accident." There was only sadness and regret in his voice.

His expression confirmed her initial conclusion. He was watching the display, but she wondered if he saw any of it.

"I'm sorry. It must've been very hard." She watched him for a moment more, hoping his expression would betray his thoughts, but nothing surfaced. She watched white sparks sizzle across the sky. She couldn't waste this opportunity. How often were they alone?

"I saw her photo in Maddy's room. She looked happy." She felt his appraisal and looked at him.

He looked away. "She was, early on, when we were close. But after Maddy came along . . . things changed."

"Too wrapped up in motherhood?" Abigail clutched the quilt, afraid if she so much as moved, it would spoil things.

"She was never wrapped up in Maddy. She was too . . ."

She was sure he'd been about to say something important. "Too . . . ?"

She waited for his reply. Two fireworks flared in the sky, three booms sounded.

"It's in the past. Gotta keep moving forward. Nothing you can do about what's already done."

Abigail kept the disappointment from her face. "True." No reason his reply had to be a dead end. "Is that why you moved to Montana?"

"Needed a fresh start."

She nodded. "Sometimes it's easier to leave bad memories behind."

"Exactly."

The song on the loudspeakers wound

down, and strains of "God Bless America" began.

She sensed Wade shutting down, so she attempted to lighten the mood. "Why Moose Creek, Montana? I mean, it's charming, but it's barely a dot on the map."

"That was part of its appeal." He paused for a thunderous boom. "Dylan's grandfather had a ranch here, and Dylan brought me here when we were boys. I loved it. The wide-open spaces, the sky stretching on forever. Not to mention the horses and cattle and mountains. When I needed a place to start over, it seemed ideal."

"Didn't you feel like an outsider at first? It's a close-knit community."

"A little. Dylan's grandfather took me under his wing and introduced me around. He was highly respected around these parts."

"He passed away?"

"Circle D was his ranch. Dylan inherited it."

"How did you come to own Stillwater?"

"It was on the market when I was looking to make the move. I bought it before we came out here, stock and all. Best thing I ever did."

Most men only dreamed of the life Wade had had in Texas. He was a rodeo champion, a celebrity, and he made a bundle of money. Why was he so glad he'd exchanged all that for an endless job that barely paid its way?

"Why's that?"

He shot her a look. "'Bout as nosy as Maddy."

"Sorry," she said, though she wasn't really.

"Been good for Maddy. A safe, God-fearing community. Wouldn't trade what we have here for everything I had back in Texas."

Abigail was more aware of all he'd given up than he knew. She had to respect that he didn't regret leaving it. She wished she could return to the topic of Lizzie, but she didn't want to press her luck.

"Still having headaches?" he asked.

"Not today." Abigail propped her elbows on her folded knees.

"If you need a break from Maddy, let me know. I'll work something out."

His concern tweaked her guilt. "Thanks, but I'll be fine. My mom is the one who insisted I take some time off." She shifted to a new subject quickly to avoid questions about her job. "My dad's health woes started with hypertension, so she's worried mine'll progress like his did."

"Understandable."

"I don't like being idle. She asked me to come out and check on Aunt Lucy. Mom was afraid she might be losing her faculties."

"Lucy Bowers? She might be a little eccentric—"

Abigail shot him a look.

"Okay, a lot eccentric, but she's right as rain."

"I hope so."

The song built to a crescendo and the fireworks came in quick succession now, booms reverberating through the night, flashes and sparks lighting and sizzling. Families around them began gathering their things, but she sat still, content to watch to the end. Wade was motionless too, apparently in no hurry to beat the crowd.

When the display came to a noisy end,

the crowd cheered and whistled. Abigail smiled at the enthusiasm. The music and fireworks over, quiet fell over the hill.

Abigail pulled the blanket from her shoulder and stood.

Wade retrieved the sparklers and gathered the blanket. "Need a ride?"

"You mind?"

He shrugged. "Going there myself." He set the blanket around her shoulders. "Save me from carrying it."

Abigail wrapped up in the quilt, glad for its warmth, and they started down the hill. It seemed darker than ever with the flare of fireworks gone. Thick clouds of smoke hung overhead, veiling the moon and stars, and carrying the smell of fireworks. She breathed deeply.

"You might want to pull the blanket up off the—"

Abigail's foot caught on the quilt and she stumbled. She caught herself easily and snatched the blanket higher. Her face grew warm. "You just had to jinx me."

"Yeah, it was all my fault." Wade's lips twitched.

She made it to the bottom without further incident, and when they reached the boardwalk, they joined the crowd. The streetlamps lit their way now. Decorative flags fluttered in the wind overhead, and the sounds of idle chatter and footsteps on the boarded walk filled the night.

Wade greeted friends with a wave or a tip of his hat. As they neared the fringe of town, the crowd dwindled. Families called good night to one another and went toward separate vehicles, and the sounds of the crowd were replaced by the chirping crickets and the whispering wind.

They left the walk and cut through a park on the edge of town. Soon it was just the two of them. Abigail was conscious of their isolation, of their lone footsteps swishing through the tall grass. She took two steps for every one of his.

"Not much farther," Wade said. "What I get for arriving after the parade started." He seemed to realize she was trailing and slowed his pace.

"Won't Maddy beat us home?"

"Doubt it. The fairground was packed, and Shay had the kids with her and all the stuff that goes with it."

Moments later the truck came into view at the edge of the park. Any cars that had been parked nearby were gone. A lone streetlamp shone down on the old red Ford.

Wade opened the passenger door, made sure she and the blanket were tucked in, then shut the door. She appreciated the gentlemanly gesture, couldn't remember the last time someone had opened her car door.

She buckled her belt. The cab smelled like Wade. Leather and earth and some indefinable masculine scent. She pulled in a lungful of the fragrance. Nice.

The driver's door opened and Wade got in. One jangle of the keys later and the truck turned over.

Abigail felt a yawn coming on and covered her mouth. Many nights in the city she stayed up well past midnight working, yet it was barely past eleven and she was fighting sleep. She'd become accustomed to the different routines here. Life on a ranch had a way of aligning with nature's rhythms and cadences.

She settled into the seat, leaning back. As Wade pulled onto the street, she smothered another yawn.

"Past your bedtime?" Wade asked.

"I can't believe I'm so tired. I'm a night owl."

"Used to think I was too. Now I get my best work done in the morning."

"Think it has something to do with the slower pace? I mean, there's not much night-life in Moose Creek."

"God probably intended people to retire at dark and rise at light, don't you think?"

"Probably. I guess the body has a way of resetting its circadian rhythms. I'll have to ask my sister."

"The doctor?"

"*Mm-hmm*." The hum of the engine and slow rocking of the truck weren't helping. It had been a long, full day, and she'd been on her feet most of it.

Wade turned onto the main road that would take them to the ranch. Abigail closed her eyes and drew the blanket tighter even as she felt heat blowing through the vents. It felt good to have someone else in the driver's seat. To let someone else take charge, and to know she was in good hands.

It was a strange thought to have about someone whom she was investigating. Deep down, at the core, she didn't believe he'd had anything to do with his wife's death. How could she feel so safe if she thought him guilty? She took a deep breath and let it out. No need to think about this now.

She pulled her arms from the quilt, sank deeper into the seat, leaned her head against the door. She just wanted to rest her eyes for a few minutes, then she'd feel recharged. Maybe she could do some research once she got back. Maddy would probably sleep in tomorrow since she'd stayed out late.

Abigail rewound her thoughts to the fireworks, to her conversation with Wade. He was nice to talk to. Nice to be with. Nice to look at.

She didn't even chide herself for the thought. She was too tired. Besides, he *was* nice to look at. He was a good dad, a good friend, a gentleman. She couldn't believe he hadn't been snatched up by some woman from the Big Sky State.

Her thoughts swam through her head, growing fuzzier and more ambiguous until they were gone altogether . . .

"Abigail."

She barely heard the warm, low drawl.

"Abigail."

Her eyes popped open.

Wade was staring. "Wake up. We're home."

She looked around, orienting herself. "I wasn't asleep."

"Truck's been off two minutes."

She had dozed off then. What had Wade been doing those two minutes? Watching her sleep? She nearly asked, but the look on his face answered her silent question. The same look he'd had on the hill. His eyes, shadowed under the brim of his hat, were heavy-lidded, pensive.

She drew in a lungful of the musky scent that was all Wade. She was wide awake now. Her gaze fell to his slightly crooked nose, to his chiseled jawline, covered now with a day's growth of stubble.

Must touch. The pads of her fingers tingled under the prickly scruff. She met his eyes again and knew he welcomed the touch. An ache formed in the middle of her stomach, burning for him to do everything his look promised.

Then his jaw clenched under her hand, and he closed his eyes as a look of torment passed over his features.

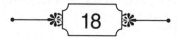

18

Abigail watched Wade open his eyes, watched regret replace the wanting.

Her hand fell to her side.

"We can't . . ." he whispered.

She fought against the pull of reason. She didn't want to think past the yearning, she wanted to surrender to it.

"You work for me," he continued. "It's just not . . ." He seemed to struggle with his thoughts, his words. "You're Maddy's nanny."

"So . . . ?" She placed her hand over his and found it knotted in a fist.

He tore his eyes from her. "Not looking

for a relationship." Something in the way he said it made her think it was more than a temporary condition.

Abigail wondered why, wondered if the reason was buried somewhere in the secrets of his past. Her own reasons were starting to surface, beginning with the conflict of interest. "Fair enough." He was right. She knew it, but she didn't have to like it.

"It would just be—"

She waved him off. "I get it. You're right." She said it with more conviction than she felt. She wondered if he was aware that his fist clenched repeatedly.

"All right, then."

"All right." She pulled her hand from his.

He gave her a tense smile. "I mean, we can handle this."

Living under the same roof. Chemistry galore. "We're both adults."

"And it's only . . ." He swallow hard. "Eight more weeks."

Eight weeks. Fifty-six days. But who was counting? "Exactly."

Wade shifted awkwardly, seeming to realize that his calculation made it seem even worse.

A moment later, Abigail opened the truck door. "Well. Thanks for the ride."

"You're welcome." He didn't seem to be going anywhere.

Abigail exited the truck and dashed toward the house. She needed space. Space between her and Wade. It had been an atypical scenario tonight, she reassured herself as she bounded up the porch steps, entered the house. Dark night, romantic fireworks, handsome cowboy. It would all seem different come morning.

*

It didn't seem different come morning. Or night. Or the night after that. Even though Wade wasn't around—had made a point of not being around, Abigail suspected—she couldn't seem to forget. Her traitorous mind relived the night in minute detail, slowing for her favorite parts, then rewound them again, just for torture's sake.

She thought when she got back to her research, her feelings would change. But no matter what she read, no matter how much speculation the media had cast upon Wade, she couldn't imagine him doing anything as horrific as murdering his wife. She remembered the look of regret in his eyes when she'd asked about Elizabeth's death.

Her instincts said he wasn't responsible. But was her intuition clouded by feelings? She'd never wrestled with this before, had never gotten too close to her subject, and hated that now, of all times, when *Viewpoint* was on the line, her feelings were muddying her judgment.

She needed to be impartial. And while Wade's absence might help her peace of mind, it wasn't helping her investigation. And it wasn't helping Maddy either. He'd missed dinner two nights in a row, returned after Maddy's bedtime, and Abigail felt responsible.

She wondered how long he'd keep this up. Didn't he know his daughter needed him? Apparently it only took one little moment of chemistry to scare him away from his most important job.

Which brought up the other point Abigail had been wrestling with. What was it exactly that stopped Wade from pursuing their relationship? Sure, Abigail worked for him, and sure, she was only there for the summer, but those were issues people worked around.

Was there something more? Was he scarred from having lost his wife so suddenly? Afraid of his past catching up with him? Or had his relationship with his wife—which apparently hadn't been all that great—sworn him off women for good?

And why was Abigail speculating about a relationship that was doomed from the start? Doomed by the column she was obligated to write? And she *was* going to write it, one way or another.

Somehow, she had to get back on a regular footing with Wade. Both for Maddy's sake and for her column's. It was obvious now that she had to aim for friendship. Anything more would send him running. Not to mention mess with her own peace of mind, distract her from her job, and cloud her judgment.

No moony looks, no flirting, no sauntering, and no touching. She thought of his clenched fist under her hand the night before. He'd definitely been pushing the boundaries of his restraint. Definitely no touching.

You're the Truthseeker. You can do this.

Wade's stomach rumbled. He was half tempted to ignore it the way he'd been ignoring his feelings for Abigail. He lifted the saddle and pad from Ace's back, set the saddle in the tack room, then brushed the underside of the pad.

Who was he kidding? He may have avoided her for two days, but he'd hardly ignored his feelings. Truth be told, thoughts of Abigail rattled around his brain all day, and there didn't seem to be a thing he could do about it. Avoiding her might feel safer, but it also meant neglecting Maddy. He hadn't seen her in two days. What kind of father was he?

He stored the pad, then began brushing Ace with short, quick strokes. Wade had to go in for supper whether he wanted to or not. It was the mature thing to do. And if he could manage forty cantankerous bulls, surely he could handle one harmless woman.

He pressed his lips together. *Harmless, my foot.*

He finished grooming Ace, checked the horse's hooves, then led him to his stall. After the horse was settled for the night, Wade walked toward the house with the eagerness of a man approaching his final meal.

Cowboy up, Ryan. Focus on something else. He was eager to see Maddy and he was hungry. He'd start with that. The kitchen was lit, and through the window he saw Maddy and Abigail already eating at the table. After two nights of eating without him, they'd given up waiting, he supposed.

He drew a deep breath, then opened the door and stepped inside.

"Daddy!" Maddy's chair squawked across the floor as she popped to her feet and gave him a hug, making him feel even guiltier.

His eyes met Abigail's over her head. She gave a benign smile, then fetched him a plate. When Maddy returned to her seat, Wade hung his hat and removed his boots.

"We just started." Abigail set his plate and silver at his spot.

"It's your favorite," Maddy said. "Greta let me make the mac and cheese! Well, Abigail helped."

Moist-looking slices of ham were stacked on the serving platter, and a bowl of creamy mac and cheese sat beside it. "Looks great."

"We already prayed." Maddy took a mouthful of pasta.

"Guess I'm covered then." Wade served himself. He wondered if Abigail was looking at him. If Abigail was thinking about the Fourth. If Abigail knew how close he'd come to placing a kiss on those lips even as she'd slept in his cab. Of their own volition, his eyes darted her way.

She looked away, stirred her mac and cheese.

He smothered a sigh. If they could just get through this meal, then things would return to normal. Whatever that was.

"What's wrong?" Maddy was looking at him.

"Nothing."

"You're frowning."

He had to pull it together. "Just thinking." Wade faked a smile, then cut into his ham. Tender, like always. Greta might have the disposition of vinegar, but there was a reason he kept her around.

They ate in silence. Wade chewed faster in an effort to speed the meal along. Maybe he and Maddy could play a game, or maybe Abigail would go to bed early. *Please, God.* He could imagine the bubble of tension bursting with her exit.

"What's going on?" Maddy looked between them.

Abigail took a bite of ham, dropped her eyes to her plate, and chewed slowly.

Thanks a lot. "Nothing," he said.

More chewing. He could feel Maddy's appraisal. She was no dummy, and his acting skills apparently needed work.

"Did you two have an argument?"

He gave his daughter a look. "No, we did not. Finish your supper." He was sure Abigail was looking at him now. A fine sheen of sweat broke out across his forehead.

He wished the meal were over. Why had he loaded down his plate? And why had he initiated the clean-your-plate rule with Maddy?

"'Cause it was just like this last summer when Miss Greta and Mr. Pee Wee had that argument over his new truck. They wouldn't even look at each—"

Wade gave Maddy a stern look.

"What . . . ?" Maddy's eyes widened.

Abigail's lips twitched.

He pressed his lips together, drilled Maddy with a look. "Eat your supper."

Maddy looked contrite. "Sorry."

Wade felt a prickle of guilt for his firm tone, but daggonit, the girl could be so nosy, and did she have to put him on the spot in front of Abigail?

They finished the meal in silence. When they set their dishes in the sink, Maddy asked them to play Operation, and Abigail declined. Relieved, Wade agreed. Anything to get things back to normal.

They set the game up on the coffee table in the living room, taking seats on the floor, and when Abigail left the room, Wade could've sworn he heard the balloon of tension pop.

*

Abigail took the stairs slowly, her muscles protesting. She almost hated leaving the room when she'd had so much fun at dinner. Listening to Maddy question her dad had been amusing, especially when he'd gotten so uptight about it. Seeing the flush crawl up his neck had been rewarding.

She turned at the landing and took the next flight. She would've gladly stuck around for the game if she hadn't been in the saddle so long that evening. Her muscles would hate her come morning if she didn't give them a long, hot soak.

When she rounded the corner on the second floor, Maddy's not-so-quiet voice carried up the stairwell. "Sorry . . . embarrassed you."

Abigail stopped and strained to hear Wade's response. The pause lasted so long she thought she'd missed it.

". . . have questions, at least wait until we're alone," Wade answered.

"Sorry."

A faint buzz sounded.

"The bread basket's the hardest one, Dad."

"Now you tell me."

With his large hands and those tiny tweezers, the game was probably impossible for Wade. There was a pause, and Abigail imagined Maddy reaching for one of the pieces.

She should draw her bath. She took a step.

"So . . . really have an argument?" Maddy said.

"Maddy."

"You said to ask when we're alone." A pause. "Got it!" she said louder.

"Good job." He lowered his voice. "And no, already told you we didn't have an argument."

"Well . . . really strange. Don't you like her, Dad? Is that why you haven't been home?"

Abigail covered a smile.

"'Cause I like her a lot," Maddy continued. "She's the best nanny I ever had."

Abigail's heart warmed at Maddy's words.

"Like her just fine." A buzz sounded again, and Wade's sigh carried all the way up the steps.

"Boy, Dad, you're not very good at this."

Abigail smiled all the way to the bathroom, where she drew a warm bath and wondered what challenges tomorrow would hold.

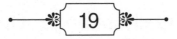

19

What was she doing wrong? Abigail surveyed the vegetable garden—or rather, the rectangle of dirt where the vegetables were supposed to be sprouting. Greta said gardening was easy, but if it were so easy, where were her seedlings? They'd worked hard, had taken two afternoons just for planting, and that didn't count the tilling and soil preparation.

Abigail squatted in the dirt, hoping for a microscopic sign of green. Nothing. Stupid sprinkler. She gave it a glare. What was she doing wrong? She'd ask Aunt Lucy for help, but the woman would probably advise her to stick plastic vegetables in the dirt.

"How's the garden?"

She hadn't heard Wade's approach. She stood and turned, glad things had grown less awkward over the past two days. She couldn't help but notice that he cut a fine figure against the Montana skyline in his Western shirt and faded jeans.

"Nonexistent," she said. "Don't know what I'm doing wrong. I picked a sunny spot and followed the planting directions. Guess I really am a city girl."

He surveyed the barren soil. "What'd you plant?"

"Potatoes and corn mostly."

"Maddy's favorites."

She shrugged. "How do you think I got her to help?"

He grinned. "You watering?"

"Every day."

"How long?"

"Timer's set for fifteen minutes."

"Not long enough. A shallow watering dampens the soil but won't reach the roots. Run it an hour every few days. A thorough soaking makes for strong, healthy roots."

"Oh." Abigail looked at the damp soil.

"Is it too late to fix? It's been almost three weeks since we planted."

He shrugged. "Try and see. Where's Maddy?"

"Upstairs, cleaning her room."

Wade's brows lifted. "How'd you manage that?"

"I told her we were going to redecorate." She hoped he remembered her asking a few weeks ago. "That still okay?"

He shrugged. "Fine by me." His eyes grew shadowed, and he frowned. "Guess her room is kind of bland. Probably should've done it before now."

"It'll be a fun project for us. Hopefully it'll go better than the garden."

"Just cosmetic stuff?"

"That's the plan. Can I borrow the truck when Maddy's finished? I thought we could run to town and pick out the paint."

He tucked his hands in his pockets. "I was just headed there."

"Can we can come along? I can get Maddy now if you're in a hurry." Two birds with one stone.

"I can wait. It's not every day my daughter cleans her room."

Abigail changed the timer on the sprinkler, then went to tell Maddy her dad was waiting. Forty minutes later they were tucked into the truck's cab, an excited Maddy fidgeting in the middle.

"I can't get over your room," Wade said. "Hasn't been that clean since we moved in."

Maddy's smile made her face glow. "I can't wait to redecorate!"

Abigail noticed a new bracelet on Maddy's wrist. "Hey, it matches your necklace." She turned the knotted hemp on the girl's wrist.

"Olivia made it for me. She's really good at jewelry."

"That was nice of her," Abigail said. Olivia was sure a giving little girl. She was glad Maddy had given her a second chance.

"What about lime green paint?" Maddy asked a moment later.

"On the walls?" Wade frowned as he turned onto the main road.

"That might be a little . . . bright," Abigail said.

"But it's my favorite color, and you said I could pick."

Rats. She had said that.

Wade's scowl passed over his daughter's head and landed on Abigail.

"What if we make lime green your accent color?" Abigail said.

"What's an accent color?"

"The color for things like throw pillows, lamps, your new rug. Things like that. That way if your favorite color is purple in two years, you can easily change it."

"Rug?" Wade asked. "Her room is carpeted."

Whoops. "I was thinking we could pull up the carpet and see if there's hardwood underneath."

"And if there isn't?"

She shrugged and winced. "Cross that bridge when we come to it?"

"Please, Dad? I hate that old brown carpet. And I want a rug with my accent color." She looked to Abigail for approval on her new word.

Abigail winked at her.

"I can see when I'm outnumbered." Wade shifted in his seat. "Guess I should be glad she's not wanting lime green carpet," he mumbled.

"Thanks, Daddy!" Maddy wrapped her arm around his bicep and held on.

Abigail watched Wade melt under his daughter's affection. Abigail had known her dad was putty in her hands, but Maddy seemed unaware of her influence.

"So what about the walls?" Maddy asked.

"Well, since you want a horse theme, maybe you can make your accent colors lime green and brown. Then you can choose something more neutral for your walls."

"Where you going to sleep while all this painting is going on?" Wade asked.

Abigail hadn't thought about that. "I guess we won't be able to get it done in a day's time."

"Not hardly."

"She could sleep in my room," Abigail offered. "I have a full-sized bed."

"Maddy thrashes when she sleeps. Trust me, you don't want that."

"Heeey . . ." Maddy gave him a mock frown.

Wade shrugged. "I call it like I see it."

"Fine, I'll sleep on the couch," Maddy said. "I can see where I'm not wanted."

"Better you than me," Wade said.

Maddy poked him with her elbow.

An hour later, after finally choosing beige paint and a border from the scant selection at Timberline Hardware, Abigail and Maddy stood in front of the store with a sack of supplies and two gallons of paint.

"There he is." Maddy looked both ways before darting across the street toward the truck.

Wade eyed the paint cans as they piled into the cab. "Tell me it's not lime green."

"Plain ol' beige, Dad, but the horse wallpaper is sweet!"

"Wallpaper?"

"Just a border." Abigail patted his arm and found it rock solid. "Relax, Dad."

"Can we start today?" Maddy asked.

"It's almost suppertime," Wade said. "And you'll have to move your things away from the walls and tape off the trim first."

"Sounds like you've done this a time or two," Abigail said.

"Don't tell me you haven't." Wade turned out of the parking lot.

Abigail lifted her chin. "I'll figure it out."

"Like you figured out the garden?"

She sent him an exaggerated glare, which he missed entirely. "Low blow, Ryan."

"We can move furniture and stuff tonight and paint tomorrow," Maddy said.

"Tomorrow's Abigail's day off, squirt."

"Will you help me, then?" Maddy asked her dad.

Abigail started to speak, then decided to wait for Wade.

Maddy nestled against Wade's arm. "Please, Daddy?"

Maybe Maddy was starting to realize her power. Abigail suppressed a smile.

"Suppose we could trim after church and chores."

"Thanks, Dad!"

"I guess I could help too," Abigail said.

Wade's lips pressed together.

Well, tough luck, cowboy. She had to get to know him better if she wanted the truth, and the only way to get to know him was to spend time together. *Besides*, she thought, assuaging her guilt, *it'll be good for Maddy*.

※

"Can we pull up the carpet?" Maddy asked after they'd piled most of her belongings in the hallway.

Abigail surveyed the ugly carpet. She hadn't noticed the stains until the room was cleared. "I think we'd better leave it, to catch the drips."

"Just a peek?"

Wade dumped the painting supplies from the bag. "Suppose so." He got on his knees and ripped the carpet from the tack strips with ease.

Abigail and Maddy peeked over his shoulder as he pulled the stained pad back.

"Hardwood." Abigail sighed with relief.

"Yay!"

"Hope it's in decent shape." Wade put the carpet back.

"Of course it is. What are you thinking?"

"I'm thinking there must be a reason someone laid carpet."

"Oh, Dad."

Wade and Abigail taped off the wooden trim while Maddy paced the room, eager to wet the first roller. But by the time they finished taping, it was after ten, and Wade declared it quitting time.

"Please, Dad? Can't we paint a little while? Just one wall?"

Abigail stepped in. "We'll have all afternoon tomorrow, Maddy. Your dad's had a long day."

Maddy's shoulders drooped. "All right."

"Let's grab your pillow and blanket and make up the sofa," Abigail said.

Maddy exited the room and Abigail followed. She didn't miss the gleam of appreciation in Wade's eyes as she squeezed past.

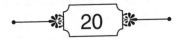

20

Abigail went to church with her aunt, then they grabbed a quick lunch at the Tin Roof. As they were about to leave the café, Aunt Lucy couldn't find her car keys. They searched her purse and the booth area for ten minutes and finally found the keys in the car's ignition. On the way back Abigail dropped a hint about a checkup, but her aunt didn't pick up on it. She just talked about her latest idea for a Colonial doll. Next time, Abigail resolved, she would outright suggest Aunt Lucy make an appointment.

By the time Abigail returned to the house,

Wade and Maddy were already in their paint clothes and wielding wet brushes.

Abigail didn't have an old shirt, so Wade offered a gray Texas Longhorn T-shirt, which was long enough to cover the shorts she hoped to preserve. She'd hardly started painting when Olivia called, and Maddy took the phone downstairs. Ten minutes later she was still chatting with her friend.

"So much for her eagerness to paint," Wade said.

"I think she's more eager to have the room done than to actually do the work." Abigail wet her brush and swept it along the window trim.

"You don't have to stick around," Wade said from his spot on the floor. "You should be resting."

"I think painting is soothing."

"If you say so."

They worked in silence, then a few minutes later they reached into the paint can simultaneously.

Wade gestured for her to go first. "How's Miss Lucy?"

"Good, I think. I enjoy her company— you never know what she's going to say next." Abigail swept the brush across the can's rim, removing the excess paint.

"She's a character."

"You have any colorful relatives back in Texas?"

Wade wet his brush, then went back to the trim. "Not really. A few cousins running around, an aunt and uncle, but they're relatively normal."

"I always wanted cousins."

"You have a sister."

"She's a few years older, so we didn't play together much. I always wanted those big family get-togethers with kids running around everywhere."

"Know what you mean, being an only child. That's where neighborhood friends come in, I guess. I'm thankful I had Dylan."

"Yeah." She thought of Julia. "I had a good friend who lived two doors down. We walked to school together, played at recess together . . . she loved to play in the rain. Used to say it was just like taking a shower except for the clothes." She wasn't aware of the sadness in her voice until she noticed Wade studying her.

"What happened?" he asked.

Abigail's brush paused. She'd never told

anyone outside her family about Julia. She sneaked a peek at Wade and got caught in the warmth she found in his earnest gaze. She somehow felt he'd understand. She reached for more paint. "One day I was going to her house, and Julia was in the garage with her father. He was hitting her."

"You saw it?"

She squatted down and swept the brush under the window trim. "I heard it."

"How old were you?"

Abigail smoothed out a few brush lines. "Ten."

"A year younger than Maddy."

Abigail loaded her brush.

The action seemed to set Wade in motion. He wet his own brush and started back to work. "That's terrible. What happened?"

Sometimes she still wondered if she'd imagined it, and she'd replay the scene to confirm her conclusion. She replayed it now and found the recollection fresh and raw and convincing.

Abigail pulled herself from the virtual nightmare. "I sneaked away before they saw me. She never mentioned it, but I think he abused her regularly. I saw bruises on her arms sometimes." Her mouth was dry as sawdust. "I never told."

She couldn't believe she'd told him. She hadn't even told her sister and mom until she was an adult.

"You were only ten. Must've been afraid."

Why had she started this? She cursed herself for bringing up the subject.

She was making a mess of the trim, but loaded up again anyway. If she stopped, she'd have to look at Wade. And if she looked at Wade, she'd see accusation or disappointment or some other emotion she couldn't bear.

"I should've told anyway. She was my best friend." She clamped her mouth shut, wondering why she was going to this place, with Wade of all people.

"What happened to her?"

Abigail shrugged. "She moved away when we were thirteen. Kept in touch awhile, but then I lost track of her."

A few moments later, Wade lowered himself to the floor next to her and wet his brush. "Don't know how someone could do that to a child."

"I don't either." She didn't want to talk

about this anymore. It made her feel too raw, too vulnerable.

"Wasn't your fault, you know."

The words were balm to her wound, but she didn't let them soak in too far. "Well, I can't do anything about it now." She couldn't go back and fix it. She'd always regret that she hadn't told, would always carry the weight of knowing she could've stopped it.

She felt Wade's perusal but wasn't about to look his way and fall into those eyes again. "Everyone has baggage, I guess. I do, you do, Maddy does . . . You just put it behind you and move on, right?"

❧

Wade fought the wave of sympathy. He imagined Abigail at ten, knowing her best friend was being abused, and couldn't stop the shudder. She must've been confused and afraid. To say nothing of the guilt she obviously carried. It radiated from every pore. He was on a first-name basis with guilt himself.

But Abigail was done talking about it. He could see that much and respect it.

"I mean, that's what you did," Abigail

said. "Moved to Montana and started a new life—put the past behind you."

Wade reloaded his brush, then swept it along the trim. If only it were as easy as changing locations. "Hard to put the past behind you when your daughter's a living reminder of it."

"She's like her mother?"

Wade shrugged. "Some things. Her smile. The way her eyes light up when she's excited, the way she tucks her hair behind her ears—that's all Lizzie."

"Must make it hard."

"Wouldn't change it for the world. Maddy's all I have."

Her eyes were crystal green in the light that flooded through the window. He saw compassion and understanding and so much more hidden in their depths.

Wade felt connected to her. Maybe it was the way she'd bared her soul, the fact that he'd just shared something he'd never told anyone, not even Dylan. Maybe that's why his next words tumbled out.

"I was the one that found her—Lizzie." Wade started to wet his brush, then realized he'd made a complete line around the room. The trim was finished. He set the brush on the can's rim.

"You found her?" Abigail's voice was gentle, coaxing.

"We'd argued earlier, before I left the house. There was a party. I wanted to go, she didn't. I was young and selfish. I left for the party, left Maddy with her."

The familiar pang of regret hollowed his stomach. If only he hadn't gone. If only they hadn't argued. If only, if only . . .

"What happened?"

Her question pulled him from deep inside himself. Why was he spilling his guts to someone he'd known barely over a month? What did he know about her— really know—that he'd trust his deepest secrets to her?

He rose and grabbed a paint tray. "Like you said. Past is the past and ought to stay there."

Abigail finished the last part of the window and stepped back. "I'm sorry for what you went through. Maddy too. Losing a parent is hard."

Wade set their brushes aside and poured the paint into the pan while Abigail unwrapped the rollers. "I worry about her. She's at that age where she needs a mom."

Abigail handed him a roller. "You're doing a great job. She loves being with you."

The sound of Maddy's feet on the stairs halted their conversation.

When she entered the room, she grabbed a roller and unwrapped it. "Olivia said lime-green and brown are really popular colors. I can't wait 'til it's finished."

"Me neither," Abigail said.

Wade's mind was stuck on his conversation with Abigail. His daughter did need him. But what if he failed Maddy the same way he'd failed Lizzie? It was why he held himself back—that fear that maybe she was better off without him.

And Abigail didn't make it easy. Between picnics and projects—case in point, he thought, looking around the room—both of them were becoming a regular part of his daily routine whether he liked it or not. And he wasn't sure which of them scared him more.

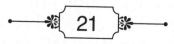

21

One week later, Maddy's room was finished. The walls were painted creamy
beige, the equine border was applied, the
wood floor gleamed like honey, and her new
lime green pillows and shaggy rug completed the look.

After replanting their garden, they
watched new seedlings spring from the
ground and inch higher each day. Like-
wise, Abigail's relationship with Wade
grew. Roots of friendship sprouted easy
conversation and laughter. Dinnertime,
and the moments afterward, had become
her favorite time of day. Wade's quiet

strength soothed her, his humor tickled her funny bone, and his tender, awkward way with Maddy only endeared him to Abigail.

Her column had become an afterthought, though the reality that she must at least notify her mother about the story was a constant nagging itch. While the writing of the article could wait, the cover had to be laid out well in advance of publication, and that deadline was quickly approaching.

As the day drew closer, Abigail found herself hoping something would change. That BlueFly Publications would rescind their ultimatum, that another story would materialize for one of the other reporters, something amazing enough to rescue *Viewpoint*. Because the closer the cover deadline grew, the more attached she became to Wade and Maddy, and the more she recognized her own truth.

She didn't want to write the story.

She still didn't know the details surrounding Lizzie's death, but she knew one thing. Wade wouldn't have hurt his wife—not on purpose.

The story was still a story, however, even without that bit of information. Because every fan in the continental United

States, every publication, every tabloid, was interested in the whereabouts of J. W. Ryan. Interested enough to buy any magazine with his picture splashed across the cover. It would be their best-selling issue since her mom exposed a senator's affair back in the eighties, back in *Viewpoint*'s heyday.

But knowing this didn't make it easier.

Abigail changed into her pajamas, washed her face, brushed her teeth, booted up her laptop, and responded to e-mails. She took her blood pressure medication, cleared the junk off her nightstand, then set the stuff back out again.

Today was the day—the day of no turning back—and she'd waited until the last minute. Because, though she might see the story as the magazine's one hope for salvation, she knew Wade would only see it as betrayal.

Abigail stared past the sheers into the dark night. Her own reflection stared back. She looked so innocent in her pj's, her hair still sporting a youthful ponytail. She tugged the band, setting her hair free. *Innocent, my fanny*. She was about to betray her new friends. What would they do when they discovered what she'd done? How would they feel then?

They'd hate her, that's how they'd feel. Abigail ran a hand over her face.

She was thinking like a woman, letting her feelings muddy the facts. *Think like a journalist. You're the Truthseeker. Remember who you are.*

And she wasn't just any journalist. She was the one who was about to save her mom's magazine. Her job and many others. That was the key—to focus on what really mattered.

Her mom needed all relevant cover material for the September issue by tomorrow morning. Abigail eyed her cell phone, nested in the pocket of her purse. Her pulse hammered in her ears.

She retrieved the phone and dialed her mom's cell. She was doing the right thing. The only thing she could do in this situation. The story had fallen into her lap. It was a gift from above, and who was she to thwart—

"Abigail. I was just thinking about you, sweetie."

"Hi, Mom."

"E-mails are nice, you know, but I wouldn't mind hearing your voice more often."

"I know you're busy."

"Never too busy for my girl. How's Aunt Lucy?"

"I'm not sure. There've been a couple things that worried me, little things really. I'm going to try and get her to have a checkup."

"Well, good luck with that if she's anything like your father. I hope you're enjoying your time with her."

"She's a delight, just as I remembered. Her church ladies love her. They're like a little flock of sheep all gathered around her every Sunday. You should see it; it's so cute." She was stalling and she knew it, but couldn't seem to help herself.

"I'm glad you're going to church."

"It's been good. Long overdue."

"And are you finding time to rest?"

"I am." Abigail nearly added that she felt fine, but she'd had headaches the last two days, and she was sure her blood pressure was up—though she'd avoided checking it.

Before she told her mom about Wade, she had one last hope. She said a quick prayer and crossed her fingers to cover all her bases. "How's the September issue shaping up? Going to start laying out the cover tomorrow?"

"Oh, the usual. A look at the economy from the small business perspective, an interview with the president's photographer . . . Hendrick is doing an interesting piece on childhood celebrities . . ."

She heard the false enthusiasm in her mom's voice. So much for her last hope. Abigail had to tell her mom about Wade, but first she had to come clean. "Mom, I know about the ultimatum from BlueFly."

The sigh was loud. "I swore Reagan to secrecy."

"Yeah, I swore her to secrecy on my health, and you see where that got me."

"I didn't want you to worry."

Mom probably wondered why she hadn't already rushed back to Chicago. She'd understand momentarily.

"Have you been feeling okay?" her mother asked. "I really didn't want you stressing about *Viewpoint*."

Here goes. "I'm fine, Mom. I called to tell you I'm in a position to help the magazine. To rescue it, actually." Abigail wadded the material of her pajama top in her fist, clenching until her nails bit into her palm.

"Go on . . ."

Abigail closed her eyes and gathered her courage. *You're a journalist. You're the Truthseeker. You're going to save* Viewpoint.

She lowered her voice. "I found J. W. Ryan." There. She'd said it. She exhaled, waiting for the relief she'd expected and finding none.

"J. W. Ryan, the rodeo celebrity?"

"The very one."

"No one knows where he is—what do you mean you found him?"

"I mean I'm living in his house." She was careful to keep her voice down. "The girl I'm watching is his daughter."

"You're living in—Addison is the girl—oh my word."

"*Madison.* Maddy." The name conjured Maddy's face, and the image of Maddy's face conjured guilt.

Abigail shoved her emotions aside. *Truthseeker.* "J. W. goes by Wade now. Wade Ryan. He and his daughter own a ranch here in Moose Creek, keep a very low profile."

"Are you sure? How can you be sure it's J. W.?"

"I'm sure, Mom. I've been doing some research. He hasn't changed much in looks, and from what he's told me of his past, it lines up with what we know of J. W. It's him, no doubt in my mind."

"Oh my word! This is perfect. Abigail, do you know what this means?"

"It's a new day for *Viewpoint.*"

"And just in time. Oh, Abigail, it's an answered prayer—I have to talk to Larry about the cover—this is the last issue we're working on—well, not the last issue now! The Truthseeker column is going to save the day! We'll plaster J. W.'s image on the cover with the words *Celebrity Cowboy Found* or maybe something catchier, and we must use a baby blue background to set off those eyes! What about his wife's death—have you discovered anything—oh, Abigail, you could be living with a murderer!"

"No, Mom. Wade's no murderer. I don't know exactly what happened to his wife, but he didn't kill her."

"You can't know that. I mean, your instincts are great, but you can't be too careful. Maybe you should move back in with

Aunt Lucy . . . we can come up with a reason—"

"Living here puts me in the perfect spot to do my research." *The perfect spot to betray my new friends.* "Really, Mom, I'm safe. I promise."

"What's wrong?"

"Nothing."

"You sound, I don't know . . . strange. Are you sure you're all right? So much for a relaxing vacation—you've been working all this time."

"I'm fine. I get plenty of rest."

"Well, put your health first, sweetie. *Viewpoint* is important to me, but nowhere near as important as you."

"I know that. I'll keep trying to get more info on Elizabeth's death, but one way or another, I'll get the story to you on time. Just save space for my column."

"Be careful. I don't like you living in his house."

"I'm completely safe. Besides, they don't know who I am. As far as they're concerned, I'm just Lucy's great-niece, filling in as nanny for the summer." And that's all she'd been when all this started.

"Do be careful. Don't press so hard that

he gets suspicious. Oh, what am I saying? You're a better investigator than I ever was."

"But you're the best editor-in-chief a magazine could ask for. And BlueFly is going to realize it come September."

"Take your time with the article. You can have until mid-August if you need to. Everyone will pick up that issue, Abigail, you realize that? And once they do, once they see our fresh new format . . . I can offer a subscription discount to entice new readers . . . We've got to make this the best issue ever."

Abigail couldn't help but smile at her mother's enthusiasm.

"You have made my week—no, my year! I've been so worried about the staff—do you know how many jobs you're saving?"

"The story presented itself. I'm just doing my job." That's all she was doing. Her job. And it wasn't like she was doing Wade and Maddy any real harm. Wade was innocent, and she'd make sure that fact rang through loud and clear in her column.

22

Abigail's laptop was driving her crazy. It had been running slow for the past few weeks, but now it was really trying her patience. She could bake a cake in the time it took for a page to load.

She shut the thing off and went downstairs. Maddy had ridden her bike to Olivia's, where she was spending the night, so Abigail had the evening off. Computer shops would be closed tomorrow, so if she was going to get it repaired, the time was now. If only she could find one that stayed open late.

She opened the phone book to the yellow

pages and set it on the kitchen table. If she was lucky, they could fix it while she waited. She scanned the list for a shop in Moose Creek and found none. They were all in Bozeman, a forty-five-minute drive. Terrific. It was almost seven already.

She called the first shop on the list and was told they closed at seven; besides which, it would take three days for them to even look at her laptop. She called the next one on the list, and the next one. Finally, on the fifth try, she found a shop that was open until nine and would diagnose it on the spot, maybe even fix it, depending on the problem. She took down directions to the shop and hung up.

Now for a vehicle. Aunt Lucy was off work, but she played bridge at her friend's house on Saturday evenings. Abigail retrieved her purse and laptop and then dialed Wade's cell, hoping he had reception.

"Yeah?"

"Hi, Wade, it's Abigail. Wondered if I could borrow the truck to go to Bozeman . . . unless you have plans."

"No plans. Go 'head. Keys are on the hook."

"Great, thanks."

Abigail left the house and started the vehicle. The thing was so old. She wondered why Wade didn't get one of the shiny new trucks that seemed to be so popular with the cowboys around town. She was sure he could afford it.

The drive to Bozeman took forever, but she finally reached the town as the sun was sinking over the mountains. She found the shop after getting lost only once, and the repairman was able to free up some space on her hard drive—which was apparently the problem. She was out the door with a faster computer in less than sixty minutes, just in time for the man to lock up behind her.

She headed out of town. The sun was long gone, the moon rising in the sky, and the mountains to the north were only shadows on the horizon. Streetlamps flickered on, and college students walked the sidewalks, hurrying toward the restaurants and bars that lined the main street. Her stomach rumbled, and she realized she'd skipped dinner. With Greta off and Maddy gone, she hadn't even thought about eating. She considered stopping at a drive-thru, then heard Reagan's voice chiding her and decided to have something healthier back at the house.

When she made it to the highway, Abigail turned east and pushed the pedal, waiting for the delayed acceleration. The highway was all but deserted, a long stretch of road winding around buttes and rolling hills. She settled back in her seat, content to have her laptop in top order again.

She could stay up late doing research. Or she could spend time with Wade, since he didn't have plans. All alone with Wade. The shudder of her nerves had nothing to do with fear and everything to do with a whole night alone with the cowboy who'd wedged his way into her heart.

Still, it wasn't often they had a chance to talk without Maddy around. She couldn't waste the opportunity. Almost a week had passed since she'd told her mom about Wade, and she hadn't learned anything new.

She wished she could forget the story and enjoy his company—because she did enjoy his company. More than was healthy, given the circumstances. If only things were different. If only he wasn't the subject of her investigation. If only the story wasn't necessary to save *Viewpoint*.

Abigail sighed hard. *If only you could focus on your job and forget about your feelings for Wade.*

The thought stopped her cold.

She did have feelings for Wade—feelings that went beyond friendship. The truth hit her, the weight of it a sinking reality in the pit of her stomach. Somehow, being near him, sharing with him, watching him parent Maddy, she'd lost her way. Somehow, on the way to doing her job, she'd let Wade in, and she wondered now how she'd get him back out. Could feelings be reversed? She didn't think so.

And yet she was stuck here. She had a job to do—two, actually. Somehow she had to complete both while guarding her heart. Because she could see now that this path would only end in heartache for both of them. It would be hard enough to betray a friendship, but to—

The engine made a funny clunking noise. As soon as it sounded, it was gone. She hoped everything was okay. She looked around at the surrounding darkness. How long had she been on the road? Fifteen, twenty minutes?

Another clunk sent Abigail's nerves into overdrive. Was she out of gas? She hadn't checked the gauge once. But no, there was almost half a tank. The engine sputtered and the truck began decelerating.

Oh no. She pressed the gas pedal to the ground and got nada. There was an exit ahead, veering off to the right. She saw no lights, but it was her only hope of a service station, or at least a store where she could wait.

Abigail turned down the ramp, pulling hard on the wheel, which had lost its power steering. The truck coasted down a slight incline that led only to a long, desolate road. Maybe she should've stayed on the highway. It was so dark out here, and not a car in sight.

She pulled the truck to the side as it coasted to a stop. It gave a final shudder as she turned off the ignition. Darkness pressed against the windows and silence shrouded the vehicle. *Relax. You're in Montana, not Chicago.* In Middle-of-Nowhere, Montana, with no sign of life anywhere.

But she had her cell. She pulled it from

her purse and dialed Wade. She wasn't sure how he'd come for her since she had his truck, but surely he could borrow a friend's car or Aunt Lucy's if she was home now.

There was no answer on his cell, so she tried the house. The phone rang once. Twice. *Come on, pick up.* Who would she call if he didn't answer? What if Aunt Lucy wasn't home yet?

I need some help here, God. I know we haven't talked in a while, but—

"Yeah?" Wade's voice had never sounded so good.

"Wade, it's Abigail. The truck broke down."

"Where are you?" The instant alert in his tone calmed her.

"Well . . . I was on I-90, and I coasted off an exit when the truck started sputtering."

"Which exit?"

Hmmm. She looked around, hoping something—like a sign—had materialized since last time she looked. "I'm not sure. There's a fence along the road . . ." How lame was that? "I think there's a building way back off the right side."

"You were coming back toward Moose Creek, traveling east?"

"Yes. Wait—I passed a sign a few minutes ago that said something about grizzly bears." The thought had her scanning the darkness.

"I think I know where you are. Be there soon—maybe twenty minutes. Keep your phone on and lock your doors."

"Are there grizzly bears around here?" She failed to keep the squeak from her voice.

"They're enclosed. You have nothing to fear, city girl. Sit tight."

Abigail hung up, feeling stupid for the question. She turned off the headlights and gazed out the window. Man alive, it was dark out here. Even the moon was hiding. It was like being in a darkroom. What animals were out there? Bobcats or wild things that preyed on humans? Could they smell her fear?

She turned the headlights back on. Two beams shot out about twenty feet, their cones fading into darkness. Maybe someone from the highway would see her lights and come help. Then again, maybe someone would see them and take advantage.

She quickly flipped off the lights. What had gotten into her? She was a woman who could walk the streets of the third largest city in the US without thought to her safety, yet she freaked about being stranded on a dark country road?

Still, there were those bears. *Enclosed bears*, she reminded herself.

Abigail sighed and shifted, unbuckling her seat belt. Well, she'd wanted something else to worry about other than her infatuation with Wade. She'd gotten it.

It hadn't taken him two seconds to respond to her call for help. She was relieved he hadn't sounded irritated. They had a long night ahead of them. A long night at home, just her and Wade.

Home? She was calling it home now? *You're leaving Moose Creek in a month. Then you'll be going to your real home. Your real job.*

Even so, she was eager to get back to the house, Wade or no Wade. Anything to be out of this broken-down rattletrap in Nowheresville.

Where was he anyway? It had been at least ten minutes, hadn't it? A screech of some kind pulled her eyes toward the window. It was an animal sound, but what kind? And how close? And more importantly, could it get through the door of a broken-down Ford?

Her heart kept time like a tightly wound clock. She was safe. Wade had said so himself—hadn't he?

She needed something to do. Something to occupy her mind until he arrived. She opened her laptop. The screen seemed bright in the confines of the cab, but she held it down low so it wouldn't shed enough light to draw attention from the highway.

There was no Wi-Fi of course, but she could do something else. She opened her picture files and browsed those for a while. Christmas last year at her mom's, several pictures from her last story. New Year's dinner with Reagan at Follia.

Reagan. She could call her sister to pass the—no, she couldn't. Wade might call, and she didn't want to risk missing it. What was taking him so long?

She closed the photos and was just browsing her documents when her cell rang.

"Think I might be close to your exit. Are your lights on?"

"No."

"Turn them on so I can find you."

She flipped the old switch and looked behind her for Wade.

"I see you," he said and disconnected.

Abigail saw his lights turning down the ramp. *Thank You, God.*

By the time she gathered her laptop and purse, a truck was beside her.

"Hop in," he called from the window of the silver truck. She took the keys and switched vehicles.

"What about your truck?"

"Get it later." He put the truck in drive and started off. "You cold?"

Abigail realized she was shaking, but it wasn't from the chill in the air. Still, she wasn't about to admit it. "I'm fine."

He flipped on the heat anyway and took the other ramp onto the highway. "Sorry it took so long. Had to hunt down Dylan."

She'd recognized the silver Chevy. The cab's new-car smell mingled with the faint scent that was all Wade.

Abigail bucked her belt. "Sorry you had to come all the way out here."

"Not your fault."

Abigail relaxed into the seat as the heat warmed the cab. Her heart slowly settled.

She inhaled a deep breath and whispered another prayer of gratitude.

A country singer crooned softly on the radio about a lost love, and Abigail sneaked a peek at Wade. She remembered her mom worrying for her safety, and the irony struck her. She felt safer with Wade than she'd felt with anyone in a long time. There hadn't been any doubt that he'd come for her, one way or another. He was that kind of man. The kind of man she could count on, lean on.

A good man. Her story would reflect that. She'd see to it. Just because she had to betray his whereabouts, and hopefully the cause of Lizzie's death, was no reason he had to be cast in a negative light.

"It make any kind of noises?"

"What?"

"The truck, before it died."

"Oh. It sort of went *klunk, klunk, klunk*, gave one last shudder, then it was gone. You know, it's none of my business, but you could kind of use a new one."

"She's a workin' truck."

"Well, she ain't really workin'," Abigail said in her best Texas drawl.

Wade smirked. "Kick a man while he's down, why don't you."

Abigail's stomach let out a ferocious growl, and she crossed her arms over her middle.

"That your stomach?"

"Forgot dinner."

"Want to stop somewhere?"

She shrugged. "I'll just grab something at the house."

"Suit yourself."

When they pulled up to the house, Abigail was struck by how dark and vacant it looked. Not even the porch light on. They'd be all alone in that house all night for the first time. If she had trouble maintaining a professional distance with Maddy around, how was she going to manage when they were alone?

It's an opportunity, she told herself. She could get to know Wade better without letting him in any further. Besides, it was late. Must be after ten by now, and Wade rose early to tend to the animals.

"What about Dylan's truck?"

"I'll pick him up for church in the morning."

Wade opened the front door and let her

by. Abigail flipped on the lamp, set down her things, and headed straight for the kitchen. She opened the pantry and paused in front of the half-empty shelves, then heard Wade's footsteps following her into the kitchen.

23

Wade opened the fridge door, feeling guilty about the paltry selection. "Guess Greta needs to hit the market."

"It is kind of sparse." Abigail reached into the pantry. "I'll have some peanuts."

"We've got eggs and stuff. I could make an omelet. I skipped dinner too."

"You cook?"

"Cowboys have many hidden talents." Omelets were the only thing he cooked, but she didn't have to know that.

Abigail set the table while Wade cracked the eggs into a bowl, adding cheese and ham. The quiet of the house without Maddy rang in his ears. A cozy supper with Abigail was the last thing he needed. What was he doing? It was hard enough to keep his distance as it was.

When the omelet was finished, he served it and sat across from Abigail. She'd taken Maddy's usual spot across from him, which put more distance between them. Fine by him.

After a silent prayer, he dug in. He thought of his daughter and hoped she'd be okay at her friend's all night.

"I wonder what Maddy's doing." Abigail scooped egg onto her fork. "Has she spent the night away before?"

"No. Was wondering the same thing."

"Eggs are good." Abigail saluted him with her empty fork. "The girls are probably having so much fun, she won't think twice about being away."

"Probably." He'd slept over at Dylan's many times by age eleven. They used to practice their roping, sometimes on Dylan's dog, Moe. When they tired of that, they amused themselves by putting frogs in Dylan's sister's bed or sneaking matches from the kitchen and starting fires behind the barn. He wondered what kind of mischief two little girls could make. He should've spoken with Shay personally. He hoped she was keeping an eye on them.

"What's that face for?"

"Remembering the antics me and Dylan used to pull at her age."

"And hoping Maddy isn't doing the same?"

"Maybe."

"Girls aren't as mischievous as boys, in general. They're probably doing each other's nails and soaking their feet."

"Soaking their feet?"

"Pedicures, silly."

He wasn't even sure what that was. Boy, did he have a lot to learn. "Maddy's never painted her nails." At least, he didn't think so. Would he have even noticed? "Hope that's all she's doing."

"Can't keep her on a leash, you know. Kids need a little space. Besides, you survived your childhood antics."

"As did you."

Abigail smiled, and Wade was struck by her beauty. So much for sitting across from her.

"Manicures and bead-making can hardly be counted as antics." Her smile slid slowly from her face, then she took a bite of omelet, her eyes taking on a faraway look.

Wade wondered if she was thinking of her friend, the one who'd been abused by her father. He was sorry he'd mentioned it.

"She'll probably stay up all night and sleep all day tomorrow," Wade said.

"Probably. Guess you're in for a quiet day."

"Have to work on the truck anyway."

"You'll fix it yourself?"

"Me and Dylan." Wade was good with the basics, but Dylan had never met a mechanical problem he couldn't fix. Saved Wade loads in repair bills over the years.

"He'll probably give you the same advice I did."

That he should sell his truck? Never. "He knows better."

"What is it with men and their trucks anyway?" Her green eyes twinkled.

Her teasing boosted his spirits, and he told himself it was just the pleasure of friendship. "We get attached. Perfectly normal."

"It's a chunk of steel. Well, steel and rust, in your case."

"Hey . . . below the belt."

Abigail shrugged. "Call it like I see it." Her full smile was dazzling. There was no other word for it. Wade couldn't look away if he wanted to. And he didn't.

"So what else are you attached to?" she asked, her tone light.

"My ranch and my daughter . . . God." All he needed, right there.

"You never go out on weekends. No woman in the wings? Like Marla from Pappy's Market? She's crushing on you, you know. Asks about you every time I'm in."

Knowing Marla was prying Abigail for information embarrassed him. He wiped his mouth, then sipped his milk, trying to hide his discomfort. "Not seeing anyone at the moment."

"You're blushing."

Daggonit. "Cowboys don't blush."

"Au contraire."

She didn't have to enjoy it so much. "Marla's not my type." He couldn't shift the limelight soon enough. "What about you? Someone waiting for you back in the Windy City?" His intense longing for a negative answer surprised him. Abigail hadn't mentioned a boyfriend, and she didn't give off taken vibes, though she had turned down Dylan.

"Not at the moment," she said after she swallowed. "Haven't dated seriously since college, but I do date." She stabbed her empty fork at the air. "What's your excuse?" That flirtatious smile again.

"I need an excuse?"

"You're a healthy, virile single man. Do you know your market value out there? It goes up each year, you know. Women get more desperate as the good ones get taken."

He refused to admit how much that word *virile* pleased him. "You don't exactly seem on the hunt for a 'good one.'"

"I'm looking, but I'm picky. Haven't found one that matches up to my daddy yet. 'Course I may just pick my way into perpetual spinsterhood."

He smiled. "Can't see that happening."

"You didn't answer my question." She forked a piece of ham.

"Which was . . . ?"

"Why don't you date? Moose Creek is small, but there's a handful of pretty single women. Or have you dated them all?"

He hadn't dated any of them, but wasn't

about to admit it. "Too busy with the ranch and Maddy. Relationships take time."

"The good ones are worth it. Your busy schedule aside, don't you think Maddy would like a mother?"

He pressed his lips together. Their conversation had taken a bad turn. She was getting personal. He ignored her question and took another gulp of milk instead.

She didn't take the hint. "You hire people to do the things a mother would do. If you found someone you loved, it would remove a burden, not add to it."

"You applying for the job?"

Abigail sputtered on a sip of milk.

Look who was blushing now. He probably shouldn't have said it, but she'd asked for it. He was feeling a little uncomfortable himself after the leading question—what if she said yes?

"No . . ." Abigail said after recovering from her coughing spell. "I am not applying for the job. Sheesh. Clearly a touchy subject."

"Very discerning."

She made a face that reminded him of the one Maddy made when she was about to stick out her tongue.

They finished eating in silence, and Wade regretted putting her on the spot. Now things felt awkward. Well, what did he expect? There was enough friction between them to start a forest fire, always had been. From day one, he'd been attracted to her. What did he think he was doing, hiring someone like Abigail to live under the same roof? Like playing with fire. A subject he knew a little about, he thought with a self-deprecating smirk.

At least the night was almost over. They'd go to their separate rooms, and tomorrow Maddy would return and things would go back to normal.

Abigail stood and placed her dishes in the dishwasher. "Thanks for the omelet. It was good." She rubbed her bare arms.

Probably cold from sitting in his broken-down truck so long. "You can turn up the heat." Wade stacked his dishes in the dishwasher.

"You don't mind? Or, hey, how about a fire? I've never had a fireplace. On cold Chicago nights I fantasize about curling up in front of a big stone fireplace."

Wade followed her into the living room,

trying to curb his own fantasies, which had nothing to do with a fireplace.

Get a grip, Ryan. "You'll be up awhile?"

"Couple hours. I can start it."

"No offense, Grace, but I want to wake to a standing house."

She made that face again, but it was starting to grow on him. She could stay up all she wanted. Soon as he got this fire going, he was heading for the hills before he did something stupid. He brought wood in from the pile out back, opened the flue, and started stacking.

"I can't believe how chilly it gets at night," she said, settling on the sofa. "Summer nights back home are mild, but it must be in the forties tonight."

"Temperatures vary more here. It was a change for me too." One last log, then he'd get this puppy burning and skedaddle.

"You must've been a Boy Scout."

Wade struck a match and lit the newspaper wads on the bottom. "Not even close." He encouraged the flame with a breath until it caught on a dried twig.

Rising to his feet, he drew the mesh curtains, then set the screen in front of the opening. "Leave the flue open when you go to bed. Just make sure the fire's died down."

"Where you going?"

"Bed."

"Oh." She sounded disappointed. "I thought we could talk."

She was curled into the corner of the sofa like a lazy cat, an afghan wrapped around her shoulders. Her beguiling eyes, wide and innocent, tempted him.

Talk about playing with fire. "Have to get up early."

"I thought you might want to talk about how Maddy's doing, since she's not here."

She knew all his buttons. The fire crackled and popped as the kindling caught fire. "What about her?"

"She's hitting that, uh, awkward stage. Lots of changes are coming . . . ?"

Son of a gun. His knees gave out and he sank onto the chair. He did not want to go there with Abigail. "Changes?" His voice produced a squeak he hadn't heard since puberty.

Abigail laughed. "It's coming soon enough, ready or not. Has anyone had those talks with her?"

He knew he should've, but . . . "The school?"

"You can't leave it up to them. You haven't addressed the topic?"

He was a bad father. "Not really." She used to ask him questions about sex, but he'd mostly dodged them. *Not good, Ryan.*

Maddy must've given up, because she hadn't asked any of those questions in a while. Maybe now she was too embarrassed. Abigail was right. The kid was nearing that age. But how awkward would that be? What would Maddy even say if he tried?

"I take it by the terrified look on your face that you wouldn't mind my addressing such issues with her."

Whew. "Be my guest."

"Happy to be of service."

When he darted a look her way, the corner of her mouth was tipped up. *Fine, be amused.* She didn't realize how hard it was being a single dad to a daughter. Harder than it looked. Especially when it came to touchy topics.

"The fire's nice," Abigail said. She stared into the glowing grate as if lost in thought. "Reminds me of camping out when I was young."

"You camped?" He couldn't picture it.

She tipped her chin over the afghan. "Yes, I camped. Well, only once, but we did have a campfire."

"What's wrong, the bears scare you away?"

"Actually, a rainstorm came and flooded our tent. We had to pack up and leave in the middle of the night."

"Maddy loved camping when she was little. I haven't taken her since we moved here."

"You should. She'd enjoy that."

He really should. In a couple years she probably wouldn't want anything to do with him.

"Maybe we could all go."

Trapped in a tent with Abigail all night? He didn't think so. The thought made him squirm. Even from across the room, the subtle scent of her perfume summoned him.

"We can be friends, right?" she asked.

Was he that transparent? She must not feel the same stirrings he did if she thought they could be friends.

"Nothing personal, Abigail. I just don't let women too close." He felt her eyes on him and wished he hadn't said it, was afraid he'd given too much away.

"Strange thing for a man to say."

"Not a man with my past." Too much again. Who was this woman who always managed to loosen his tongue?

"Is this about your late wife?"

She wasn't going to leave it alone. Irritation kindled inside, but then he looked at her and saw nothing but compassion in those shadowed eyes. She wasn't trying to conjure up bad memories, she just wanted to understand. Besides, the soothing tone of her voice drew it from him.

"Losing Lizzie was hard. After she died, I decided it's best I just keep to myself, for everyone's sake."

The fire crackled and sizzled beside him, and its golden glow danced and shimmied over Abigail's features.

"It was terrible, what happened to your wife. But you can't let that keep you from living."

"I am living." He was just doing it alone. Just him and Maddy.

"Most men wouldn't call it living," she said. "Most men wouldn't make it a year."

"Most men don't have my self-control."

"How do you do it?"

"I don't touch." He set his jaw. Couldn't believe he'd let that slip out. Judging by her look, she couldn't either.

"Not at all?" What was that in her tone? Compassion? Pity? Great, just what he wanted.

Maybe now she'd understand. Maybe now she'd stop looking at him in a way that made him wish he'd never put that rule in place at all.

She let the subject die, and he was grateful. Just as well he went to bed before he spilled anything else, before the compassion in Abigail's eyes pulled him over to the sofa and made him forget his rule.

"Think I'll turn in now." The recliner groaned as his weight left it.

Her lips turned up in a sad smile. "'Night." Her soft reply was like a beckoning finger, but he resisted. All the way up the stairs. All the way behind his bedroom door, which he locked for good measure. Keeping Abigail out of his room was easy. Keeping her out of his heart was a whole other matter.

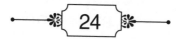

24

After church and lunch with Aunt Lucy, Abigail walked toward the ranch, down the long, winding lane. Aunt Lucy had offered to drive, but Abigail needed the exercise. Besides, the day was mild and sunny, and she was in no hurry to reach the ranch.

Even though she hadn't gotten any real answers last night, it was clear that Wade was hurting. After he retired, she'd read the *Moose Creek Chronicle*, then picked up Wade's current issue of *Livestock Weekly*, which sat on the oak coffee table. The format was boring, and the cattle business was more complicated than she'd thought. She didn't understand half the articles but sifted through them anyway to help her understand the man she was so drawn to.

No, she corrected. The man she was writing about. The man who was the subject of her investigation.

When the fire had died to an orange glow, Abigail retreated to her room and turned on her laptop. She needed to start her column even if she didn't have all the details. She opened a Word document and started typing. She had no more than a paragraph when Wade's words flashed in her mind, stopping her fingers.

"After she died, I decided it's best I just keep to myself, for everyone's sake."

The way he'd said it made her heart ache. It was as if he thought he was contagious. Did he plan on staying single forever? Sure sounded like it. She admired his restraint, but not his reasoning. Sounded like he feared he'd taint any female who came within arm's length.

Which was silly, especially since his child was female. It wasn't as if he could avoid Maddy.

But he did avoid Maddy, didn't he? Wasn't

it one of the first things Abigail had noticed about the pair—that there was a wall between them? Was it possible Wade held back because he feared he'd somehow harm his daughter?

Wade was a good man. He would never hurt Maddy, or any female, intentionally. It was a crazy thought, but she'd heard crazier. People got silly notions in their heads sometimes. That would explain not only why there was a wall between father and daughter, but why Wade didn't date or seem to have female friends. Why he avoided Abigail at every turn. Like last night, when he'd run for his room when the conversation turned personal.

How could she ever find out what happened to Lizzie when he wouldn't even accept Abigail's friendship? Though, if she were honest, that was only half the reason for the heaviness weighing her steps now.

What she'd said about not finding a man who matched up to her dad was true. But also true was the growing recognition that Wade might be the first man who'd reached those heights. He might have hang-ups and misconceptions, but he was a man of integrity. He was strong and courageous. She pictured his blue eyes always hiding in the shadows of that sexy cowboy hat, his masculine frame moving slowly and purposefully. He wasn't afraid of hard, honest work. In fact, he enjoyed it, had a quiet passion for it. Yes, he measured up.

She'd finally found a man who passed muster, and a relationship was impossible. Doomed before it began. Because she couldn't have both: the story and Wade. He'd hate her in the end. How depressing was that? She rubbed her temples, where a headache had begun to throb. Her hypertension was acting up again. Too much stress.

Her stride grew shorter as the house came into view. She was in no hurry, especially now, with guilt and dread dragging each step. Dylan's truck was there, and Wade's truck was parked near the barn, the hood up. She wasn't in the mood to face either of them—wanted to hide in her room and be alone with her laptop. Maybe she could sneak inside unnoticed.

She quickened her pace as she neared the truck. The engine wasn't running, and the sound of her footsteps on the gravel seemed loud. She didn't even look at the truck, just shot past, eyes on the front door.

"Abigail, hey . . ." Dylan straightened, barely missing the hood.

"Hi, Dylan." She tossed him a smile and continued. She didn't see Wade.

"Hey, can you come here a minute?" Dylan asked.

Rats. Resigned, Abigail headed back to the truck where Dylan held a tool and a dirty rag.

"You look fetching today," he said as she approached, his dimple making a divot in his cheek.

Abigail was in no mood for his flattery, but she smiled anyway. "Thank you."

He gestured toward the truck. "Wade said she made some kind of noise before she bit the dust."

"There was a *clunk*ing noise right before I lost power."

"Nothing before that?"

"Not that I noticed. It kind of shuddered when I shut off the engine, and that was it. Sorry I can't be of more help." She turned toward the house.

"Wait, Abigail." Dylan wiped his tool on his rag. "You like country music?"

She could see where this was headed. "Not really. More of a classical music gal myself."

"Give me a chance to win you over. We have a great local band, the Silver Spurs, and they're playing at the Chuckwagon Saturday."

"Marla's brother's band. Tina from Mocha Moose told me about them."

"You're getting around."

Not in the way he hoped. "I like meeting people." She knew it was the wrong thing to say as soon as she said it.

"Then come with me Saturday. Everyone from town'll be there, and it'll give you a chance to hang out with the home crowd." He winked.

"Thanks, but I don't think so. Have fun, though." She turned toward the house.

"I won't give up, you know," he called, teasing.

"I'm getting that impression."

She heard his chuckle before she took the steps and escaped into the house. She went to the kitchen and gulped down three Tylenol. It was quiet inside. Wade wasn't around, and she found Maddy passed out on top of her new quilt. Her overnight bag sat inside the door, spilled onto her new rug. She looked sweet, her dark lashes fanning the tops of her cheeks, her hair splayed across the pillow. Abigail smiled as she pulled the door closed quietly.

She needed to get back to her article. She had all afternoon and could probably get a large portion of the first draft done. After settling on the bed with her laptop, she checked her e-mail. Her mom had written. The layout team was excited about designing the cover for Wade's story, and Mom would send the cover proof as soon as she had it.

Abigail went online and looked for a tidbit about Wade's past for her article. Along the way she got sidetracked by other articles, stuck looking at the plethora of rodeo photos. Mercy, he was gorgeous.

He'd smiled more in those days, or so it seemed. Life must've sucked the joy from him. She understood it, wished she could relieve him of the load he carried. He seemed so carefree in the pictures.

A warning box appeared on her screen. She was almost out of battery power. She looked on her nightstand, but her cord wasn't there. What had she done with it? It had been in the case she'd taken to the computer store the night before. She checked the case and found it empty. It must've fallen out in Wade's truck.

Rats. She needed the cord if she wanted to write. But she didn't want to face Dylan again, not to mention Wade.

She closed her laptop and peeked out the window, realizing the headache had finally faded. Dylan was rooting through a toolbox in his truck. Wade was nowhere to be seen. Maybe if she hurried . . .

She slipped on her sandals and trotted down the stairs. If she could just get into the passenger side, grab the cord, and return to the house before Dylan spotted her. She hustled down the porch steps and across the grass. All this to avoid Moose Creek's own Don Juan.

Dylan's back still to her, she slipped around the fender, between the truck and barn, and pulled open the door. Spotting the black cord coiled on the floor, she reached for it just as she heard the toolbox lid slam closed.

Abigail peeked out the back window, saw him coming. Then she realized the barn door was at her back. She could slip through and enter the house through the kitchen door. She made the decision in a split second.

Abigail pushed the truck door closed quietly and turned toward the barn door with the cord in hand. A few steps and she'd be in the barn, free and clear.

She checked behind to see Dylan rounding the back corner of Wade's truck just as she entered the shelter of the barn. She turned the corner. Almost there, almost there . . .

Thud. Her body smacked into something hard and unmoving. The cord fell from her hand. It hit the dirt with a dull *thunk* as she looked up into the surprised eyes of her favorite cowboy.

25

Abigail meant to pull away. Had every in-tention of pulling away once she gained her balance. Then she felt the warmth of Wade's hands on her arms, the warmth of his hard stomach against her. She inhaled the musky scent of him.

And those eyes. Shadowed under the brim of his hat, they were the color of new denim. They caught her and held her in a grip as firm as that of his hands on her arms. His initial surprise had given way to something else. Something that held her rooted to the ground. Something that made her ache for more.

Then his fingers were loosening, and she wanted to cry out her disappointment. His words echoed in her mind. *"I don't touch."*

But instead of drawing away, he slowly lifted his hand to her face. His calloused fingertip trailed down her cheek in a touch she felt clear down to her toes. It was tentative, a measure of her response.

He was touching her. A simple touch, and yet she realized it was more than that to him. So much more.

She couldn't breathe. Couldn't move. Wanted to get lost in those eyes. She wondered if he felt her reaction, then realized she didn't care. Didn't care about anything, so long as he touched her again.

His eyes locked on hers, conveyed what he wanted, asked permission.

The answer was *yes*. Unequivocally, undeniably *yes*.

His arm moved around her, then he lowered his head, tipped her chin. His lips moved across hers as softly as butterfly wings, tasting, testing. She trembled in response. She hadn't known he was capable of such gentleness. It only endeared him to her more.

She wanted to stay in his arms all day. Maybe forever. He fit against her like he was made for her, like he was her cowboy and hers alone. She remembered his words about women from the night before. Was he willing to take the chance?

Was she? Abigail shushed the thought— didn't want to think about any of it.

His hat nudged her forehead, tipping back as he deepened the kiss and drew her closer. His jaw was rough against her palm, and she savored the feel of it before slipping her fingers through the soft waves at his nape and straight up through the back of his hair. His hat hit the ground.

"Abby . . ." he whispered. It was a plea, and she gladly answered it with her mouth.

She loved the raspy drawl of her shortened name on his lips. Her hands moved down to the breadth of his shoulders, feeling the hardness of his muscles under his cotton—

"What's taking so—" Dylan's voice.

Wade jerked back. The cool barn air took his place, and Abigail nearly whimpered.

Dylan shuffled to a halt. "Whoops. Sorry for the, uh, interruption." Dylan sounded amused. "Guess I know what's taking you so long now, buddy."

Heat crept into Abigail's cheeks. She put her fingers to her swollen lips.

"Be out in a minute," Wade said.

"Take your time." Dylan winked at Abigail. "Guess Saturday night's out for sure, huh?" he said as he left the barn, ruining any chance she and Wade might pick up where they left off.

She closed her eyes for a heartbeat, unsure.

"You have a date?" Wade asked.

Abigail darted a look at him. His hair was disheveled, poking out at the sides, sticking up on top. She could still feel the silky weight of his hair between her fingers.

"It's nothing. He asked me out."

Wade picked up his hat, taking his time. He dusted it on his thigh, then eyed her, his jaw set. She knew that look.

"Well." He set the hat on his head. "Have fun." He turned to follow Dylan.

"Wade . . ."

He didn't stop.

"I'm not going," she called after him.

"Don't back out on my account." And like that he was out the barn door.

Abigail barely suppressed the growl that worked into her throat. How could he think she'd go out with Dylan after his kiss? After his touch? Did he think she kissed any ol' guy? It had been months, okay, years, since she'd let a kiss go that far. Since a man's touch alone had stirred her to want so much. Even now the memory of it warmed her cheeks, made her legs go weak. How could he kiss her socks off, then swagger away like that, like it meant nothing to him?

She sent a glare toward Wade's retreating back, then scooped up her cord.

❀

Wade leaned over the truck's engine and inspected the flywheel teeth. He could hear Abigail's footsteps marching right past the truck, across the lawn, and up the porch steps. The front door slammed and he cringed.

What was she so sore about anyway? He was the one who was honkin' mad. Mad that he let temptation steal his good sense, mad that she stirred things he hadn't felt in too long, made him want things he couldn't have. His anger had nothing to do with Dylan. Nothing to do with the fact that his best friend was going out with the woman he'd just kissed.

Dylan whistled. "That was some kiss."

"Shut up."

"Thought you said there was nothing between—"

"I said shut up." Wade knew the shuddering from Dylan was suppressed laughter, and there wasn't a blame thing he could do about it.

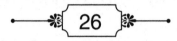

26

Marla from Pappy's Market talked Abigail
into it, then when Shay invited her, it sealed
the deal. Wade had Maddy and Olivia for
the night, and Shay was in need of a night
out. Abigail felt obliged to give her one.
Besides, she needed to get away from the
house in the worst way. Wade had been
unbearably testy all week.

On Saturdays the Chuckwagon served
food and rolled out the dance floor. Kids were
welcome, though the crowd was largely adult
tonight, Abigail noted as she and Shay
walked across the peanut-strewn floor.

From a large table at the edge of the

empty dance floor, Marla waved them over. They headed her direction, squeezing past tables and chairs. The air was thick with the smell of grilled steak and onions, and the din of chatter made it hard to converse.

The Silver Spurs were setting up on-stage, and Abigail was glad Marla had saved them seats because the place was packed.

"Hey, everyone," Shay yelled, taking a seat next to Marla.

Abigail took a seat on her other side and saw Dylan across from Marla. "Hey," she called.

"I can't believe my luck." Dylan's eyes swung across the three of them. "I have the prettiest view in all Montana."

Marla rolled her eyes. "You are so full of it."

But Abigail could tell she enjoyed the compliment. Marla and Shay did look nice tonight. Shay had taken a little time for makeup, and her hair, normally pulled back in a functional ponytail, now flowed over her shoulders like a glistening waterfall. Abigail had drawn the line at mascara and lip gloss, but she had to admit her hair had cooperated.

Dylan received an onion blossom from the server and set it in the middle of the table. "Help yourselves," he said to the others. He looked at Abigail. "Where's Wade?"

She arched a brow. "How should I know?"

His lips twitched.

Abigail felt Shay's questioning eyes and was relieved when Marla introduced her to the others at the table. Abigail waved and smiled. It was too loud for a long-distance conversation.

A microphone squealed, and the manager announced the Silver Spurs. After roaring applause, the lead singer began a foot-stomping tune.

"That's Marla's brother," Shay fairly shouted into Abigail's ear.

The singer smiled in Shay's direction and winked.

"I think he likes you," Abigail said.

Shay gave a wry smile. "One musician was enough to last me a lifetime."

"Your ex?"

"He left me and Olivia high and dry."

Abigail cringed. "Sorry."

When the server appeared, Abigail ordered fries and a soda. She remembered

Aunt Lucy saying something about Shay never getting over her first love, not even after she'd married. She wondered what had become of him.

The first song ended, and Dylan asked Marla to dance. Soon other couples crowded the floor, none of them better than that pair. Despite his bulk, Dylan could bust a move, and Marla had no trouble keeping up. They were fun to watch, made Abigail want to get up and dance a jig herself, though she'd never danced to country and western music.

Three songs later, someone cut in on Dylan, and he returned to the table and took the seat across from Abigail.

A spry, elderly man Abigail didn't recognize asked Shay to dance. She slid gracefully from her chair and joined him on the floor. Despite his age, he had nimble feet.

"Who's that?"

Dylan leaned in. "Pappy Barnes."

"From Pappy's Market."

He nodded, then gestured toward the band. "What do you think?"

Abigail nodded. "They're good."

"Good enough to sway you over to country?" His eyes twinkled.

"Maybe for one night." The band struck up another tune, and Marla's brother sang into the mic with his raspy voice.

"Dance?"

She'd been eager for the chance, but she didn't want to lead Dylan on. It was only a dance though. "I'm not very good," she warned.

"I'm up for the challenge if you are."

She shouldn't pass up the opportunity. It would give her a chance to question him about Wade. "Well, I *was* starting to feel like a wallflower."

He stood, chuckling. "Perish the thought!"

She accompanied him to the dance floor where he took her into his arms, maintaining good space. He guided her fluidly, and after a few minutes, Abigail relaxed and enjoyed the rhythm of the music.

"You lied," he said. "You're a good dancer."

"You make it easy."

He spun her around the floor until she was dizzy, her white skirt floating around her legs. They talked as they danced. Dylan was like an older brother, she thought, quick-witted and fun to spar with.

When the moment seemed right, Abigail changed the subject. "Does Wade ever come?"

Dylan shrugged. "Sure, when I can drag him out."

"Why's he reluctant? This place is pretty fun, plus he could bring Maddy along."

Dylan spun her around, then picked up where they left off. "He went through a lot when his wife died."

"He told me. It must've been terrible."

Dylan seemed to take measure, like he was unsure Wade had really confided in her. "It was."

"What was Lizzie like?"

Dylan opened his mouth, then closed it. He spun her slowly, then pulled her toward him. "You should ask Wade."

Abigail admired Dylan's loyalty even while she fought disappointment. "Not asking him anything right now. He's been so grouchy this week."

"You don't say."

She looked at him, waiting. There was more to that comment, but he wasn't talking.

The song flowed into another, and they naturally changed their pace. When Marla's partner left the floor, Abigail offered to step out, but Marla fanned her flushed face and shook her head.

"Did Marla come with you?" Abigail asked.

He grinned. "Don't tell her I asked you first."

"Must be hard juggling so many women."

"You're each so special, I just can't get enough of you."

"Oh brother." Abigail rolled her eyes. Shay and Pappy floated by to her left.

Dylan spun her in a circle, and the room whirled. Her gaze floated past their table, then stopped and fixed on the seat across from Marla.

Wade was there—and he was staring right at her.

He looked away, back toward Marla, who was talking.

Abigail focused on the wall behind Dylan. Great time for him to appear.

Dylan spun her in another circle, and her feet got bungled up.

"My fault," he said smoothly.

Abigail glanced toward the table. Maddy and Olivia were there, too, sipping what looked like Shirley Temples. They must've talked Wade into coming, because he sure didn't look happy to be here.

She hated to imagine what Wade must be thinking—but then, he'd thought it anyway, hadn't he? Assumed she was keeping a date with Dylan after that kiss—a date she'd never agreed to in the first place. She was growing tired of his testiness. He'd been insufferable all week, ignoring her until he had to speak, and snapping at her even then. How could one little kiss cause such a change?

"What's wrong?" Dylan followed her eyes. "Ahhh . . ."

"Ahhh . . . what?" Now who was testy?

He cleared his throat. "Soorreey. What's with the two of you?"

Abigail clenched her teeth. It wasn't her; it was Wade.

"Look," Dylan said. "I know it's none of my business, but he's been through a lot and—shoot." He spun her the other direction, led her toward the back of the stage. "If looks could kill."

She darted a look toward the table. "He doesn't own me." He didn't even claim her, not even as a friend, by her last count.

One of the women from their table nudged Wade with her shoulder, laughing. Marla leaned across the table so far, she was in danger of plunging into his lap.

Abigail looked away. "Besides, looks like he has plenty of company." She dreaded returning to the table. The night had gotten complicated fast, and just when she'd been having fun.

The song morphed into another, and Dylan pulled away.

"Don't." Her heart quickened at the thought of returning to the table. "I don't want to go back."

He sighed hard, then took her in his arms again. "Can't stay out here all night, you know."

Maybe she could call it an early night. She spotted Shay, who'd found another partner. She was smiling, and the man dancing with her couldn't seem to take his eyes off her.

So much for an early night.

Dylan twirled her around. The space between them had widened since Wade's arrival. Then she spotted Wade dancing with Maddy in the opposite corner of the dance floor.

"Look," Dylan said. "No offense, but when this song's over . . ." He raised his shoulders.

"Fair enough." Wade wasn't at the table now anyway. Her fries were probably cold and soggy by now, but at least she could keep Olivia company.

The song began to wind down, and Dylan led them in a series of turns toward the other corner. She tensed. "What are you doing?"

They were side by side with Wade and Maddy as the band hit the last note and struck up a slow tune.

"Cut in?" Dylan asked Wade.

Abigail shot Dylan a glare that went unnoticed.

"Sure, Uncle Dylan!" Maddy sailed into his arms, leaving Abigail and Wade alone in the corner.

"I was just—"

"Dance?"

Even though they spoke simultaneously, she heard reluctance in his request. The fact that he didn't want her in his arms made her want to be there even more.

She raised a brow. "Sure."

Wade's jaw twitched. He took her into his

arms, holding her stiffly. An average-sized barn could fit between them.

Can't dance without touching, now, can you? Abigail looked at the band. At the tin corrugated siding on the walls. At the dark beams running across the ceiling. At the crowd. People seemed to be staring at her.

"Thought you weren't coming with him," Wade said.

She darted a glance at him, but he was looking over her head. "Thought you didn't care."

"I don't."

"Good." So she was being childish. Why'd he ask her to dance if he didn't want to? And why was he so mad when he didn't want her for himself?

His hand barely held hers, and she could scarcely feel the weight of his other hand on her waist. It was like he couldn't stand to touch her. It was a sharp contrast to the poignancy of his touch six days ago. But he'd made it very clear that he regretted it.

An ache started behind her eyes, and she bit her lip hard. She wasn't going to cry. She was angry, daggonit. How dare he kiss her and then treat her this way. So he regretted it—did he have to be so mean? Rejection was bad enough without his passive-aggressive behavior.

It hurt that he'd ignored her, that he'd snapped at her for no reason. It had hurt all week, and she didn't stop to question why until now. People didn't have the power to hurt you unless you cared about them. The truth was, her feelings for Wade had gone deeper than she'd realized.

How deep?

She didn't want to think about it right now. Didn't want the *L* word to so much as enter her mind when Wade so clearly didn't return those feelings, wasn't even willing to pursue them.

But denial wouldn't change the truth. The irritation she'd felt all week had only been a front to cover the fact that she was falling in love with him. She hadn't fully admitted it until now, when being in his arms was more pain than pleasure.

From across the floor Maddy caught her attention and waved. Abigail returned it, trying for a smile and failing miserably. But Maddy didn't seem to notice. She laughed as Dylan picked her up and spun her around.

Abigail fixed her eyes on the third pearly

button of Wade's shirt. What did her feelings matter anyway? It wasn't like their relationship could go anywhere. Hadn't she been over this a hundred times already? Was she that hardheaded?

The song began winding down, and Wade stepped away before the last chord struck. He ushered her off the floor, and Abigail tried not to care that he couldn't seem to escape soon enough.

She took her seat as Wade disappeared into the crowd. Two women from the next table stared at her, and she resisted the temptation to stick out her tongue. *Wow, Abigail, you really are childish.*

The table was empty until Dylan returned a moment later and sat beside her. "Having fun?" he asked.

"A blast." Abigail pulled her plate of soggy fries closer and dumped ketchup on the pile. She wanted to go home, but she'd come with Shay. And asking Wade for a ride would only defeat the purpose of leaving.

She bit into a cold fry and glanced over Dylan's shoulder. A woman she didn't know stared back. Abigail glanced around the room. "What the heck? Do I have ketchup on my face or what?"

Dylan followed her gaze, and his lips twitched. "You're Moose Creek's new Natural Wonder."

She frowned. "What?"

"Wade hasn't been on the dance floor since he's been here—and not for lack of willing partners."

The news was a warm injection in her heart. But what did she expect? He could hardly dance without touching—which he avoided at all costs. Although he'd come pretty close to it just now.

"They're just jealous," Dylan said. "And curious."

"Well, they shouldn't be. He was forced into it." Abigail bit into another fry.

"Ha! Wade's not forced into anything. If I know anything about him, it's that."

Wade reappeared, squeezing between tables with a soda in his hand. His eyes narrowed when he saw them. Then he set his jaw and walked deliberately toward them.

"Shoot," Dylan said. "You did tell him I'm not your date, right?"

Abigail shrugged. "He didn't ask."

Dylan frowned at her, the dimple nowhere to be seen. "You're as bad as him, know that?"

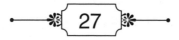

27

Wade steeled himself as he approached Abigail and Dylan. Why had he let Maddy and Olivia talk him into coming tonight when he knew Dylan and Abigail were here? He'd all but asked for it, hadn't he?

Now he wished he could be anywhere else, especially when he'd seen them on the dance floor. Maddy's words from earlier that week buzzed in his ear. *"Wouldn't it be great if Uncle Dylan and Abigail got married? I could call her Aunt Abigail!"* The innocent comment had haunted him all week.

Now the two lovebirds were huddled together at the table. If there were anyone else he could sit with, he would. But all his friends were on the floor. He took a gulp of his Coke, then squeezed between two chairs. He was going to accept the first dance offer, he didn't care who it was. Had half a mind to go find a partner right now.

He seated himself on the other side of Dylan so he wouldn't have to look across the table at Abigail. A line dance had formed on the floor. So much for dancing. He watched Maddy hook her thumbs in her belt loops and perform the steps like a little cowgirl.

"Some onion bloom left." Dylan slid the plate toward him.

"No, thanks." Wade took a long drink of Coke. He could feel Dylan's eyes on him. Was it hot in here?

From the floor, Marla gestured to Dylan, trying to get him onto the floor. Wade gritted his teeth, praying Dylan wouldn't leave him alone with Abigail. It seemed to work.

"I was telling Abigail about coming across that wolf pack last summer," Dylan said.

He should just go home. Pack up Maddy and Olivia and head for the ranch.

"She didn't realize we had wolves 'round here," Dylan continued.

Wade would go if they hadn't just arrived. He watched his daughter sashay across the floor, smiling widely. Olivia turned the wrong way and they collided, laughing. Maddy was having a good time.

"Maybe I should just leave so the two of you can talk," Dylan said.

That got his attention. "Talk?"

Abigail leaned around Dylan. "You know, talk. That thing people do when they want to communicate."

That thing he hadn't been doing all week. Well, neither would she if he'd kissed her, then gone off with *her* best friend. "Maybe I don't want to communicate."

She stared him down, and he didn't give an inch. Not even when the stubborn glint was replaced by something else. Something he couldn't quite define.

"I need air." Abigail left the table, headed for the door.

Wade watched her go, her lithe figure skimming between chairs. He wondered about that look he'd just seen and wished he knew her well enough to interpret it.

"What's your problem?" Dylan asked.

Wade clenched his jaw. His problem? Last he checked, friends didn't date their best friend's—

What? Abigail wasn't his girlfriend. Still, Dylan had seen the kiss. He knew.

Knew what, Ryan? That you're smitten with her? It was the same revelation that had disturbed him all week. The kiss had been a real wake-up call. Heck, the touch before it had been enough.

"You're being a jerk," Dylan said.

"You got no room to talk, *buddy.*"

Dylan gave a sardonic laugh, the kind he saved for when he was ticked off— which wasn't often. "She didn't come with me, *pal.* She came with Shay. Marla's my date."

A knot formed in the pit of Wade's gut. Dylan was right. He was being a jerk. Had been one all week. The knot tightened into an ache, the kind of ache he felt when he made a stupid parental decision and was left feeling like a heel.

"If you want my opinion," Dylan said, "I don't think you're mad at me or Abigail. I think you're ticked off at yourself for kissing her. But that's just my opinion."

Marla appeared at their side, grabbing

Dylan's hand. "Enough talking already . . . let's boogie!"

Dylan sent Wade one last look as he followed Marla to the floor. Olivia and Maddy returned to the table long enough to swipe their drinks, then headed across the room to join their school friends.

Dylan was right. He owed Abigail an apology. He shouldn't have kissed her, but his regret shouldn't have led to him being a major jerk all week. She hadn't deserved it.

Before he could talk himself out of it, he stood and made his way toward the exit. Outside, the night air was cool against his skin. The streetlamps twinkled on the deserted street. He looked down the boardwalk, wondering if Abigail had done something foolish, like try to walk home.

Then he saw a dark form on a bench down the block and headed that way.

Her head leaned against the building behind her, her long legs stretched out in front, her feet crossed at the ankles. She was probably wishing she were home—and not his home. Back in Chicago. Far, far away from him.

She didn't see him until he was upon

her, and then she crossed her arms over her stomach and pulled her legs in, a protective posture. It made him feel like a heel all over again.

The bench groaned as he dropped onto it. He tugged his hat down, then rested his forearms on his knees, wishing he'd given some thought to what he'd say.

He made eye contact. It was the least he could do. "Sorry I was a jerk back there."

Son of a gun, she was beautiful. The lamplight glowed dimly on her skin. Perfection.

"I didn't come with Dylan."

He didn't want to admit he had no say in who Abigail dated. He wanted to have a say, but he had no right. "Even if you had . . ." He let the sentence trail. "I've been a jerk all week. Sorry about that too."

There was a long pause. He studied the brick hardware store across the street. Watched a couple park their car and walk arm in arm into the Chuckwagon. The only sound was the heavy thumping of the band's bass.

"Should I go?" Abigail asked.

She wasn't talking about a ride back to the ranch. She was talking about going home. To Chicago.

The thought of Abigail leaving was like a sucker punch. The air left his lungs, and he sucked it back in, tasting dirt and smoke from someone's burn pile.

He looked at her. "No."

"I'm confused." She had the same look in her eyes she'd had back in the restaurant.

"Last Sunday . . . shouldn't have happened."

Her eyes dropped, and she turned away.

"Look, it's not . . ." He tried again. "No one has . . ." The words clogged in his throat like hay in a chute. He sighed. Why couldn't he just say it?

She turned his way as if she could read in his face what he couldn't bring himself to say. It was no good.

"Stop it," he whispered.

"Stop what?"

"Looking at me like that."

"I'm trying to figure you out."

He looked away. He was a goner where she was concerned, and her knowing it wouldn't help.

"But you don't want me to," she said. "Because then I might realize you actually enjoyed that kiss."

He set his jaw.

"That you might even want it to happen again."

"Told you how things are." Then he'd gone and muddied his message with that kiss. "Not interested in a relationship," he said, just to clear things up.

"You're done with women."

"Exactly." He'd already failed one woman. He didn't want any harm to come to Abigail— she didn't deserve it. She'd been nothing but good to him and Maddy.

"Wade."

He felt her eyes on him and leaned back against the wooden slats. He had to protect her from himself. It was the least he could do. He'd managed for five years, he could get through one measly summer.

"It's awful what happened to Lizzie. You and Maddy have been through so much. Wade, look at me."

He felt her fingers on his chin, turning him toward her. Those olive eyes held compassion and something else.

"Honey, it wasn't your fault."

The endearment made him go soft inside, but the words that followed sucked the moisture from his mouth. It shamed him to hear his innermost feelings on her lips. He wanted to crawl under a haystack and hide.

"It's not your fault," she repeated. "You didn't fail her and you aren't failing Maddy. Don't you believe God is in control of everything? Don't you believe He has a plan?"

Her words were like salve on a wound, yet he rejected them. He looked away before he lost his resolve, before her words made sense.

"You think you're defective or something," she said. "I refuse to believe that. You're a good man, Wade. Do you think God made you incapable of having a healthy relationship? He wouldn't do that. You're believing a lie."

He hadn't thought of it like that. He wanted to believe her—she'd never know how much. He'd tried so hard to protect others—Maddy, other women . . . Abigail.

She was so tempting, but what if she was wrong? What if he took a leap of faith and failed her too? He'd never forgive himself. He was already half in love with her.

"What are you thinking?" she asked.

"I don't want to be stupid. Or careless."

"You're neither of those things."

"What if you're wrong?"

"I'm not," she said. "I've kind of been out of the God-loop for a while, so maybe it's crazy to mention this, but have you asked God about this?"

"Not really."

"Don't you think you should? If you're going to give up women, maybe you should check with your Creator first."

He released his breath with a grunt. For a woman who was out of the God-loop, she made a lot of sense. It was something to think about—pray about. Some Christian he was, not even praying about something so crucial. Maybe she was right—maybe it was a lie. But he'd believed it so long.

Wade was suddenly aware of her thigh touching his. Of the faint scent of her sweet perfume. It was becoming as familiar as the fragrance of a summer meadow, and just as welcome. She smelled so good, so . . . Abigail.

"Is it true you don't dance with other women?"

He nodded slowly, the memory of holding Abigail stiffly in his arms so fresh. Not his finest moment.

"Got the ladies in there jealous. Now they're all going to hate me."

She was teasing, but it was a ridiculous thought. He'd seen Abigail in there tonight. In two months she'd managed to charm not only him and Maddy, but the whole town of Moose Creek.

"Nobody could hate you, Abby."

As the seconds ticked by, the twinkle in her eyes faded.

And then he was gone. Gone in so many ways. Not just lost in the moment, but lost in Abigail. She'd come into his home and found her way into his boarded-up heart. She'd pulled off the sheets, dusted the corridors, and let the sun in again.

It felt good. He felt alive. *She* made him feel alive.

With his eyes, Wade followed the line of her nose down to its curved tip, to the fullness of her lips. Six days were too many. How'd he live so long without touching her that way again?

He leaned in, and she came to him willingly. She was soft and pliable. She touched the hair at his nape, and he shivered. He pulled her closer, and she fit like a missing puzzle piece, right into his chest. Right into his heart.

You love her, Ryan. No denying it. God help him, it was true, whether he wanted to believe it or not. He'd meant to shut her out, had tried to shut her out, but there was no stopping it.

His old fear surfaced, poked its sharp claws into his flesh. What if something happened to Abigail? What if she was wrong? What if it *was* him? What if, in the moment she needed him most, he failed her?

No.

He tightened his arms around her and deepened the kiss. It was too late to turn back now. Even if it was true, he wouldn't let any harm come to Abigail. He'd protect her with his life if necessary, same as Maddy.

Abigail framed his face with her soft hands before plowing them through his hair again. Her touch was getting him. His heart galloped in his chest, setting off tremors through his body. He had to call it quits before he did something they'd both regret.

Wade drew back, setting her away with hands on her shoulders. Abigail's eyes opened, questioning. If only she knew how much strength it had taken. "Know what you do to me, city girl?"

The question seemed to ease her mind. The corner of her lips curled up. "Good to know."

Wade pulled his gaze from hers before he got stuck there again, then retrieved his hat from where it had fallen. He set it on Abigail's head and looked at her appreciatively. She made one heck of a cowgirl. "You were born to wear that thing."

"A little big."

He gazed at her face, loving the planes and curves that were becoming so familiar. "Fits just right."

Abigail smiled. Her eyes told him she agreed.

"Go back inside?" he asked.

"Sure." Abigail removed his hat and set it back on his head. She held his eyes for a long second. Just before she turned away, he thought he glimpsed a shadow passing over them.

28

Abigail woke early the next morning, despite her late night. She stretched from her prone position, reveling in the feel of her muscles lengthening after being still all night.

She pulled the quilt to her chin and reviewed the kiss in her head just one more time. Who was she kidding? She'd revisit that one all she liked. And she liked it plenty.

She'd apparently danced with Wade enough times to stake her claim, as Dylan had put it, since no one else vied for his attention. She wondered what Maddy thought of them spending so much time together and realized it was a conversation they'd need to have. She hadn't seemed bothered. She'd smiled and waved across the floor a few times.

Wade had loosened up once they went back inside the Chuckwagon, and the group had cut up together at the table. Abigail hadn't laughed so hard in ages. And then the slow dances would come, and she'd feel as if she were in a dream, his strong arms around her, her head tucked into the nook under his chin. She wanted to stay there forever.

And maybe she would. Maybe her story wouldn't come between them the way she feared. Maybe he was tired of hiding here. Maybe it would come as a relief. Especially when he saw the good things she was writing about him.

And there were so many good things about him. A smile curved her lips, just thinking about him. Something she'd said last night must've made sense, because gone was the guarded Wade, and in his place was a man Abigail could spend the rest of her life getting to know.

So this is what it feels like, she thought, sighing. This warm feeling that flowed through her at the very thought of him. She bent her knees, tenting the quilt. After church she'd have lunch with Aunt Lucy, then she'd spend the afternoon with Wade and Maddy. Maybe later they'd pack a picnic and head to Boulder Pass. She envisioned the kisses she and Wade might sneak under the weeping willow and let out another contented sigh.

First, though, church. She had a few minutes before she had to get ready, so she propped up on the bed and grabbed her laptop. Reagan was supposed to go out with Dr. Steve again last night, and Abigail wanted to see how it had gone.

Nothing from Reagan, only an e-mail from her mom. She clicked on it.

What do you think? her mom had written.

Below the message, an attachment was embedded. Abigail scrolled down.

Her stomach dropped to her toes. The mock-up of the *Viewpoint* cover filled the screen. Wade stared back at her with those startlingly blue eyes and cocky smile.

Cowboy Corralled, the blurb said in a large, bold font. *Where has J. W. Ryan been hiding, and why did he disappear after the mysterious death of his wife?*

Abigail stared at the cover. Reread the

words, seeing it as Wade would when it hit the newsstands. He wouldn't be relieved at all when he saw this cover, read those words.

Was there any way he'd forgive her? Any way his feelings for her would remain steadfast in light of such a betrayal?

The warm pleasant feeling that had flowed through her was replaced by a heavy weight. The flip side of love: loss. She couldn't bear the thought of losing Wade. Couldn't stand the thought of him and Maddy feeling she'd betrayed them.

Abigail slapped the laptop shut, not wanting to see the image, not wanting to think about the story from Wade's perspective. She sprang from the bed and paced the confines of her room.

What could she do? What would happen if she told him the truth? If she told them how the story had fallen into her lap?

But what if Wade told her to leave? How could she leave when she'd only just discovered she loved him? And more than that, she loved Maddy. They were good for each other. She'd begun to think of them as a family, had begun to imagine that they could become a real one. How could she hurt them?

She couldn't. She had to get out of this.

Abigail retrieved her cell and dialed her mom. While the phone rang, Abigail looked at the laptop sitting innocently on the night-stand. She thought of the magazine and its precarious position. She loved Wade, but she loved her mother too. The column was scheduled, the cover designed, the marketing planned. How was she going to get out of it?

Her mom answered groggily.

"Hi, Mom," Abigail said quietly.

"Abigail. Did you get the cover?"

Abigail ran her hand over her face. "I did."

"And . . ."

She didn't know what to say or how to say it. How could she let her mother down? The whole thing had been Abigail's idea. She'd started this chain of events, and now she was going to bail? No matter what she did, it seemed like the wrong thing. Abigail nearly moaned.

"Abs? You didn't like it?"

"Mom, I . . . I don't know if I can do this."

"What do you mean?"

"The story, Wade, the magazine . . . I'm so confused."

"You're scaring me, honey. Tell me what's wrong."

Abigail smothered a hysterical laugh. What's wrong was that she was in love with the subject of her investigation. What's wrong was that he was going to hate her when he found out.

"Mom, I have feelings for Wade—for J. W. Ryan. Real feelings."

The pause rang loudly over the phone. "I see."

"I know everyone's counting on me, on this story, but—"

But what? She was ditching her mom and the entire *Viewpoint* staff in favor of a new guy in her life?

"You've never had trouble separating your emotions from a story. Is your hypertension acting up, affecting your work? You're under too much stress."

"It's not my health, Mom. I'm just having second thoughts."

"Honey, I sympathize, really, I do. But these things have a way of working themselves out. *Viewpoint*'s future is dependent upon this story. The cover gets finalized to-morrow. It's too late to go back to the drawing board."

"I've barely started the article anyway. And I still haven't gotten to the bottom of Elizabeth's death."

"I don't mean to play the guilt card, but a lot of people are counting on this story, Abs."

"I know, I know." So many jobs at stake. It was selfish to back out.

"There's still time to get the rest of the facts. And you're a talented writer, sweetie. You said you were sure he had nothing to do with her death. You could cast J. W. in the role of hero. By the time you're finished, he'll be thanking you."

Ha. She doubted that. But maybe she could paint him so favorably he'd come off, well, just like he was. She'd only have to tell the truth.

"Tell him about the story before the issue hits the stands. Surely he'll see your side. It's not like you went there intending to deceive him. You happened upon the story and agreed to it before you had feelings for him. If anyone understands what it's like to be backed into a corner, it's him."

That was true. "But the media, Mom.

You know they'll descend on this town for interviews. He and Maddy came here to get away from all that. He just wants to be left alone."

"Well, there's nothing we can do about that. A press conference might get them off his back—wait a minute. Didn't you say Moose Creek was struggling financially? Something about trying to become a tourist destination?"

"It's a failing town. The mayor wanted to restore its position as the Gateway to Yellowstone, but it's not working out."

"Wouldn't the media's presence benefit that effort? With so much publicity, people would rediscover Moose Creek. Wade's living there would kind of make it the chic new rustic getaway destination."

Abigail hadn't thought of that. Could her article possibly save Aunt Lucy's shop, the Chuckwagon, Pappy's Market, the other shops? Wasn't a little unwanted publicity for Wade a small price to pay to benefit the whole town? She hoped he'd see it that way.

"I've got it," Mom said. "We can feature Moose Creek as a destination in the travel section for the October issue. Elaine had a piece on New Orleans, but we'll table that. You can write the article yourself if you'd like."

"That's not a bad idea." Maybe by the time this was over, the town would thank her. Surely Wade would forgive her when he saw how hard she was working to help Moose Creek.

"I know J. W. might be angry at first, but a lot of good will come from this. If he has feelings for you, surely he'll understand."

Maybe he would. If she wrote the biggest story of her life and handled it with care. The publicity would be short-lived, a small price to pay for the benefit to the whole community.

"All right, Mom. I'll write it."

"You won't regret it, honey. I'm sorry you're going through this, but try to relax and believe in yourself. This is going to work out. We can accomplish a lot of good for everyone with this one column."

Her feelings somewhat settled, Abigail hung up and changed into her church clothes. Her mom was right. She needed to have confidence in the process, in her skill as a writer. Everything would work out for her and Wade, and it would work out for Moose Creek. It had to.

29

Abigail shifted on the hard pew and resettled her Bible in her lap. The choir loft behind the pastor blurred until she saw nothing but basic shapes and colors. Her mind wasn't on Pastor Blevins or his message. It was on Wade.

She'd seen him briefly that morning after Aunt Lucy tooted her horn outside the house. As Abigail had hurried down the stairs, he'd appeared in the kitchen doorway looking all sleepy-eyed in his T-shirt, jeans, and bare feet. His hair stood up on end as if she'd already run her fingers through it.

He met her at the bottom of the stairs. The step put her eye-to-eye with him, and the look he gave her made her heart catch in her throat. He caught her chin and gave her a kiss she knew she'd carry all day long, pulling away all too quickly.

"Save the afternoon for me?" he asked.

She found her voice. "Uh-huh."

He rewarded her with a sexy smile she would've emptied her wallet for, then she made her way out the door on shaky legs. The way he made her feel . . . she wondered if he had any idea . . . and if she made him feel the same way.

". . . Truth seekers."

The pastor's words pulled Abigail from her thoughts. Was he talking about her? She glanced around, relieved to find no eyes on her.

"That's exactly what the disciples were," the pastor said. "They left their families, their occupations, their homes in order to follow after this man called Jesus. They were truth seekers because Jesus is Truth and that's who they sought. Jesus said, 'I am the way, the truth and the life . . .' What does that mean?"

The pastor continued, but Abigail was

lost in his previous words. If Jesus was Truth—and she believed He was—and if Abigail was the Truthseeker, why hadn't she been seeking Him? Instead of pursuing Him, she'd been pursuing her career. Chasing story after story as if finding the next truth would somehow scratch an itch that never went away.

The Truthseeker had forgotten what the Truth was. Who the Truth was. How blind she'd been! She knew Christ was the one Truth that mattered the most, but somehow she'd lost her way, had put that Truth on the back burner while she went in search of a lesser truth.

She remembered her words of wisdom to Wade the night before. How easy it was to identify someone else's issues and overlook the obvious in her own life. All these years of being the Truthseeker, and she'd never put the two together. Well, she was putting it together now. From now on, she'd seek the real Truth first, just like her dad. That was being the ultimate Truthseeker.

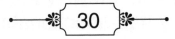

30

Abigail exited the house and shut the screen door softly behind her. There was an empty spot on the swing next to Wade, and she planned to claim it. The porch light made his skin glow, his dark hair glisten. She loved looking at him. Did it every chance she got. The past week she'd spent every waking moment thinking of him. Her days had never lasted so long.

Abigail smiled as she settled next to him. The swing creaked with the rhythmic motion. The night smelled like sagebrush and freshly mown grass. And Wade.

"Maddy asked about us," Abigail said as she snuggled under his arm.

They'd been careful to save the displays of affection for when they were alone, even though she knew Wade had told his daughter they had affectionate feelings for each other.

"What'd you say?"

"That I like you very much." She nudged him in the side.

"That so?"

She curled her arm around his waist and dropped her head on his shoulder. "And here I thought I'd been so obvious."

Wade dropped a kiss on the top of her head. Abigail turned her face into his shirt and inhaled a lungful of his scent just to tease her senses. He smelled so good. He ran his hand down her bare arm, and gooseflesh pebbled her skin.

"What else she say?" Wade rubbed her arm, warming her.

"She asked if I had to leave . . ." The thought caught her in the gut.

His arm tightened. "When's your flight?"

"The twentieth."

Two weeks. It wasn't enough, not even close. She didn't want to go. But he hadn't asked her to stay. Hadn't even told her about Lizzie or his brush with fame. She tried not to let that cast a damper on this otherwise perfect evening.

"Can't believe summer's almost gone," he said. "Sure went fast."

"It's been amazing. I came for Aunt Lucy and found you and Maddy instead."

"You've been good for her. Just what she needed. Just what I needed. You were right before . . . Should've trusted God to work out my future instead of trying to fix it."

"You're trusting Him now. That's what matters." Abigail gave a contented sigh and snuggled into his side. She was proud of him for admitting he'd been wrong. They were both growing spiritually. They were good for each other.

She wished she could just enjoy his company tonight and forget the story. But she had to write it next week, and she was still missing crucial material. She swallowed hard and forced herself to ask, hating herself for doing it.

"You mentioned something before about Maddy's mom—that she was never all that wrapped up in Maddy. What did you mean? I hope you don't mind my asking."

Wade was still for a moment. Then he kissed the top of her head. "Another time, okay? It's been a long day, and I just want to enjoy the feel of you in my arms."

Abigail tipped her head back, looked him in the eye. He'd been through so much with Lizzie. Could she blame him for wanting to forget? For wanting to enjoy a few moments of intimacy on this mild summer night? One of their last.

Abigail drew her fingers down the angular plane of his jaw. When Wade lowered his face, she met his lips, responded to his tender ministrations, wanting to help him forget all about Lizzie and his painful past. She was with him now. Whatever had happened, no matter how horrible, had somehow led to this point. Led them all to this point.

This was going to end happily, she could feel it. He deserved a happy ending. Maybe if she did as her mom suggested and told him in advance, he'd understand. She could tell him right now. Right here on the swing.

But he hadn't even wanted to talk about Lizzie tonight, hadn't wanted to spoil their evening. News like hers would definitely spoil the evening. She'd tell him later. Later would be soon enough.

Abigail deepened the kiss and felt a tremble pass through Wade.

He drew away, reluctance filling his eyes. "Woman, you're killing me."

His admission made her heady, made her want to press her luck. But he pulled her against him and tucked her head under his chin.

Abigail buried her face in his chest and nestled into the softness of his cotton shirt. Yes, there was going to be a happy ending for sure.

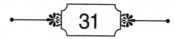

31

The article deadline was approaching, and as it did, Abigail's anxiety rose. Despite her mom's assurances that everything would work out, her blood pressure was out of control, and her daily headaches had returned. Sunday afternoon she knew she should be writing the story, but it was Wade's only day off, and she couldn't resist spending time with him and Maddy.

Because of her procrastination, she was forced to write all week at night after Maddy and Wade were in bed. She worked late into the night crafting the story, one she thought would both do justice to Wade and satisfy *Viewpoint* readers. Once the first draft was finished, she spent hours checking the facts and honing her words. She'd read the story so many times she nearly had the thing memorized.

She finally finished on Friday around three in the morning. It was her best writing. Abigail had poured her heart into it, and she thought it showed. She decided to let the story rest a day, give it a final read-through Sunday morning, and then send it to her mom.

The week had been long on work and short on sleep, and by Saturday night she was ready to drop into bed, exhausted.

"I've been keeping you up too late," Wade said after she yawned. He set the swing in motion and pulled her into his arms.

"You're worth it." He *was* worth it. Worth sleep deprivation and so much more. She hoped he'd understand, once she explained, once he read the story. She'd decided to tell him Friday, the night before she left. But now, with his thigh pressed against hers and his heart thumping against her cheek, she didn't want to think of it.

"How's your headache?"

She loved the deep drawl of his voice.

"Better." She'd been living on Tylenol all week. But truth be told, it wasn't working like it used to. Maybe she needed something stronger.

"You need to take care of yourself." He ran his hand down the length of her hair, then toyed with the ends.

His touch sent a shiver down her spine, and she nestled closer.

"Maybe Greta can watch Maddy next week so you can rest up before . . ."

Before you go home. He didn't want to say it. Neither of them did. Abigail didn't even want to think about it.

"I'm fine. I want to spend the week with Maddy." One week from tonight she'd be back in Chicago—would have told him everything. What would their relationship look like in a week? Would he ask her to stay?

Because she would, in a heartbeat.

※

Wade tightened his arms around Abigail and wondered if she could feel his heart hammering in her ear. All he could think about was her leaving in a week.

He didn't know how she'd done it, but

she'd stolen his heart. He couldn't bear the thought of her leaving, the thought of going back to life the way it had been before she came. He'd been praying, just as she'd suggested, and somehow the more he prayed, the more his heart had opened. An answer to a prayer? He had to believe it was.

He'd made the decision the moment she'd settled in his arms tonight. It felt like she was coming home, and he knew he wanted that every night for the rest of his life. He thought she wanted it too, but there was much to be said, much to be decided. He had yet to profess his love or tell her about his time in the spotlight. He was ready to do so.

Abigail rubbed her temple, and he realized her head hurt more than she let on. He moved her hand and rubbed it for her. Poor darlin'. He wished there were more he could do. He'd tell Maddy to stay close to home next week. No running off on horseback or dragging Abigail all over the ranch. If she stayed, she'd have all the time in the world to rest. He'd see to it personally. Maybe he could just keep Maddy with him, a little father-daughter time. They'd both enjoy that, and Abigail would get her rest.

Ten minutes later Abigail's body had relaxed against his, and her breaths had deepened. She barely stirred as he carried her to her room, removed her sandals, and tucked the covers around her.

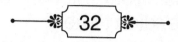

32

The next day Abigail read and sent off the article, went to church and then over to Aunt Lucy's for coffee. With the article out of her hands, a weight had lifted from her weary shoulders.

Now she only had the matter of Aunt Lucy's health to resolve. She handed a mug of freshly brewed coffee to her aunt, moved the dolls that occupied the recliner, and took a seat catty-corner to the other woman.

"Aunt Lucy, there's something I need to ask you about. You might think I'm prying, but Mom and I are concerned—"

"You can relax, dear. I already went to see Dr. Garvin."

Abigail met her gaze. "You did? Why?"

"Well, for heaven's sake, I'm old, but I'm not oblivious. Your mother sent you to check on me, didn't she?"

Abigail looked down at her ring. "Sort of. But she really did want me to take a break too. What did Dr. Garvin say?"

"He said I'm crazy as a loon. But that has nothing to do with age. I'm fit as a fiddle, so you and your mom can relax."

"I hope you're not upset with us."

Her aunt's big eyes softened. She leaned forward and laid her wrinkled hand over Abigail's. "All done in love, I know that. I may be as old as the hills, but I still got plenty of life in me."

"I know, but I'm still relieved Dr. Garvin gave you the all-clear. Mom will be too. And, Aunt Lucy . . . I've so enjoyed my time here with you. I'm glad I came to Moose Creek, and I'm proud to be your great-niece."

Her aunt blinked back tears. "Now you stop that or you're going to make me fog up my glasses. You don't fly home till

Saturday. Maybe we can squeeze in another visit."

"You can count on it."

❀

When Abigail returned from Aunt Lucy's, Wade took one look at her sleepy eyes and delayed the picnic.

"Upstairs, right now," Wade said. "You need a nap."

"No, I don't, I'm—" A deep yawn cut off her words.

He held up his hand. "Don't want to hear it."

"Better do it," Maddy added. "When he uses that voice, there's no changing his mind."

Wade cornered Abigail upstairs and gave her something nice to dream about before joining Maddy in the living room. Today he was going to tell Abigail he loved her, was going to ask her to stay, but daggonnit, she wasn't going to be falling asleep in his arms when he did.

Wade played Operation with Maddy. He was losing soundly for the fourth time when he realized he was having fun anyway. Seeing the smile on his daughter's face was enough for him. Abigail had been right. Maddy needed him as much as he needed his daughter.

"You know, Maddy, next spring when we do the branding . . . well, you're old enough to help."

"Really, Dad?"

He nodded, and she sprang across the game and hugged him. "Thanks, Dad!"

His daughter was growing up, like it or not, and he planned to enjoy her company while he still had her.

After the game, Wade started on the dishes. Figured if he didn't, he'd find Abigail in here later. When the dishwasher was humming, he dried his hands and joined Maddy in the living room where she was playing a game on Abigail's laptop.

"Whoops," Maddy said as he entered the room. "I accidentally hit something. I don't want to mess it up; can you fix it?"

"You get Abigail's permission?"

Maddy shrugged, handing him the laptop. "She always lets me."

"Doesn't mean you can sneak into her room and take it. Find something else to do until she wakes."

Maddy made a face, then started up the stairs.

"Quiet up there," he reminded his daughter. Abigail had had a solid hour, but he wanted her to be good and rested.

Wade set the laptop on his thighs. He hoped his daughter hadn't messed it up. Looked like an e-mail had just popped open. He was set to minimize it and exit Maddy's game when the subject line caught his eye. *J. W. Ryan Cover Proof.*

He frowned. The e-mail was from mjones@Viewpoint.com.

He scanned the message.

What do you think? it read.

Dread swept through him, almost stopped his fingers from scrolling down the page. But he had to know. He scrolled down.

His own image stared back. An old photo from his rodeo days, the one they'd run in that ridiculous magazine contest.

Had Abigail found an old cover? If she knew he'd been a celebrity, why hadn't she said something?

He scanned the headline beside the photo. *Cowboy Corralled*, it said in a large, bold font. *Where has J. W. Ryan been hiding, and why did he disappear after the mysterious death of his wife?*

It wasn't an old issue. The date on the cover corroborated the thought. His image blurred as the significance hit him like a hoof in the gut. Someone from *Viewpoint Magazine* had sent it to Abigail. The head-line promised answers . . . He read it again, hoping he was wrong, that somehow this was a misunderstanding he'd laugh about later with her. She'd said she was a writer. Was this the kind of story she wrote?

Cowboy Corralled. That pretty much said it all, didn't it? And if his suspicions were true, Abigail wasn't who he thought she was. He was tempted to snoop through her e-mails, but he couldn't bring himself to do it without more evidence.

He'd investigate on his own computer. Wade dumped the laptop on the couch and went to his office. He typed Abigail's name into a search engine. If that was even her real name . . .

The first listing was on *Viewpoint*'s web-site. He clicked on the link. The feeling of dread spread through him like venom.

Abigail's photo stared back and beside it, the title of a column. *The Truthseeker.*

Was that what she was? There was a headline and an article underneath, something about a corrupt politician. Those weren't *stories*. Those were investigative reports. She was a blasted investigative reporter.

He clicked on her name and was directed to a bio. She'd written for *Viewpoint* for six years, earned her own column three years before, and had since collected awards for her exposés.

Well, bravo for her. She was here to "expose" Wade—for what? What had he done except try to make a decent life for his daughter? He'd opened up to this woman about his deepest fear. Had trusted her with something he'd never told anyone, not even Dylan.

He was a fool. He'd seen enough to know that. He pushed back from the desk. Needed to get out of there. He stormed out to the barn, his mind spinning with the events of the past three months. Something dark and ugly swelled inside.

He needed air. He needed . . .

When he entered the barn, he stopped in the cool musty shade. His breaths came and went with effort. He wanted to hit something, anything. He balled up his fist and swung for the nearest object, a saddle hanging on its peg.

He was so angry, choking with it. She'd played him for a fool. Had used him and his daughter, an eleven-year-old, for heaven's sake. Who did she think she was, coming into his life, into his house—

Into my heart.

He couldn't go there right now. Didn't dare. It was too much to swallow at once. Way too much.

He had to think. Had to digest what this meant for him and Maddy. Abigail was writing an article, obviously. She'd come here to spy on them, and he'd kindly let her right into their home. So much for protecting his daughter. He'd let her down again. Let her down just as he'd let Lizzie down.

He took another swing at the saddle, knocking it to the floor, letting out a roar that clawed up his throat.

At least he hadn't told her the details of Lizzie's death—thank God for that. But she knew where they lived. What more did she need? She had everything she needed to sell tons of magazines. She'd get herself a little recognition for her big scoop, maybe even a nice bonus from her boss.

Focus, Ryan. He had to think about Maddy. What could he do? No way could he stop the article. If she'd come here to do something so duplicitous, so heartless, she wouldn't back down now. Wouldn't throw away a summer's worth of work and lies. He pictured her face, the way she'd looked at him when he'd kissed her before the nap. So convincing. Oh yeah, she was good all right.

Think! He had to make a plan. There'd be a media frenzy when this hit the news. Other magazines, even the newsmagazine shows, would pick up the story. They'd descend on Moose Creek like mosquitoes on a wet dog.

He'd be back to hiding in his house, screening his calls, and how would he shield Maddy from it all, especially with school starting? The bloodsuckers in the media wouldn't think twice about hassling a kid if it got them what they wanted. Case in point: Abigail.

Wade paced the length of the barn, churning up straw and dirt with his angry strides.

The media would stir up all the things he'd worked so hard to put behind them. They'd trigger memories, remind Maddy of her loss.

They'd have to move again. Go someplace and start over again, just as they'd done in Moose Creek. The thought made his stomach turn over. This was their home, where they belonged. Abigail had no right to chase them from it.

And yet, what choice did he have? He didn't want to be in the spotlight anymore, didn't want to be gossiped about, especially didn't want Maddy subjected to the cruelty that could come from such gossip.

But Abigail Jones had spoiled their safe haven. He wondered when the story would be published. How long did they have before life as they knew it was over?

Wade turned and paced the other way. His horses stared at him wide-eyed from over their stall doors. Ace whinnied, sensing his agitation.

A shuffling at the doorway pulled his gaze toward the opening. Abigail was silhouetted there, leaning lazily against the door frame.

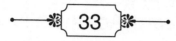

33

Abigail hated to admit it, but Wade had been right. A nap was just what she'd needed. Her headache was gone. Maddy had fallen asleep in her room, which gave her and Wade a few minutes alone. She searched the house, and when she didn't find him, she went outside.

Abigail felt downright springy as she took the porch steps and made her way to the barn. The bright blue sky yawned overhead and the sun beat down, warming her bare arms. She glanced back at their vegetable garden, and the sight of new life put an extra bounce in her step.

The memory of Wade's kiss just before her nap was fresh on her mind as she neared the barn door. She intended to pick up right where they'd left off.

When she entered the coolness of the barn, she heard Ace's whinny and knew she'd found her cowboy. She stopped at the entrance, waiting for her eyes to adjust from the harsh sunlight. She heard Wade's boots shuffle to a stop a short distance away.

"Feeling rested and frisky," she teased. "You were right, I needed a nap." And right now she needed his arms around her. She took a few steps in as her eyes adjusted. In front of her, a saddle lay in the dirt.

"Wade?" She saw him now, in front of Ace's stall, and she smiled. "I found you." She walked toward him, could almost feel his lips on hers.

"Reckon you did."

He sounded odd. Her steps stuttered. His form, his features grew more defined as she neared. His jaw was set. His eyes, shadowed under the brim of his hat, revealed nothing.

"Wade?"

"I know who you are."

His cold tone stopped her in her tracks, sent a shock of dread through her. *Please, be wrong.* "What?"

Ace whinnied again, scuffled his hooves in the stall.

"I know about the article." He spat the last word like it left a nasty taste on his tongue.

No. Please, no. It wasn't supposed to happen this way. "How—"

"You think I'm some ignorant cowboy?"

"No, I—Wade, you don't—"

"Understand? I understand just fine, *Abby*." The way he snarled her pet name was a slap in the face. "You get extra points for stringing me along?"

"Please, Wade, just listen . . ." She reached out to him.

He jerked away from her touch. "You used us."

"No, I didn't—"

"Used us, lied to us, *exploited* us." He hit a stall door, and Abigail jumped. "You weaseled your way into my home and manipulated us into telling you things!"

"That's not—"

"Tell me I'm wrong then!" His brows pulled tight. "Tell me you're not writing some article. Tell me you're not the 'Truthseeker.' That you don't work for *Viewpoint Magazine*. Go on, Abigail, tell me." He gave a harsh laugh. "Truthseeker. You don't know the meaning of the word."

A roaring filled her head. There was no breath left in her lungs. No words on her tongue. They all jumbled into a mass and clogged her throat.

"Yeah, what I thought." He turned and walked away, his body rigid.

"You don't understand. I know it looks bad, but I care about you, Wade. I care about you and Maddy both—"

He whirled and glared. "Heck of a way to show it."

"I didn't know who you were when I came here—I swear it! I was only applying to be your nanny. It was only later I realized who you were. My mom's magazine was going under, September was our last issue, our last chance, and we needed a miracle to save it. I did it to save the jobs of all those people, and I hated what I was doing—I wanted to tell you the truth so badly! The article is very favorable, I promise, and I know—"

"There's not going to be an article."

"I wish there were a choice, Wade, I really do, but I'm backed into a corner."

"You got nothing on me, Abigail. You don't know squat about Lizzie. All you know is where I live, and by the time that issue hits the stands, we'll be long gone."

She froze. Gone? They were moving? Or had she heard wrong, for all the roaring in her head? "What?"

"You heard me. We're moving."

No. It wasn't supposed to happen this way. "Oh, Wade, don't—"

He jabbed his open hand into the air. "This is how it's going down. I'm taking Maddy to town for a while. You're going into the house to pack, and when we come back you're going to be gone—"

"No, please—"

"You're going to leave, and you're not coming back." He drilled her with a look so cold she shivered. "You're not welcome here anymore."

His words knocked the breath from her. Not see him, not see Maddy ever again? Worse, he thought she'd betrayed his trust, that she'd manipulated him into revealing his most private thoughts.

And worse yet . . . wasn't it true?

She should have told him. She never should have done the story to begin with. It wasn't worth losing the man she loved, worth hurting a little girl who'd already been hurt so much.

"I can't just leave," she whispered, her voice breaking. "I love you."

Wade turned his face, looked away. His jaw twitched. "Stop it."

Footsteps sounded behind her. "Ready to go, Dad!"

No, not Maddy. Abigail couldn't deal with her, too, couldn't process it all.

"What's wrong?" Maddy asked, no doubt feeling the tension that cut through the building.

Wade closed the distance between himself and Abigail. She met his cold gaze, begged him to change his mind.

"Tell her you're leaving," he whispered, for her ears only. His eyes were shiny black pebbles set in a face of granite.

Her eyes stung with tears. "I don't want to leave, Wade. *Please*."

"Tell her you're leaving and not coming back." His calm doggedness was unnerving.

She couldn't tell Maddy that, couldn't let

her think she didn't matter to Abigail. She couldn't bear to hurt her.

She wouldn't do it. Wouldn't hurt Maddy even more. "No."

He lowered his voice again. "Should I tell her what you did? I'll do it. I'll do it right now, Abigail." He left no doubt in her mind he'd carry out the threat.

She couldn't let Maddy find out like this. She'd know the truth eventually, but it wasn't going to be now, with Wade breathing fire.

"Abigail?" Maddy was closer now. "Daddy? What's going on?"

Wade looked at Abigail. Hiked his brows. *Tell her*, his eyes said.

Abigail sucked in a breath of musty dirt and blinked away her tears. She turned, tried for a smile and failed, then took Maddy's hand instead. "Honey, I'm afraid I have to leave." Her voice was broken and small.

"You can't go swimming?"

This was so hard. Abigail tried to swallow the lump in her throat, cleared her throat. "No, I mean I have to go back to Chicago."

Maddy looked between the two of them. "Your plane leaves Saturday. I know that."

"I . . . I know. It does, but I have to go earlier. Now."

"But why?" Maddy whined.

"I . . . I can't explain right now. But maybe I can come back later and—"

Wade cleared his throat pointedly.

She squatted to Maddy's level. "Honey, no matter what happens, I want you to know that—"

"Are you coming back?" the girl asked.

Oh, God, what do I say? What could she say with Wade standing over her shoulder editing each word?

"You are coming back, aren't you?" Maddy's volume increased frantically. She looked at her dad, then back at Abigail. "Aren't you?" Her eyes filled.

"Maddy, I—" The words caught in her throat. What could she say? She couldn't admit Wade was making her leave, wouldn't let her come back. What good would it do to turn the child against her father? Better that she thought it was Abigail's fault.

After all, it really was, wasn't it?

"I hate you!" Maddy fled from the barn.

The words cut into her. She couldn't leave Maddy feeling that way. Abigail started after her.

Wade blocked her path, stared down at her with those cold, hard eyes. "You've done enough."

She wanted to comfort Maddy, tell her she loved her, that she hadn't meant to hurt them. But maybe Wade was right. Maybe that was best left for him to handle.

Abigail met his eyes and felt them slice clean through her heart. He was right. She'd done way more than enough.

34

Abigail woke early the next morning, her eyes swollen, her heart heavy. She showered, returned her belongings to her suitcase, then crept into her aunt's kitchen where she forced down a slice of toast. Her new flight to Chicago left in three hours from Bozeman, and the cab would be arriving soon.

She couldn't believe her time in Montana had come to this. She wanted to collapse onto the sofa, pull the quilt over her head, and stay there. She glanced out the kitchen window toward Wade's ranch. She wanted to go see him, wanted to set things right between them. But the memory of that cold look in his eyes was enough to shatter that fantasy.

She'd been a wreck when she'd shown up on her aunt's doorstep the previous day. Aunt Lucy had listened patiently as she'd poured out the whole story, from the article to her feelings for Wade, her words tumbling out in a jumbled mess.

Now the overhead light flipped on as Aunt Lucy entered the kitchen, knotting the belt of her robe around her thick waist. "'Morning, dear."

Abigail looked away from the pity in her aunt's eyes. "Hope I didn't wake you."

"I wanted to see you off. Are you sure I can't drive you?" Aunt Lucy sank into the nearest chair.

"I'm sure. The cab'll be here any minute."

"I'd ask how you're feeling, but it's all over your face."

Abigail swallowed the last bite of toast and pushed back her plate. "I don't know what to do. I've made a mess, and it's too big to . . ." A lump swelled in her throat, forcing off her words.

"There's only one thing you can do at a time like this, honey: pray hard. God knows all you've done, and He knows your heart. Trust Him to lead you."

Abigail wanted this fixed. She wanted to go back in time and do things differently, but that wasn't possible. "You're right. I know you are, it's just hard—" She swallowed against the lump.

"Love is never easy."

A car horn tooted outside.

"My ride." They stood and hugged. Abigail kissed her aunt on the cheek. "Thanks for everything, Aunt Lucy. I love you."

"Love you too, child. I'll be praying for you."

Abigail gathered her things and started for the door.

"Oh, one more thing." Aunt Lucy waddled across the room and plucked a doll from the sofa. "Take Lydia." She handed the doll to Abigail. "She's my best comforter."

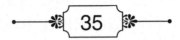

35

Abigail stared at the blinking cursor. The page was blank except for the title. Every now and then she wrote a sentence, re-read it, then hit Backspace.

The hum of the computer was the only sound in the office. Beyond her cubicle, the room was empty.

Just like her heart.

Outside the shaded windows a car roared past, the bass thumping from its stereo. A distant car alarm shrieked.

She missed the sound of the wind rustling through tall grass. Missed the big blue sky that stretched as far as you could see.

Missed the hills that rolled like waves in a never-ending ocean.

Stop it. She had to stop this incessant torture. Get back to work.

Her column for the last issue of *Viewpoint* had been canceled and the cover was undergoing a hasty redesign. It was over. She'd let everyone down. Her mom, all the employees, and most of all, Wade and Maddy.

Her eyes swung to the title in the header of her document. *Moose Creek.* She was going to squeeze the travel article into the September issue in place of her column. Since Maddy and Wade wouldn't be there, what could it hurt? At least a little good might come from her ill-fated stay in Moose Creek. Only trouble was, she couldn't find the words. Couldn't find a way to describe the town, the people. Couldn't find a way to explain how special it was, how much they'd all affected her.

A pounding on the front door broke the silence. She pushed back from her desk and walked toward the entry. Reagan waved from the other side of the glass door. She looked nice in her trendy jeans and red blouse.

Abigail twisted the two deadbolts and opened the door.

"You look awful," her sister offered by way of greeting.

"Thanks."

"Why are you here?" Reagan tucked her brown hair behind her ears.

Abigail locked the door and started for her desk. "Working on an article."

"It's Saturday. By the looks of you, you should be home taking a nap."

Abigail shrugged. "Can't sleep." She'd had a constant headache since her return to Chicago five days earlier. If her thoughts of Wade and Maddy didn't keep her awake, her palpitations did. The bags under her eyes could hold her wardrobe.

Abigail dropped into her chair and rolled close to her desk. The screen saver had kicked on, mercifully sparing her those two words.

Reagan perched on the corner of her desk. "You didn't answer your cell."

Abigail pulled it from her purse. "Oh. It's dead." Not like Wade was trying to reach her. "Thought you were having lunch with Dr. Steve."

"Just got home and tried to call you. I

was worried when I couldn't get through. You have a headache, don't you? Are you taking your meds?"

"Yes, Mother." She was getting what she deserved for hurting two people who least deserved it. Ironic how exposing truth had always felt so satisfying. This time it only felt wrong.

"You're scaring me, Abs."

There was already enough guilt flowing through Abigail to float a boat. "Sorry." She was getting good at letting people down.

"The cowboy really got to you, didn't he?"

The word put an instant image of Wade in her mind. Hat tipped low over his blue eyes, lips curved in a barely-there smile. The shallow cleft in his chin. The image was so real, she felt like she could reach out and touch him.

Then he was gone. She'd dreamed about him last night. It was as close to him as she was getting. The thought weighed her down.

"Don't want to talk about it," Abigail said.

"Have you tried calling him?"

Abigail frowned, crossed her arms.

"Talking is therapeutic." Reagan crossed her own arms and waited. "Well, have you?"

Her sister wasn't going away, wasn't the least bit intimidated by her best angry look. "Yes, Dr. Freud, I have. Many times. He doesn't answer. Doesn't want to talk to me, obviously, and can you blame him? I left a message telling him not to move, that we weren't publishing the article, but do you really think he'll believe me at this point? You think he'll chance their future on my promise? 'Cause I don't."

She'd wondered a thousand times what he'd told Maddy. If the girl hated Abigail as much as Wade did. But hadn't she said as much?

"You really do love him."

A familiar ache filled her stomach—filled the hole that had been there since she'd left Wade standing in the barn. When Abigail was packing, she'd heard Maddy crying outside, had watched from her window as Wade put his daughter in the truck and drove away, his tires spitting up dirt and gravel. It was the last time she'd seen them.

"You were only doing your job, honey," Reagan said.

Her job. A lame excuse. "I let so many people down. My work has always left me fulfilled. After I finish a column, I'm almost overwhelmed with a sense of justice. It's what keeps me going . . . it's why I write."

"But now you feel . . ."

"Empty." No other word for it. She'd never had a story go so wrong. The column had failed, *Viewpoint* would be canceled, and she'd hurt two people she loved. "I never should've gone after this story."

"It fell into your lap—what were you going to do? It was right up your alley."

"No. My column exposes wrongs. I investigate, get the facts, then I expose the evil or immorality. But Wade's not evil or immoral. He did nothing wrong. He was just trying to move on with his life after his wife died, trying to protect his daughter."

She remembered what he said about letting Lizzie down, how he felt he'd failed her. Was he feeling that way about Maddy now? All because of her? She palmed her eyes. "And now they're moving because of me."

Reagan's hand smoothed Abigail's hair. "You didn't plan for that to happen."

"I told myself that if the article showed him as the hero he is, everything would be okay. I was kidding myself. I should've told him the truth." She gave a wry laugh. "The Truthseeker. I'm beginning to hate that word." Wade was right. She didn't know the first thing about truth.

"Is it okay if I say something here?"

"Can I stop you?"

"Probably not." Reagan shifted, her hand dropping from Abigail's hair. "Sometimes I wonder if you write what you do because of Julia."

Julia? Abigail lifted her head. "What does Julia have to do with my writing?"

"I think you've carried a lot of guilt about her abuse—about not telling. It changed you."

"I was a child."

Reagan waved her words away. "I'm not saying you had reason to feel guilty. I probably would've done the same thing, Abs. You were scared, rightfully so. The man was a monster."

How could Reagan bring this up now when she was reeling over Wade and her horrid story? "And this has to do with my writing, how?"

"Think about it. You *didn't* tell the truth

then, and you've regretted it ever since. Now your life's work is to expose wrong-doers through your column. You don't see a connection?"

Abigail didn't even want to think about it. "No, I don't."

"You weren't responsible for her father's behavior."

"I know that, Reagan."

"If you'd told, he might've come after you."

Abigail shuddered at the thought. She had no doubt he'd been capable—it was one of the reasons she'd kept silent all those years ago.

"I think you're trying to redeem yourself through your column," Reagan said softly. "But there's no way you can. That's like trying to earn salvation, and you know that's impossible. Let it go. You've carried it around too long."

"I'll think about it," Abigail said to appease her sister. She would think about it later. Much later, when she didn't have all the other stuff hanging over her head.

"Promise?"

Abigail sighed, impatient. "Yes, I promise." She propped her elbow on the desk, bumping the mouse. The screen saver disappeared, revealing the title of her blank document. She wished she could go back to Moose Creek and do things over. She'd handle it all so differently.

"I hate regrets," Abigail said. But she'd made her bed, and now she had to lie in it, as her dad used to say.

"Maybe he'll forgive you in time. Once the anger fades, he might listen."

"Only I won't know where to find him." Abigail remembered the confrontation in the barn. Maybe if she'd been the one to tell him the truth, if he hadn't found out on his own . . . "You didn't see his face, Reagan." The way his jaw was set, that hard look in his eyes. She never wanted anyone to look at her that way again, much less the man she loved.

"And I can't blame him," Abigail continued. "He's losing his home, his ranch. Maddy'll have to make new friends, go to a new school—all because of me."

"You were caught between the proverbial rock and a hard place."

"And I chose the wrong one." She'd never known that hurting someone she loved could hurt so much.

"It'll get better, honey. I promise." Reagan gave her a sympathetic smile.

The words sounded nice, but right now, sitting in the eye of the storm with her eyes closed, it was hard to believe she'd ever feel better again.

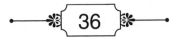

36

Abigail decided to take a break from the Moose Creek article. The words weren't coming anyway, and she was weary of staring at a blinking curser. She locked up the office and drove from the parking garage, turning onto the empty street. The sun had gone into hiding behind a thick bank of gray clouds.

She pointed the car toward her apartment, wondering what she'd do when she got there. She'd skipped lunch but wasn't hungry. Couldn't stomach the thought of eating. She could use a nap, but her bed had become a place to avoid. A place where memories haunted her until she slept, and then the dreams started. Dreams that made waking up painful.

She wondered what Wade and Maddy were doing right now. Probably packing their belongings and talking about how awful Abigail was, how glad they were she was out of their lives. Where were they moving? Once they left Moose Creek, they'd be lost to her forever.

Who are you kidding, Abigail? They're already lost to you.

The thought knotted her stomach. Why was she torturing herself?

She made a turn and kept driving. She'd drive around all afternoon if she had to, but she couldn't go back to those four walls. She had to stay busy.

Noise. She needed noise. She flipped on the radio, and a country and western tune filled the car. The song reminded her of riding in Wade's pickup truck. Of that Saturday night at the Chuckwagon in Wade's arms.

Abigail changed the channel. The sound of peaceful strains of strings and flutes filled the car. Maybe classical music would soothe her.

Leaving the city, she turned toward the suburbs and a succession of sleepy streets. She passed a group of neighborhood children running through a sprinkler, enjoying the last days of summer, a precious weekend after a week in a new school year. Maddy would start school on Monday, her first day of sixth grade.

Under the shade of a giant oak, a young girl wearing a helmet wobbled down the sidewalk on her pink bike.

Pink. Like Maddy's.

Stop it, Abigail. Don't go there.

She turned the corner, down a lane lined by small brick homes, similar to the street where she'd grown up. A middle-aged woman, down on all fours, weeded her burgeoning flower bed. Abigail thought of Aunt Lucy's plastic flowers, and a tiny smile formed. She thought of her vegetable garden, and the smile slid from her face. It would die now. The plants wouldn't stand a chance under the August sun without the sprinkler. Not that it mattered, since there'd be no one around to harvest the vegetables. Soon there'd be a big commercial *For Sale* sign at the end of the drive, under the Stillwater Ranch archway.

There she went again. Why was every image, every thought, a direct highway to Moose Creek?

Abigail turned at a four-way stop and progressed down the next street. Hedges and low fences divided the small lawns. Sidewalks stretched out on both sides of the narrow street. Children played games of street hockey and kickball in the cul-de-sacs.

Reagan's words about Julia rang in her head. Did she still carry guilt? Why else would the memory of Julia be painful after all these years? Yes, she did carry guilt. It surfaced sometimes when she least expected it.

And she subconsciously chose to expose truth now to make up for the one time she hadn't? Is that why she experienced that satisfying sense of justice when she finished a column? Was there a connection?

It made sense, though she hated to admit it. She was driven in her job. Her mom had called her a workaholic on more than one occasion. Was she so driven because she enjoyed her work, or was she trying to earn her own redemption?

Maybe I am. The words rang of truth, a subject she was only just beginning to understand.

Only One could redeem a person, and He was the same One who called Himself Truth. The irony didn't escape her.

She reached the end of a street and turned right. The sign in front of a low sprawling brick building caught her eye. She hadn't been here in years. And yet it looked just the same. Well, maybe a bit smaller.

Abigail parked the car along the grassy curb and exited the car. She hadn't meant to wind up here, but it seemed appropriate somehow. The gray clouds swallowed the sky now, hiding any trace of the sun, shading her from its punishing heat.

She followed the curved walkway to the back of the building, passing her dad's old classroom. Colorful construction paper pictures adorned the windows. Everyone had loved her dad. He'd been the best teacher in the school.

The walkway led to the empty playground, and Abigail followed it until she reached the metal swing set. Fresh wood chips covered the base now, a safety precaution that had been added since she'd been in school.

How many hours had she and Julia spent on this swing set? Every recess from kindergarten until fifth grade. They'd pump their legs to see who could go higher, then coast for a while playing Would You Rather. *Would you rather eat a whole jar of peanut butter or walk all the way home barefoot on the hottest day of the year? Would you rather tell Mr. Lugwig that you love him or kiss Scottie Bowlen?*

Abigail lowered herself onto the rubber seat. It cradled her hips tightly, forcing her knees together, her ankles apart. She grabbed the cool metal chain and pushed off.

Would you rather clean the whole school or hitchhike to Canada?

Julia had been better at Would You Rather, making them so equivalent in difficulty it was nearly impossible to choose. They'd debate forever which exercise was worse, but in the end they'd usually agree.

Abigail pumped her legs, and the air whipped through her hair, cooling her skin. The metal links creaked and groaned rhythmically, the sound taking her back years.

She extended her arms, leaned back, and watched the leaves overhead shimmy and shake under the breeze. Beyond them, the sky was a gray abyss.

I'm sorry, Julia. I wish I'd told somebody. You were a good friend to me, and you deserved a better childhood.

A drop of rain hit her forehead, followed by another on her arm. She dragged a foot in the wood chips on her next pass, wanting to escape before it started raining in earnest.

Then she remembered Julia's love for playing in the rain. How she'd stay out until she was soaked to the skin and say it was no different from taking a shower except for the clothes.

A moment later a steady drizzle began to fall from the sky, wetting Abigail's skin, her clothes. She extended her legs and leaned back again until her arms straightened. Then she blinked up at the sky.

It was time to move on, to forgive herself. She needed to lay it down and let Jesus take it, stop trying to make it right. Because no column could erase the past.

Reagan was right. She was tired of dragging a load of guilt. The stories had alleviated the feeling, but only temporarily. Abigail was ready for a permanent fix. She was tired of feeling restless. She wanted peace, and she wouldn't have it until she found redemption. She'd spent most of her life seeking self-redemption instead of Truth. Redemption was free; how had she forgotten that?

You can have it, God. I'm giving it to you, and I'm not taking it back. I can't work my way to redemption, and I don't need to when you already did that for me.

She didn't know what that meant for the future of her career and didn't care at the moment. She was making the choice to forgive herself and was going to move forward however God wanted her to. Abigail began pumping her legs, working higher and higher until she reached the pinnacle, then she leaned back in the rain and smiled.

37

Wade's fork scraped across his plate, gathering the last mound of macaroni and cheese. "It's good, Maddy," he said, breaking the silence that had strung on for several minutes. There'd been a lot of that lately. Silence.

"Abigail taught me."

Her name still sucked the air from his lungs. After the first couple days without her, Maddy hadn't brought her up again. Instead, she'd suffered in silence the rest of the week, a persistent frown etched between her brows. Greta, who'd looked after Maddy all week, had expressed concern.

Wade didn't know what to do. He yearned to see her smile again, had brought home a pack of Twizzlers the day before. But there weren't enough Twizzlers in the world to cheer her up right now.

It was easier to stay busy than to see her forlorn. And between cutting out the cantankerous bulls from the cows, moving the cattle, and planning for their move, there hadn't been time for anything but work.

And thinking of Abigail.

He'd thought staying busy would make the time pass quickly. Instead, the week had felt like a month. A long, slow, painful month.

He'd begun the process of putting his ranch on the market. Dylan had reluctantly agreed to buy his cattle and hire Pee Wee to cover the extra head. He still had to figure what to do about the house Miss Lucy rented. He couldn't leave her homeless, even if she was a relation of Abigail's.

"You need to sign a form for school." Maddy pushed her macaroni around the plate.

"What kind of form?"

"Field trip. To the Western Heritage Center on Tuesday."

"That's in Billings."

Maddy nodded even as Wade's mood dropped to an all-time low. Billings was a city. Too many people. Too big a chance of being recognized.

"You know you can't go," he said gently.

Maddy lowered her fork. "Why not?"

"We've been through this a million times."

"You never let me go anywhere!"

Wade swallowed. "We're going somewhere real soon."

Her brows knotted together. "I don't want to move! We just fixed my room, and I love it here! Why can't we be like normal people?"

She looked so much like Lizzie he wanted to scream. Instead, all his fight drained out, leaving him limp as a wet rag. "Don't have a choice, Maddy."

"If I can't go to Billings, how are we gonna travel halfway across the country?"

"Very carefully."

Her eyes filled with tears. Her lip trembled. "I want Abigail to come back."

He could feel his heart breaking in two. He wanted her back, too, God help him. "She's not who we thought she was, Maddy."

Her nostrils flared. "Stop saying that! She loved us; I know she did!" She shoved her chair back abruptly and ran toward the stairs.

Wade watched her go, wondering if he should stop her. If he should sit her down for a talk or let her blow off some steam.

Abigail would know what to do.

He scowled. He was sick and tired of thinking of Abigail. Sick of wanting her.

Wade put his plate in the sink. "Going out to the barn," he called up the stairs. When Maddy didn't reply, he went to put on his boots and hat.

Wade had found a calf with pneumonia on his swing through Wolf Ridge that day. He'd treated her, but he needed to check on her before he fell into bed, and he wanted to be dog-tired before he did that. It was his only hope for keeping his thoughts of Abigail at bay.

The cool air was welcome, and he drew in a deep breath as he made his way across the yard. Inhaling hurt his chest these days. And it had nothing to do with the love pat he'd received from an ornery bull earlier.

He kept telling himself it would get better, that if he worked hard enough, long enough, he'd feel better. Or at least be too busy to feel. But time in a saddle was nothing but a slow cooker for memories. They simmered in his mind for hour upon hour until he thought he'd go mad.

The crunch of gravel and low hum of an engine stopped him before he entered the barn. Headlights he hadn't noticed before pointed his direction, and moments later Dylan's truck pulled alongside the barn.

His friend shut off the engine and exited the truck. "Still working?"

"Sick calf."

Dylan rounded the truck in his stiff new jeans, a white collared shirt, and a snazzy black vest. "Let's go check on her, then we can get Maddy and go."

"Go where?"

"Chuckwagon."

Wade entered the barn and flipped on the lights. "Never said I'd go." Truth was, he'd even forgotten it was Saturday. Every day blurred right into the next.

"Didn't say you wouldn't." Dylan followed. The spicy smell of his cologne filled up the space, making one of his horses sneeze.

"I'm tired. When I finish here, I'm hitting

the hay." He was pretty sure he wouldn't lie awake for hours tonight. At some point the body had to surrender.

"Think of Maddy, at least. She could use some fun."

"Take her then." He squatted by the calf. She looked less droopy. The Nuflor was working—her fever was down. From a few feet away, the mother mooed softly.

"You need to hang around something on two legs for a change, buddy."

"When I need your advice, I'll ask for it." No way was he going out. Every time he did he got the same thing.

Where's Abigail been hiding? Haven't seen her around in a while. She left? Oh, I was hoping she'd stay, such a nice girl. We're sure going to miss her 'round here.

Apparently she hadn't just captivated him but the whole town of Moose Creek. Made him feel a little less foolish. Least he wasn't the only one she'd duped.

Wade checked the hay. Dry, clean. No sign of moisture in the air. The calf would eat soon. Already her eyes were brighter, more alert.

"It was a low blow," Dylan said. "What

Abigail did . . . I don't get it either. But she had real feelings for you. You'd have to be blind not to see it."

Wade grunted. Those kinds of feelings he could do without.

"From what you said, she didn't come here intending—"

"She exploited us. All I need to know." Come moving day, wouldn't matter why she'd done it. Wouldn't matter that she'd supposedly had feelings for him, that he'd loved her. All that mattered was that their life in Moose Creek was over, and it was all Abigail's fault.

Okay, and his own. How had he been stupid enough to fall prey to her feminine wiles? Might be just a country cowboy, but he thought he was savvier than that.

"I wish you wouldn't move. She said she canceled the article."

"And I should trust her? Even if she did, how can I know she'll keep her mouth shut? I have Maddy to consider."

"Last I checked, Maddy wanted to stay."

What did Dylan know about parenthood? "I have to protect her—it's my job." One he'd failed too many times before.

"Abigail's a respected journalist, by all

accounts. Not like she works for some celebrity rag. You know, maybe her boss pressured her; did ya think of that?"

Dylan's defense of her was getting under Wade's skin. He gave the calf one last stroke and rose to his feet. "Don't care about her excuses. She hurt my daughter. You weren't here when Maddy was bawling her eyes out. She had it in her head Abigail was going to be her new mom."

Dylan pocketed his hands. "And you had it in your head she was going to be your new wife."

Did he have to look so smug? Wade gave his hat a sharp tug, clenched his teeth until his jaw ached.

"Not faulting you for that, friend."

Wade was finding it hard to move on past the memories when he couldn't so much as look across the table without seeing Abigail's face. She was all around him. Under the weeping willow, in the barn, beside him on the swing. That would all change soon.

"You know, you weren't all that happy with Lizzie," Dylan said. "Not really. Not like you were with Abigail."

"It wasn't real. Not to her."

"That night at the Chuckwagon when you danced with her—the way she looked at you? I was jealous, man. For the first time in a long time . . . I wanted that too."

"That's real rich, coming from you."

"I may run through women like a bull through barbed wire, but I'm smart enough to know this: you don't throw away something like that."

He hadn't thrown it away. Abigail had stolen it, for all the good it had done her. Even if Dylan was right, there was nothing to show for Abigail's time here but broken hearts.

"Okay." Dylan held up his hands, surrendering. "I'm done."

"'Bout time."

"Sure you don't want to go? Might help to get your mind on something else."

"Got plenty on my mind." Abigail just took up the other 95 percent.

"Lots of women happy to save you a dance . . ."

The only woman he wanted wouldn't be there. "No thanks."

Dylan measured Wade's resolve, then sighed hard. "All right. I tried." He shook his head. "Ladies are going to be disappointed . . ."

"They'll get over it." Wade closed the stall door and followed Dylan from the barn.

"Care if I ask Maddy?" Dylan said.

"Won't she put a damper on your love life?"

"Kidding me? Women love a man with a kid." He flashed his dimple.

Dylan wasn't fooling anyone. The guy adored Maddy, and his time with her was short. Besides, he was right. His daughter could use a little fun. Her smile seemed to have disappeared with Abigail.

"Be my guest."

Ten minutes later Maddy followed Dylan out the door, tossing Wade a petulant good-bye. He was glad she was going. Dylan would have her spinning around the floor, forgetting her troubles in minutes.

But after the door closed, after the truck rumbled down the drive, the house felt empty. Empty and quiet. He'd get some packing done while she was gone. Maddy hadn't even started on her room, and he hadn't had the gumption to make her do it.

Even his own feet dragged on the steps, despite his plan. Every time he went in her room, he thought of Abigail. It was impossible not to, with the freshly painted walls, the lime green accents, the horse border, all those feminine touches she'd left behind. She'd spent so much time with Maddy.

What you paid her for, Ryan.

Dylan's words came back to him. Was his friend right about Abigail? Despite all she'd done, he wanted to believe it. Wanted to believe everything she'd said was true, that everything she'd done was genuine, that every touch had been sincere.

He stopped on the threshold of Maddy's room. The redecorating was only a tiny portion of what Abigail had done. She'd taught Maddy to cook, had taken her shopping, had done all the things a mother did with a daughter. She'd brought out the spunk in Maddy, had made him see his daughter's need for him, had made him believe in himself again. He'd finally been able to put his past behind him and get things straight with God. All because of Abigail.

Wade looked across the hall. The door to Abigail's room was drawn. Abigail's room—he still thought of it that way. He hadn't been able to bring himself to pack up that room yet. Was hoping the smell of her would be gone by the time he finally did.

But now he was drawn inexplicably to the room. He reached for the handle and pushed the door. It squeaked as it yawned open. He smelled her fragrance as he entered, and before he could stop himself, he drew in a lungful, allowing himself to savor the smell.

Her bed was made, not a lump or wrinkle in sight. The floor was bare, the dresser bare. There was nothing left of Abigail.

Then his eyes swept across the desk and stuck there. He frowned, walked toward the desk, and reached out for the stack of money. He counted the bills. She'd left every dime he'd paid her. Every dime.

Just when he thought he had her all figured out . . .

Dylan's words came back to him now, ringing truer now. Was it possible she had come here innocently? That she hadn't known who he was until she was living under his roof? Was it possible she'd fallen for him, despite her better judgment?

Isn't that what happened to you? She'd come right into his home and stolen his heart before he could turn around twice.

Maybe what Dylan said was true. Maybe she did love him. Maybe her heart was broken too.

He remembered the look on her face in the barn when he'd confronted her. He hadn't been able to see it at the time for his anger. Hadn't let himself remember it until now. The way her eyes had filled with fear and then desperation.

The words he'd flung at her from across the barn haunted him now. *You get extra points for stringing me along?* He winced now at his cruelty. Couldn't he have given her the benefit of the doubt? Wade forked his fingers through his hair. Had he ruined everything? Abigail must hate him.

Instead of hearing her out, he'd cut her off, then sent her packing.

"No, please"—the tears that had sparkled in her eyes tormented him now. *"I can't just leave. I love you."*

He'd cut her off again, like her profession of love was irrelevant, unwanted. And then he'd threatened her with telling Maddy.

He'd been a jerk. A first-class jerk. And she must realize it by now. She hadn't attempted to call in days, four to be exact. Could he blame her?

If he closed his eyes, he could still feel her hair against the curve of his neck, still feel her breath against his skin, still smell the sweet fragrance of sunshine and flowers.

He remembered the way she looked wearing his hat, remembered the warmth of her in his arms as they danced, their first kiss in the barn when he'd been rocked by the riot she'd caused inside him. There was nothing he didn't remember. Including the way she looked at him, like he hung the moon and the stars. It was the look Dylan referred to, the one that convinced his friend her feelings were real.

Wade would give anything to have her here now, looking at him like that. *Face it, Ryan, you miss her bad*. Regardless of everything Abigail might've done, regardless of her poor judgment, regardless of the fact that she'd hurt him and Maddy . . .

Wade loved her. He loved the way she was with his daughter. He loved the way she looked at him, the way she fit into his arms like she was made to be there. He loved the way she never gave up. Not on the garden, not on Maddy, and not on him. He loved every single thing about her, even the way she twisted that ring when she was nervous or uncomfortable.

He wished now he'd answered his phone all those times she'd called. He'd been stubborn as a bull. Hadn't given Abigail a chance to speak before she left and hadn't given her a chance to explain in the week since she'd been gone.

He'd made assumptions. But he'd had it all wrong.

He dropped into the desk chair. But what could he do about it now? He'd thrown away their relationship that day in the barn. He'd ripped her story from underneath her, in essence killing something that obviously mattered a great deal to her: the magazine. Her article about him had been her last hope, and he'd taken that from her so quickly, so easily. She didn't deserve that, not after everything she'd done for them.

He popped to his feet and paced. *How do I fix this mess, God?* Even if he agreed to the article, it was surely too late to include it now. Abigail had no doubt gone back to Chicago and worked her tail end off to change the cover and column in time. And she'd said it was the last issue, barring a miracle.

Barring a miracle.

Didn't he have everything he needed to save Abigail, save her magazine? But if he saved the magazine, he also saved her job. And if he saved her job, she'd be lost to him.

He considered the cost. Was he willing to pay it, willing to do anything for the woman who'd stolen his heart—even if it meant losing her?

38

Chatter buzzed around Abigail and her mom from their booth table. She scanned the restaurant they'd dined at many times and wondered why, for the first time, she felt out of place. She'd been back in Chicago for a week and a half, but somehow it seemed much longer.

Outside, darkness was falling against the Chicago skyline. Across the restaurant, a cheer rose from the enclosed bar as the patrons watched the Cubs score a run on the flat-screen TV.

"Eat something," her mom said.

"I am." Abigail realized belatedly she'd

only been pushing the salad greens around. She forked a cucumber and slid it into her mouth.

"You haven't heard a word I've said."

Abigail thought about disputing the statement, but who was she kidding?

"You have a headache? I have some Tylenol."

"I'm fine." Truth was, strange as it sounded, her hypertension symptoms were better. She hadn't had a headache in three days, and her palpitations were less frequent. Maybe her past had weighed on her more heavily than she'd thought.

At least something was better.

"Are you ever going to tell me what happened in Montana?" her mom asked.

Abigail flashed her a no-trespassing look, then forked another bite of the salad. She was tired of thinking about Wade. The memories only made her ache for what she couldn't have.

"All right." Her mom waved her hand. "I'll just be honest. Reagan already told me everything."

"Surprise, surprise."

"I should've warned you about J. W. I mean, heaven knows he's got cowboy charisma galore and looks that could stop rush-hour traffic on the Eisenhower."

Abigail groaned. "Moooom . . ."

"Well, I'm old, not dead, honey." She sipped her French onion soup from the side of her spoon.

"I do not want to talk about this." Not with her mom or Reagan or anyone else. Abigail set down her fork and rubbed her temple. She was done stuffing food into her mouth that she didn't even taste.

"Fine." Her mom wiped her mouth on the starchy white napkin. "Let's talk about what you're going to do next."

"Show up at the office next week and start packing up, like everyone else." She hated the thought of facing everyone again after letting them all down. It was going to be a long week.

"I mean after that."

In the last week she'd made a decision that had been long in coming. Her heart was no longer in writing, certainly not in exposés. She'd barely managed to finish the simple travel article on Moose Creek.

Simple, my fanny.

"I've done a lot of praying about it, Mom, and I've decided to give up writing. I just don't have that burning desire anymore. My reasons for writing are gone, and I'm feeling led toward something else. I think I want to be a teacher."

Her mom nodded slowly, studying her face. "Okay . . . that's not completely unexpected. You know I'll support you in whatever you choose to do."

Her mother touched her hand, which, Abigail realized, was now balled into a fist around her poor defenseless napkin.

"Is that what all this tension is about? Your career? You've dreaded telling me?"

Abigail wished she could blame it on that. Truth was, she felt total peace about that decision.

"You can't write, you're not eating, and judging by the Jones bags under your eyes, you're not sleeping much either. A few months with Aunt Lucy was supposed to give you a break, but instead you've come back broken."

"Very poetic, Mom." Had she thought her mom wouldn't notice? Abigail had always been driven. Couldn't wait to get to the next story. Now she wondered how she could even take her next breath.

"Honey, talk to me."

Abigail deliberately inhaled, just to prove she could. The tangy smell of balsamic vinaigrette turned her stomach, and she pushed her plate away. "I don't know where to start."

"Are you in love with J. W.?"

"Wade."

"What?"

"He goes by Wade." She tossed her napkin on her plate. "Oh, what does it matter? Wade, J. W. . . . it isn't like I'll be addressing him anytime soon."

"If he loves you, honey, he'll forgive you."

"It's not that simple. He and Maddy are leaving their home because of me. Everything he said was true."

"You were only doing your job. You're the Truthseeker. At least, you were."

"If the truth hurts innocent people, what good is it?" That, in a nutshell, was what bothered her so much. "My column was for exposing bad people who did bad things. But Wade didn't do anything wrong, Mom. On the contrary, he only did what was best for his daughter after the awful experience of losing his wife. That article—no matter how well written—was nothing but tabloid trash, and I'm glad it wasn't published."

"Abigail . . ."

Now that she'd stated it so bluntly, she knew it was the truth. "No, Mom. My column was for exposing wrongs. Well, *I'm* the one who was wrong. Wrong for spotlighting an innocent person's private pain."

Her eyes burned, and she blinked them clear. A familiar ache swelled in her throat. *Jesus, how can there be any tears left?*

"I'm sorry I put you in that position." Her mom's green eyes turned down at the corners.

Abigail dabbed her eyes with the napkin. "It's my fault."

"You were only trying to save *Viewpoint*. Maybe there's a way to fix things between you and Wade."

Abigail shook her head. "That's not my decision. And I feel selfish for dwelling on my own misery when so many people have lost their jobs because of me. You. Riley—she doesn't even get child support, and now she'll have no income either. Warren's fighting lung cancer and needs insurance, not to mention his salary. Evelyn's the sole supporter of her elderly mother. I could go on and on."

The server came and removed their dinnerware. Abigail drained the last of her soda and pulled out her credit card.

"Know what we need?" Her mom dabbed her lips with the napkin. "A girls' day out. It'll get your mind off your troubles. Let's do something fun, maybe tomorrow?"

Abigail shrugged. "Sure."

"We can invite Reagan if she's not on call."

"I guess the theater's out then."

"I'll plan the whole day, and it'll be a surprise. How's that?"

Abigail reached deep and pulled out a smile. "Sounds fun, Mom." She supposed anything was better than sitting around her apartment with memories of Wade swimming around her head.

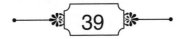

39

Abigail read the sign. *Midwestern Rodeo Grounds*.

They'd driven all this way for a *rodeo*?

"A rodeo!" Reagan said in an odd high-pitched tone from the backseat of their mom's car. "How fun!"

More like torture. Abigail swallowed the feelings that clogged her throat as her mom found a parking space. She'd wondered what her mom had up her sleeve when they'd headed north out of Chicago and crossed the Wisconsin border, then turned off at the tiny town of Manawa.

What was her mom thinking? Today

was supposed to be about getting away, forgetting her troubles. Didn't her mother know her troubles centered around a cowboy, and a rodeo would only remind her of all she'd lost?

"What do you think, girls?" her mom asked as they exited the car. "I surprise you?"

"Sure did." Abigail tried to season her words with enthusiasm.

"Who knew there was a rodeo so close to Chicago?" Reagan said.

Not Abigail. She followed her mom and Reagan toward the outdoor arena entrance. *You can do this. It's just a rodeo.* Just a few dozen cowboys showing their stuff. Soon she'd be in the car, headed back to her own world. She sucked in a deep breath for courage and was assaulted instead with familiar smells. The loamy smell of dirt. The raw smells of leather and horseflesh. The sweet scent of fresh hay.

Her heart seemed to stutter in response, and she stopped. A woman smacked into her back.

"Sorry," she muttered, stepping aside. She told herself to keep walking, to follow her mom and sister, but her feet seemed planted to the ground.

The sounds were coming now too. The country and western music blaring over the speakers. The whinny of a horse. The clopping of horses' feet.

Reagan turned and noticed Abigail had fallen behind. "Come on, Abs," she called.

Reagan worked back through the crowd, their mom on her heels.

"What's wrong?" Mom asked.

"I'm sorry, Mom. I can't go in there." She hated to ruin their fun day out, but this wasn't her idea of fun. Not anywhere close.

Her mom looked pained. "Oh, Abigail."

"It's just a rodeo, Abs," Reagan said.

But it wasn't. It was a walk down memory lane. A painful walk, one she didn't want to take today or any day soon.

"You two go on. I'll just wait in the car."

"Don't be silly! Come on, it'll be fun." Reagan took her arm, and the crowd jostled them toward the entrance. "We'll forget your diet for the day and split a funnel cake."

Sure, tempt her with food. Reagan was right, though. She was being a total sissy. It was just a rodeo. If she couldn't handle seeing a bunch of cowboy hats and trophy buckles, she wasn't worth her salt.

They hit the funnel cake stand first, then

made their way to the aluminum bleach-
ers. The sweet confection was divine, but
once it hit Abigail's stomach, a touch of
nausea set in.

They watched the bareback bronc riding,
the team roping, the steer wrestling. Every
event reminded her of something that had
happened over the summer. Watching
Wade during branding her first day at the
ranch, sitting tall and confident in his saddle. Wade sweeping her into his arms and
setting her on Ace after her fall. Dancing in
his arms that first night at the Chuckwagon.
She chided herself for her wayward thoughts
and forced her mind back to the present.

By the time two hours had passed, she
was more than eager to go home. It was
getting late. They had a long drive home
and church in the morning. "Let's leave
early," she said. "Beat the traffic out."

"There's only one event left," Reagan
said. "The best part—the bull riding."

Since when had Reagan cared about
rodeos? Abigail stifled a sigh. She'd made
it this long, she supposed she could en-
dure one more event.

One by one bulls busted from the chute,
twisting their bodies and bucking the

cowboys as the seconds ticked off time. Cowboy after cowboy hit the dirt hard. Abigail winced every time, recalling too easily her fall from Trinket and the subsequent headache. Miraculously, each cowboy got up, dusted off his hat, and exited without injury.

"Well, not quite the ride Cody wanted," the announcer said. "Let's hear it for Cody Langley!" The crowd applauded.

"Now we're ready to gear up for our last rider, and, folks, it's gonna be a doozy. Last bull out of the chute tonight is our infamous Maaaaad Hornet!"

The crowd cheered. Abigail gathered her purse, ready to leave. *Thank You, God, that it's almost over.*

The announcer continued. "Now, I always worry twice about anybody put on the back of Maaaaad Hornet. But I ain't too worried this time. I ain't worried 'cause we got a real pro riding tonight."

"Let's go now," Abigail said to her mom. "The parking lot will be a mess."

"I want to see the last rider," Reagan said.

Abigail slumped back in the seat, sighing. "Y'all ain't gonna believe this, but we got a real special treat for you tonight: a nationally renowned cowboy who's been off the circuit waaaay too long. Please welcome back . . . J. W. Ryan!"

The name snagged Abigail's full attention. She peered around the head in front of her to the chute, far away, where a cowboy lowered himself onto Mad Hornet. She must have heard wrong. Wade wouldn't show his face in public, not like this. She was losing her marbles.

Still, her heart beat wildly in her chest. The rider was broad and sturdy looking, even on the back of the notorious bull. She was aware of the crowd going mad, cheering wildly.

Was it him? Abigail squinted, focused on the cowboy. Fawn hat, black vest, fawn chaps, like the ones she'd seen him wear so many times. The cowboy wrapped the rope around his wrist, then gave his brim a sharp tug. And Abigail knew. That was his tug.

"That's him," she whispered.

What was Wade doing here? He shouldn't be in such a public place, shouldn't be risking his privacy.

The bull shot from the chute.

Shouldn't be risking his life. Abigail squeezed the straps of her purse. *Oh, God, keep him safe!* What was he doing on that bull? It had been four years.

The bull lived up to his name. He writhed and twisted, bucked and bounced. Wade's hat went flying. His body undulated with sudden jerks. One bare hand waved overhead, the other held tightly to the rope.

"Hang on," she whispered. "Hang on."

The seconds passed in slow motion. Each jolt of the bull sent shocks of panic through Abigail. She held her breath, waiting for the inevitable fall. She heard the announcer counting off the seconds, wished they'd go faster.

Eight seconds. Mad Hornet bucked, then made a sudden twist to the right. Then Wade was falling.

Abigail's fingers bit into her palms. He hit the ground hard. She winced at the sudden impact.

The rodeo clown distracted Mad Hornet, but Abigail's eyes were on Wade's still form. *Move, Wade!*

Then he shifted. He pulled himself to his feet, collected his hat, and exited the floor. Abigail let out her breath.

"You can breathe now," Reagan said. "He's fine."

Abigail set her hand against her aching chest. "Why's he—" She looked at her mom, at Reagan. "Why are we—"

"That's something you need to ask him," her mom said.

Why was he here? Didn't he know the media would be all over him? There were TV reporters here. She'd seen the vans in the parking lot. He'd never get back to Moose Creek undiscovered.

"Like, *now*, Abs." Reagan stood. "Come on." They squeezed their way down the row.

The announcer continued. "There you have it, folks; he's a man used to winning, and tonight's no different! Let's hear it for J. W. Ryan!" The crowd roared.

If nothing else, maybe they could shield Wade from the reporters. Why, oh, why had he come here? She caught snatches of conversation in the stands. Everyone was talking about J. W. Ryan, ignoring the announcer who was talking about awards.

Abigail followed her mom and Reagan down the stands and circled the arena to an entrance that said *Cowboys and Cowgirls*.

"They won't let us in," Abigail said.

But the man at the gate ushered them through. They followed the crowd of cowboys heading toward a rail that overlooked the arena. A mass of people, some with cameras, formed a throng, and she knew Wade was at the center.

"Are you back on the circuit, J. W.?"

"Where've you been the last four years?"

The reporters were relentless, yelling their questions across the heads of admiring cowboys. They'd never get in there.

Two men in orange vests pushed into the crowd. "All right, y'all, break it up! Stand back!"

"Give the man room to breathe!"

The crowd parted, drew back, but the videographers pushed to the front, still barraging him with questions.

"Hold it down now!" a cowboy shouted. "Give the man a chance to speak."

The reporters quieted. Cameras flashed, one after another.

Abigail pushed through the cowboys in front of her, needing to get to him, somehow save him from those selfish reporters. When she reached the front, the employee held her back with an outstretched arm just as Wade's eyes found hers.

His eyes locked on hers, softened. His stilted smile relaxed.

And then he spoke. "Know y'all are shocked to see me." His familiar Texas drawl was the sweetest sound. "Thanks for the friendly welcome." He rubbed his backside. "Your bull gave me a good, hard ride."

The crowd chuckled.

"Where ya been hiding, Mr. Ryan?" a reporter shouted.

His lips tilted. Flashes fired. "Getting to that in a minute." He found Abigail's gaze once again.

Her breath caught and held. *What are you doing? Why are you doing this?*

"Came out today to make an announcement," Wade said. "Know y'all have a bunch of questions, and I'll answer them. Not today though."

The crowd groaned. A reporter swore.

"Are you living here in Wisconsin?"

"I'll answer that question and a lot more real soon. Giving an exclusive interview to *Viewpoint Magazine*. It'll be in their October issue. Don't mean to tease, but that's the announcement I came to make. Promise all your questions'll be answered in that interview."

Why had he said that? The magazine was closing—there wouldn't even be an October issue.

He made eye contact with a few nearby cowboys. "I gotta run. Been nice jawin' with y'all." He started toward the exit, toward her. The security and several big cowboys held the reporters off.

Wade stopped when he reached her. His gaze burned into hers as he reached out. Abigail put her hand in his, then he turned and led her through the crowd. Her mind spun as they scrambled for the exit. What was going on? Against the back wall, Reagan and Mom watched them pass, smiling through tears. *They knew.*

"Come on." Wade pulled her down a hall and out another exit where a young cowboy stood by a big brown horse.

"Thanks, buddy," Wade said to the guy. "We'll have him back soon."

"Take your time, Mr. Ryan."

Wade swept Abigail off her feet and set her in the saddle. Seconds later he was behind her, nudging the horse to a gallop.

40

Abigail clutched Wade's arms as the horse bolted off.

"Hang on," he said.

She didn't know where he was taking her—didn't care where he was going. She was with Wade, and that was all that mattered.

They galloped through town, took a turn down a side road. After they'd ridden awhile, she felt him turn in the saddle.

"Think we lost them." He slowed the horse a bit. "There's a park up ahead. Doing okay?"

She nodded. "Yeah."

He nudged the horse into a gallop, and the scenery blurred past. Abigail held on tightly. When they reached the wooded park, he slowed, guiding the horse deeper into the park through a copse of towering evergreens. They emerged by a riverbank.

"Whoa." He pulled back. When the horse stopped, Wade dropped the reins. "Come sit by the river with me."

He dismounted, then helped Abigail from the horse. She followed him, the bed of pine needles shushing their footsteps. When they reached the grassy shoreline, they sank down into its softness.

She waited, watching him. She couldn't take her eyes from him. Was afraid if she did, he'd disappear, turn out to be a figment of her imagination. "Are we safe here?" she asked. "What if the reporters followed us?"

"Had some friends detain them. They'll find me after the interview anyway."

If *Viewpoint* published his interview, the media would be all over Moose Creek. She couldn't let him sacrifice his privacy. It was too much. "No, Wade."

"It's already done. Worked it out with your mom. I want to do this."

"But your privacy . . . Maddy."

"I'm done hiding." He looked at her, his blue eyes intense. "I want to do this . . . for you, Abby. I don't expect anything in return."

What did that mean? He didn't want her anymore? When he looked away, she was suddenly uncertain and afraid. Afraid all this hadn't been about them at all. Had she read too much into his grand gesture?

She wanted to reach out and touch him. Wished he would take her into his arms. But instead he stared over the water that rippled past.

"I want to tell you about Lizzie," he said finally.

You don't have to, she was about to say. But the purpose in his voice stopped her. It was something he needed to do.

"Go ahead," she said.

He pulled his knees up and rested his forearms on them. "I told you before that we were happy in the beginning, but that something happened after Maddy was born. Lizzie became depressed, agitated. It was subtle at first, but it got worse as the years passed. I begged her to see a doctor."

"She wouldn't go?"

Wade shook his head. "Didn't believe in drugs, and after a while she blamed her moods on me."

The sadness in his voice made her want to wrap her arms around him. Instead, she wrapped them around her knees. "Was it postpartum depression?"

"I think so. She was always the jealous sort, but after Maddy was born, it got out of hand. She imagined I was cheating on her. But it wasn't true. Even in the darkest days of our marriage, I never touched another woman, despite how the tabloids made it look." He looked at her as if he needed her to understand.

His vulnerability made her melt. "I believe you. You're not that kind of man."

Seemingly satisfied, he looked back out over the river. "Lizzie had a fit whenever I went out. But I had to get out of there sometimes—away from the dark cloud that hung over our house, over our relationship. It was suffocating. She stopped going anywhere by the time Maddy was a toddler. Our relationship was . . . strained. I almost took Maddy and left a few times, but I still loved Lizzie, worried about what would happen if we left."

"What about her family?"

"They were messed up, dysfunctional. Never even came to her funeral."

"That's awful."

"Our life looked so enchanting, but it was just painful and lonely. The day Lizzie died, I'd placed first in the qualifying rounds, and I was in the mood to celebrate. Came home, showered, begged Lizzie to come. I was meeting Dylan and a bunch of friends for supper at a local hangout.

"I was high on success when I came home, thought I had a chance of convincing Lizzie to go." He shook his head. "She was mad that I wanted to go out. When she wouldn't go, I offered to take Maddy, but she started making accusations about a certain cowgirl on the circuit. I'd admitted to Lizzie at one point that Celeste had made overtures. I never encouraged the woman, but Lizzie didn't believe me."

She could feel his desperation to make his wife believe him, and her heart ached for him. "Must've been frustrating."

"I was making more money rodeoing than I ever dreamed, but all Lizzie wanted was to move away and start a ranch somewhere. I kept putting her off, wanted to earn as much as I could while I was in my prime.

"We had a huge fight that night. I left angry and stayed out late. When I got home, Lizzie was asleep on the couch. I saw her in the darkness, thought about carrying her to bed, but I was still mad. I checked on Maddy and went to bed."

She could see the pain on his face and wanted to soothe him with a touch but wasn't sure it would be welcomed.

"I woke early," he continued. "And when I went into the living room . . ." He swallowed hard. "She was gone. There was an empty pill bottle on the floor. The woman refused to take medication to help her, but took a whole bottle to kill herself." His jaw worked.

Abigail felt his sorrow as her own. What a tragic thing to experience. "I'm so sorry."

"Called for help, but it was too late. If I'd checked on her when I came in, maybe . . ."

She set a hand on his arm. "Don't. It's not your fault. She was ill, Wade. She needed help and refused it. You can't blame yourself."

He drew in a breath and blew it out. "All hell broke loose after that. I was in shock, had Maddy to take care of—a little girl who'd just lost her mommy. Our house-keeper had heard us arguing the night before, and that caused speculation—" He shook his head.

Abigail's eyes burned at the pain in his voice. "I'm sorry. That's so unfair. It must've been horrible."

"By the time I was cleared, I just wanted to take Maddy and disappear. So I looked into property in Moose Creek. Had no ties there or anything that would leave a trail. The property was on the market at the right time, and I bought it."

"Do you ever regret leaving Texas? Leaving everything behind?"

"I brought the only thing that mattered. Moose Creek was out of touch with celebrity gossip, and the few who recognized me respected Dylan's grandfather enough to keep quiet. They gave us a soft place to fall."

Just what he and Maddy needed at the time. "Does Maddy know the truth?"

"After we settled in Montana, I told her. Didn't want her finding out some other way, and I didn't want her thinking Lizzie didn't love her."

"It's good that she knows." It would make it easier on her when the interview hit the stands.

It hit her then that Wade had finally told her, that he trusted her enough to reveal that wound. That alone meant the world. "Thank you for telling me, Wade. I know it wasn't easy."

Wade tugged his hat, a familiar move that set her heart aflutter. "I wanted to."

He looked at her again, and she wanted to drown in the warm pool of his eyes, wanted to dive right in there and wallow around for an eternity or two.

"I was a jerk that last day at the ranch. Jumped to conclusions, didn't give you a chance to explain—"

He had it all wrong. "No, Wade. I'm the one who's sorry—so sorry for hurting you and Maddy. I never meant to, it's the last thing I wanted to—"

"Hush, Abby." He reached out, laid his palm on her cheek.

She couldn't have spoken if she'd wanted to. His touch felt so good; she hadn't known how much she'd missed it until that second.

And the way he was looking at her now . . . She heard everything those eyes said, and she soaked it all in. Her lungs were ready to explode, her heart was ready to burst from her chest.

When he leaned toward her, she forgot everything. Everything but his touch. His lips found hers, brushed gently across them. They were warm and soft and everything she remembered. She touched his face, loving the familiar angles, the rough feel of his jaw.

Could he have forgiven her? Could he love her? *Please, God*. Being with him felt so right. Like she was home in her cowboy's arms.

She buried her fingers in his hair, dislodging his hat. He pulled her closer, and she relished his warmth, his strength. She couldn't get close enough. She wanted all of him and so much more. Abigail drew in a breath and savored the familiar scent of him. Heaven.

When Wade pulled away, she was breathless. His arms came around her waist, and he pulled her into him. "Ah, Abby, I've missed you so much."

Abigail leaned into his strength. It felt so good to be in his arms again. Her eyes burned with relief, and she closed them.

"Me too." The words didn't begin to describe the ache of sheer longing. She'd missed him so much. His strong hands, his gentle touch, his passionate kisses. She held on tight, not willing to let him go again.

He tipped her chin up and rested his forehead against hers. "I love you, Abigail Jones," he whispered.

"Oh, Wade." Maybe she shouldn't have needed the words, but she did. They were like fresh water for her thirsty soul. "I love you too. I've missed you something fierce. You have no idea."

"'Fraid I do." He brushed her lips, once, twice, then pulled her close.

Abigail couldn't lose the smile on her face, even when a tear made its way down her cheek. She was home, right where she belonged, and she wasn't going anywhere. But there was more to say. A lot had changed.

She hoped he wouldn't be angry that he'd saved a magazine she didn't work for anymore. It had never been her job she'd cared about.

"I learned some things about myself and about God and about the path my career's taken. I've done a lot of praying about this and—" *Just say it.* "I'm finished writing. I'm going to be a teacher."

"That so . . ."

"My reasons for writing that column were tied to my past. And now that it's resolved, the desire is just . . . gone."

"Sad about that?"

"No." Abigail leaned back, looked at him. "I'm finally discovering who I am."

He brushed the tear from her face. "I kinda like who you are." The way Wade gazed at her now was enough to make her fall in love all over again. "You'll make a great teacher, Abby."

"If you want to change your mind about the exclusive—"

He shook his head. "I know saving the magazine was never about keeping your job." He brushed her hair behind her ears. "Guess you'll be going back to school, getting a part-time job . . ."

"Something like that."

He gazed lovingly into her eyes. "You know, Montana State isn't far from my place. And I know a little girl who'd like her nanny back."

His invitation made her smile. "That sounds appealing." But she wanted so much more.

His eyes, the color of faded denim, were the softest of caresses. "Much as Maddy liked you as her nanny, she was really hoping for a mom." There was a question in his eyes.

Something bubbled up inside, something that felt like joy and peace and rightness all blended into one happy cocktail. "Really?" She felt the fresh sting of tears. Abigail ran her thumb over his lower lip.

He pressed a kiss to the pad of her thumb. "The position comes with a husband, though. Guy used to be a big-shot celebrity; now he's just a humble rancher."

She smiled through her tears. "I like humble ranchers."

Wade had never looked more serious. "I'm talking about forever, Abby. Marriage and Maddy and ranching, maybe even another baby or two . . ."

"Only two?"

"You'd have to move to the back of beyond. Leave your home, your city, your family . . ."

She shook her head. "The whole time

I've been in Chicago, all I thought about was being back in Moose Creek with you and Maddy. It's all I want." She framed his face. "*You're* all I want."

He lowered his face, and she was lost in his kiss. Lost in his love. His touch stirred her in ways she'd never experienced, this cowboy of hers, and she was going to lean on him for the rest of her life. She couldn't think of a more capable man to put her trust in.

He kissed the tip of her nose, then drew her into an embrace. "We should get back," he whispered a few moments later. "Your family will be wondering what I did with you."

Abigail wanted him to herself for a little while—was that too much to ask? But he was right.

After they saddled up, he nudged the horse into a walk and wrapped one arm firmly around her middle.

Abigail sank into his chest and rested against him. She'd never tire of being in his arms. They had a few hurdles to cross, but all that mattered was that she had her cowboy. And the sooner their forever started, the happier she'd be.

The ride back seemed too short, and when they rode into the parking lot, she could see the entrance of the arena. A horde of reporters waited, the bulky cameras ready and waiting.

"Uh, Wade . . . how are we going to get home?"

He gave her a squeeze and set a kiss on her head. "Very carefully, Abby," he drawled. "Very carefully."

Reading Group Guide

1. Though Abigail was raised in a family of faith, she gradually fell away from God as she grew into adulthood. What are some of the distractions and other reasons so many young adults wander spiritually at this time? A close walk with God is always important, but why might young adulthood be a particularly bad time for a spiritual leave of absence?

2. Why do you think Abigail's mom described her as restless? What connection did that have with her spiritual condition?

3. How is our faith like Abigail's floundering vegetable garden? In what ways can Christianity sometimes resemble plastic flowers stuck into the dirt?

4. In Abigail's profession, she's referred

to as "the Truthseeker." How is that ironic in relation to her spiritual walk?

5. Discuss (or think about) the meaning of John 14:6: "Jesus answered, 'I am the way and the truth and the life.'"

6. Something Abigail experienced in childhood shaped who she became professionally. How did significant events in your childhood shape who you are?

7. Deep down, Abigail was trying to right a wrong from her childhood by exposing truth through her column. The relief her articles brought was only temporary, however. Why is self-redemption a waste of time? Have you ever tried to "work off" feelings of guilt or remorse? What did you learn in the process?

8. Abigail's father was a spiritual role model for her. Who did God put in your life to help show you His love? Are you a spiritual role model for someone else?

9. Wade dealt with guilt over his late wife's suicide and worried about letting down people he loved. Have you ever worried you wouldn't be enough for someone? How can trusting in God help you through this barrier?

10. Despite Wade's fears, he became the kind of hero Abigail could lean on. Discuss (or think about) a woman's desire for independence versus her desire to have a real hero in her life. Are the two compatible?

Acknowledgments

I'm so grateful for the many people who helped shape this book in one way or another. *A Cowboy's Touch* wouldn't exist without the Thomas Nelson fiction team. I'm deeply grateful for the entire team, led by Publisher Allen Arnold: Amanda Bostic, Jennifer Deshler, Natalie Hanemann, Chris Long, Andrea Lucado, Ami McConnell, Heather McCulloch, Becky Monds, Ashley Schneider, Katie Bond, and Kristen Vasgaard.

Good editors are worth their weight in gold, and I'm so grateful for both of mine. Natalie Hanemann provided an objective eye and wise insight that helped me take this story to a higher level. LB Norton followed behind us and polished up the manuscript, making for a more enjoyable read.

My first reader and brainstorming partner, author Colleen Coble. Love you, friend!

My agent, Karen Solem, who handles all the left-brained matters so I can focus on the right-brained stuff.

To Billy and Marci Whitehurst, who opened their Montana home and ranch for a city girl and her husband. Thanks for taking the time to show me the cowboy way of life. Thank you also for reading the advanced copy of *A Cowboy's Touch* to check for errors. Any mistakes that made it into print are all mine.

A research trip to Montana wouldn't have been possible without my sister-in-law Gina Sinclair, brother-in-law Mark Sinclair, and niece Mindy Sinclair. Thanks so much for coming to take over our daily lives for a few days so Kevin and I could gallivant all over Big Sky Country. We're so grateful to call you family.

Thank you to author Lenora Worth, who shared her expertise in the world of magazine publishing. Thanks for all your help, friend!

To my family, Kevin, Justin, Chad, and Trevor. I love each one of you so much!

Lastly, thank you, friend, for coming along on this journey to Moose Creek, Montana. I've enjoyed getting to know so many readers like you through my Facebook group. Visit my website for the link, www.Denise HunterBooks.com, or just drop me a note at Denise@DeniseHunterBooks.com. I'd love to hear from you!

A Letter from the Author

Dear friend,

I hope you enjoyed your trip to Moose Creek, Montana, with Abigail, Wade, and Maddy. There's truly something special about the Big Sky State and the people who inhabit that part of the country.

A Cowboy's Touch is a story about a Truthseeker who winds up discovering the real Truth. She's a woman who has lost her way somewhere along the journey. I hope you're holding fast to the Truth in your life. But if you, like Abigail, have wandered a bit further than you ever intended, I hope you know it's never too late to return. Jesus is always there, waiting to love you back into his arms.

Whether you're struggling to find your way back or enjoying a close walk with Christ, I hope you'll make time to attend a

Woman of Faith conference soon. These events can refresh your spirit and bless you in ways you cannot imagine. I know they have blessed me tremendously.

In His grace,
Denise

About the Author

Denise Hunter is the award-winning and best-selling author of several novels, including *Sweetwater Gap*. She and her husband are raising three boys in Indiana.